RAVEN HOUSE

An Emmie Rose Haunted Mystery Book 6

DEAN RASMUSSEN

Raven House: An Emmie Rose Haunted Mystery Book 6

Dean Rasmussen

Copyright © 2024 Dean Rasmussen
All rights reserved.
ISBN-13: 978-1-951120-37-5

This book is a work of fiction. The characters, incidents, and dialogue are drawn from the author's imagination and are not to be construed as real. Any resemblance to actual persons living or dead, businesses, events or locales is purely coincidental. Reproduction in whole or part of this publication without express written consent from the publisher is strictly prohibited, except as permitted by U.S. copyright law.

For more information about this book, visit:

www.deanrasmussen.com
dean@deanrasmussen.com

Raven House: An Emmie Rose Haunted Mystery Book 6

Published by: Dark Venture Press

Cover Art: Mibl Art

❀ Created with Vellum

1

Someone had already broken the locks on the window, so technically they weren't *breaking into* the second-floor apartment. There were no bars or barriers of any kind, and nobody had been home for weeks, so what did it matter? If everything Tony said was true, it would be easy money.

Glancing down at Tony, who now barely held the ladder with one hand while he puffed away on an e-cigarette with the other, Damon was having second thoughts. Why had he even bothered to bring along the old man? Too late now.

Pushing up on the window's frame, it slid open with ease. No need for the tools this time. Perfect.

Who the hell leaves their windows unlocked anymore, anyway? The losers deserved it.

Damon took another step up the ladder, and it wobbled a bit, sending a wave of panic through his chest as he gripped the windowsill to steady himself. It wasn't a long way down, but he knew the old man wouldn't budge an inch to catch him.

Just think of the money.

It was the only thing that calmed him as he pulled himself up and over the windowsill. Dropping into the dark, silent home office head-first, he hit the floor a little too hard, smashing his elbow against the side. The pain swelled as he stood up and scanned the area. He regretted his decision to remove his leather jacket before ascending the ladder—he'd wanted flexibility over warmth—but at least the leather gloves had protected his hands.

According to Tony, the prize was in the closet, on the other side of the room. Damon made his way there with as much stealth as he could muster and opened the closet door while switching on the tactical flashlight he'd brought along. The stack of banker's boxes sat in the far corner.

Right where Tony said they would be.

The old man would handle everything after getting the thing out of the apartment. His connections made him an invaluable asset in the grand scheme of things, having gained the trust of the apartment's owner after weeks of careful negotiation both online and in person, but now it was time to "cut and run", as Tony had put it.

Lifting the top box first, its weight surprised him, although Tony had said the thing was heavy. He placed it on the floor of the office and kneeled in front of it like a giddy child opening a Christmas present. The lid came off with ease and he peered inside. A colorful quilt filled the box. Pushing into the fabric, his fingers touched on a solid surface the size of a football, and his heart beat faster.

This is it.

Removing the wrapped object, he laid it out on the floor and opened it carefully. Everything had gone more smoothly than he'd imagined possible. So many things could have gone wrong, especially with the old man standing guard outside—he wasn't worth his weight in manure—but elation rushed through him as he set his eyes on the polished stone figure Tony had raved about. Deep grooves etched into its form showed a workmanship rarely seen in modern design. The surreal sculpture had a freakishly large head with a tiny, squashed body at the base. Nothing like what he had imagined an Aztec god to look like.

This is what Tony had tried—and failed—to describe to him earlier. What was its name again?

Wheat sea la punch ta la... Weed seed punch ya see...

Something like that. It didn't matter. Whatever the thing was called, it was worth at least three hundred thousand dollars to some schmuck in Miami, Florida.

Lifting it with both hands, he looked at its face with a bit of trepidation. How many men had feared to gaze into its eyes? It was nothing more than heavy stone, but Tony had talked about it with such reverence. Aztec god or not, it didn't make any difference as long as Tony's connection came through with the cash.

Staring into its eyes for a long moment, the thing seemed to lull him into a brief daze, broken only by footsteps coming from the hallway just beyond the apartment's front door. Soft voices and rustling sounds.

Neighbors from another apartment passing by?

Nobody could have seen them enter the window—not from any angle—but Damon froze in the darkness and strained to hear what they were saying.

The footsteps were sparse as if they stood waiting just beyond the door. Waiting for what? The voices grew louder. Deep, commanding voices.

Fear swept through him, and his heart beat faster as he stood up with the statue and turned back toward the window. He needed to get out of there.

Cradling the statue like a baby in his arms, he hurried back to the window and used the desk chair to lift himself up over the frame just as the front door to the apartment crashed open. A flurry of voices, chaos, and pounding footsteps spread out and moved closer.

Who the hell had called the police? They had been so careful this time. Some nosy neighbor. The anger warmed his face as he struggled to get out of the window without damaging his prize.

Knocking his arm against the frame, he'd climbed halfway

out when the windowpane slammed down onto his back, sending a jolt of pain up his spine. The glass shattered above his head, and a barrage of shards rained down over his wrists, the statue, and Tony's worthless face below. Thrusting up against the frame with all his strength, it wouldn't budge. He was caught like a rat in a trap as he hung out the window face down with his crotch pinned against the edge. A flood of pain surged as blood ran down his cheeks, dripping from the tip of his nose.

But worse than that—much, much worse—blood sprayed in pulsing streams from his slashed wrist. One of the larger shards had sliced through an artery just below the edge of his glove. The pain pushed him to the edge of blacking out, but he extended the statue in the moment as if to protect it. Screaming a torrent of obscenities down at Tony, the old man only stared up at him with wide eyes and outstretched arms.

"Drop it," Tony urged in a loud whisper. "I'll catch it."

"No way," Damon said with a gasp. "Get up here, you lazy—"

The police were now in the office, pulling at his legs and screaming at him to freeze.

Are you kidding me?

Pressing one glove over the open wound, he couldn't apply enough pressure to stop the bleeding. The statue wavered at the edge of falling.

"Drop it!" Tony yelled again.

Hell with that. Damon clutched it tighter.

But another group of officers surrounded Tony only a moment later, weapons drawn. The old man backed away toward a hedge as if he might try to take off as they shouted for him to get on his knees and keep his hands behind his head. Instead of complying, he reached into his pocket and a volley of rounds took him down in a hail of gunfire.

How had things gone so wrong?

The officers twisting Damon's legs and waist also struggled to lift the broken window, but it wouldn't budge. Despite his predicament, cold metal poked against his legs with loud voices reminding him that he was under arrest.

It was too late anyway. His vision wavered as the blood flowed unabated from his wrist, splashing down over the face of the statue, flooding the grooves some ancient artist had so painstakingly carved. He watched the blood fill the tiny channels along the top of the statue and drain down across its face to collect in what looked like tiny, cupped hands seemingly designed for just such an occasion.

Staring into the statue's face while the officers raced to free him, the expression on the statue seemed to come alive. The god grinned at him. A glowing satisfaction as the blood pooled in its hands. Damon faded into darkness.

2

Emmie strained to keep from crying. They were in the third car of the funeral procession on their way to the Vista Verde Cemetery, and the weight of Finn's father's death hung in the air between them. Sarah was the empath in their group, but it didn't take a psychic to see that Finn was devastated. There was no consoling him. His father had died of a sudden heart attack, and they had all made the urgent trip to San Diego with him the morning after the news.

The seasonally mild March air of San Diego was a pleasant break from the record-breaking lows of Minnesota, but it did little to elevate their mood.

After a short ceremony in the same Presbyterian church where they had baptized Finn as a child, they headed out along the edge of the city with Jason in the driver's seat, following in the headlights-on caravan with several other cars snaking through the narrow streets. Emmie sat in the passenger seat, with Sarah comforting Finn behind them. She hadn't let go of his hand once throughout their visit, and he seemed to embrace her strength, even making small talk along the way to the cemetery.

Jason looked at Sarah in the rearview mirror. "Your hair is already channeling those beach vibes."

Sarah had added auburn highlights to her naturally light-brown hair a few weeks before, and she gave him a wry look. "Maybe it'll turn white when we head back to Minnesota."

"Let's hope not," Finn said.

But it seemed to break the tension for a moment. Jason pushed it a little further by complaining about the incessant sunlight in California and how he already missed the gloomy skies and icy roads of Minnesota. That drew a brief laugh from Finn, but the lighthearted exchange quickly faded as the entrance to the cemetery appeared ahead.

Passing through an impressive iron gate at the front of the cemetery, their rental car seemed out of place among the BMWs, Mercedes and even a Rolls-Royce as the line of cars made their way along a narrow-paved road between sprawling rows of gravestones and monuments shadowed by lines of towering palm trees and red maples. Healthy manicured lawns stretched in every direction—the perfect place for a picnic. The setting and weather were perfect, as Southern California weather never seemed to change from what she could remember having lived there years earlier. Maybe the clear skies and warmer air would help to soothe Finn's aching soul.

If there was any silver lining to the tragedy, the sudden passing of Finn's dad had brought him back home for the first time since his brother Neil's suicide two years earlier. The reunion between Finn and his mother might provide a golden opportunity to heal their strained relationship, but it could also make it worse.

After the line of cars stopped near the back of the cemetery, everyone climbed out and gathered at the gravesite. Emmie and Jason took their places behind Finn and Sarah near the front of the crowd, where the pallbearers had carefully placed the casket on a metal device surrounded by a small blue curtain blocking the open grave from view. The crowd remained hushed among the singing birds and gentle breeze as the pastor waited patiently for everyone to arrive.

Tiffany, Finn's mother, clung to the arm of her tall, dark-haired son, her face streaming with tears as she kept her chin up. Despite her outward composure, there was a tension in the way she carried herself, as if she might collapse at any moment. Her tailored black dress mirrored Finn's suit, and she adjusted her pearl necklace while glancing at Finn and Sarah, who had positioned her arm under his as he seemed to lean into her for support.

Off in the distance, a man in gray overalls and a wide-brimmed hat stood next to a black and yellow backhoe. He seemed indifferent to the proceedings but glanced over every so often until finally settling against the machine with his hands crossed over his stomach as if to show reverence. Meeting the man's gaze for a moment, he turned away.

Emmie recognized several of the attendees surrounding her. Tiffany had introduced them at the church, but the names had gone in one ear and out the other. Emmie straightened her modest lavender dress, which she'd received as a Christmas present from Jason. It was the most beautiful dress she'd ever worn—but she still felt far out of place among the other "elite" in attendance.

It was clear that Finn's family had associated with an affluent circle, judging by the sophisticated ensembles and opulent dresses adorning their guests. Each outfit radiated luxury and refinement, and their every movement exuded prosperity and poise. Their brief introductions earlier revealed a polite but pervasive impatience, although Jason seemed to do quite well in his tailored wool suit and polished leather shoes, easily schmoozing his way through the sea of egos.

The sun was still rising in the clear, mid-morning sky, but even then, its intensity would have made the event uncomfortable if it weren't for a large white canopy shielding those fortunate enough to stand within its shadow beside the gravesite.

During a moment of prayer, Emmie had the opportunity to glance around at a few mourning faces. Most of them were in their mid-fifties, the same age as Stephen Adams, Finn's dad, but guests of every age had attended. A few couples tried to reign in children who pushed too close to the casket, and a young mother further back struggled with a fidgeting baby in her arms.

The man who had given the eulogy at the church earlier now stood composed and unyielding beside Finn's mother. Emmie remembered his name. Marc Moretti. He had introduced himself as Finn's godfather in a low, firm voice that seemed to command respect, and she couldn't help but think of the movie *The Godfather*. He was undeniably handsome with a soft stare and carefully groomed light-brown hair.

Glancing toward the back of the crowd, a familiar face caught her eye. A man in his mid-fifties stood off by a tree some distance away. He was partially hidden by the tree's shade, and she couldn't get a clear view of his face. Still, she couldn't shake the sense that she'd seen him somewhere before.

Shifting and straining to keep an eye on him, she scanned her memory. Maybe she'd seen him in a photo or at the church gathering? He must have been one of Finn's relatives, judging by his resemblance to...

Stephen?

She focused more intently on his profile and compared him to the photos she'd seen of Stephen. If he would just step into the light... But he lingered in the shadows and stared straight ahead toward the casket as if he could see through the figures standing in front of him.

Because he can.

Emmie's heart beat a little faster. It could only be Stephen, and his presence jarred her. Spirits *rarely* visited a cemetery, as most of them tended to remain near the place of their final trauma, caught in the loop of despair, pain, or confusion, although sometimes they wandered. The spirit's presence wasn't enough to distract her—she had long grown accustomed to seeing them—but he shouldn't be there.

Something was wrong.

She jumped a bit when Jason squeezed her hand a little too hard, shifting her attention back to the ceremony. His expression revealed concern.

Are you alright? his eyes seemed to ask. She could practically read his mind.

With a nod of her head and a smile, she tried to calm him and her own beating heart.

When the pastor led them through a short prayer, she bowed her head like the others, but couldn't resist peeking back at the man to see if he'd moved yet.

Still there.

As they lowered the casket slowly into the grave, the pastor read from the Bible, and Emmie tried to make sense of why Stephen might have appeared at his own funeral. Finn had told her that his father had died from a heart attack, right? And those who died naturally—and a heart attack *was* in the 'naturally' category—passed on. They didn't hang around.

So why was Stephen lingering behind?

Maybe he'd wanted one final moment together with his family before passing to the other side? Or did he have something important to tell them?

Leaning back to get a better view of Stephen, Emmie was tempted to leave the group and approach him. Who could blame her for wanting to help a lost spirit? But a moment before she broke away from Jason, the man stepped around the side of the tree and into the sunlight. That sense of familiarity broke as his face became clear.

Not Stephen. Not even close.

The man had the same style of hair, but that's where the similarities ended. Had the shadows somehow played tricks on her mind? The man's brown skin was a stark contrast to Finn's Irish ancestry.

Emmie exhaled. How could she have mistaken him for Finn's father? The error unnerved her. At least she hadn't embarrassed herself by approaching him.

As the ceremony progressed, Emmie tried to put aside her mistake and focus on helping her friend. His eyes watered as the final speech drew to a close and the pastor closed his Bible.

The gravedigger finished lowering the casket into the grave and one of the children crept in beside Finn and stared down into the open hole with wide eyes before darting back into the crowd of mourners.

Marc moved in beside Finn's mother and extended his arm as she stepped forward and dropped a rose onto the casket. She wept openly for a moment before turning away and trembling in Marc's arms. Marc gazed down at her sympathetically. His eyes were full of genuine warmth as he whispered into her ear. She responded with a nod, then moved back with her head down.

Finn stood still as the crowd began to disperse, with the attendees heading to their cars to make the drive back to the church for the reception. Within minutes, only a dozen or so remained. With Marc comforting Tiffany several yards away, Finn stepped forward and dropped a rose into the grave, looking down at it for a long moment in contemplation before he stepped back beside Sarah and walked away with her toward the car.

Jason gestured toward the car. "Head back?"

Emmie responded with a quick nod, but before she could step away, her foot bumped against a solid surface. Glancing down, she spotted the edge of a gravestone flush against the ground. They had placed a green tarp around the open grave, no doubt to hide the unearthed soil, but this one gravestone poked out with the name obscured by the dirt. Brushing her foot across it, she made out the letters.

Neil Harrison Adams.

Finn's brother, who had committed suicide. From what Finn had told her, he had died in the middle of winter, a little over two years earlier, and she instinctively moved back out of respect, though she knew his spirit wouldn't be there. Neil's spirit would still be in the basement of the Adams house where he had ended his life.

"His brother?" Jason asked.

"Yes."

Jason glanced toward Stephen's grave, then back to Neil's. "At least they'll be near each other."

"In body."

Emmie turned and walked away with Jason beside her. Before she got into the car with the others, she glanced back toward the gravesite one last time with a sense of unease. There was no sign of the man she'd mistaken for Stephen. Just the gravedigger in his overalls, putting out a cigarette as he climbed inside the backhoe and started it up.

3

Emmie couldn't just blurt out to the others about what she'd thought she'd seen at the cemetery. Not even to Sarah. The mistake was embarrassing, but she couldn't shake the sense that something wasn't quite right. If she dared to mention it to her friends, especially so soon after the funeral, then the suggestion that Stephen hadn't yet passed on would hit Finn like a bag of bricks—the last thing he needed right now.

At least, she could learn more about Stephen's death, to quell her fears beyond any doubt before bringing it up to the others. Finn had gone through enough pain recently, and she didn't want to add to it. Still, the unexpected sighting gnawed at the back of her mind as they arrived at the church for the lunch reception.

The other guests were already there when they arrived, and the solemn faces from earlier that morning had given way to more light-hearted conversations as they navigated their way inside. Rows of flowers encompassed a table of photos against one wall. The sweet scent of roses, daisies and lilies filled the air, helping to lighten the mood, and the mid-day sunshine streamed in through brightly colored stained-glass windows with scenes depicting Biblical figures like the apostles Peter and Paul.

Emmie did her best to follow Jason's lead in making small

talk with a few of Finn's cousins, but eventually retreated to a table away from the others and watched the gathering from a distance. Jason stayed with her and seemed to sense her unease as they watched Sarah and Finn chatting with Finn's mother near the main door, offering their support as she embraced a steady flow of well-wishers.

The man who had given the eulogy—Emmie had already forgotten his name—Finn's godfather, stepped over with a warm smile and gestured to the chair beside Jason. "Mind if I join you?"

"Not at all." Jason shifted toward Emmie as the man sat down.

Finn had talked highly of him that morning, and now she was embarrassed at not paying closer attention as he politely shook their hands. His name hung at the tip of her tongue until he finally introduced himself and gracefully unbuttoned his suit jacket while sipping from a glass of red wine.

"I'm Marc Moretti." He stared at the glass and licked his lips. "You must try some wine. I brought my best pinot."

"You're a connoisseur?" Jason asked.

He grinned warmly. "So much that I bought the vineyard. Finn didn't tell you?"

"Not that part," Emmie said.

Marc brushed it off. "The poor kid has a lot on his mind. I invited him to stop by, and you're all welcome to join. Our vineyard is just outside San Diego, on a beautiful stretch of property south of here. A little slice of paradise."

"It'll depend on how Finn feels," Jason said.

"Of course." Marc glanced toward Finn and his mother. "I'll do all I can to help—to help him through this—but Tiffany's an amazing woman. She'll rise above this tragedy, as she's done before."

A fresh wave of sadness swept through Emmie.

Turning back to them, Marc took another sip of wine before continuing. "How do you know Finn?"

"From..." Emmie hesitated, catching herself before answering. Better to keep the topic of ghost hunting under wraps for the duration of their visit. "...Minnesota. I went to high school with Sarah, and I met Finn in the local library. He was researching something for an article he was writing."

He looked at each of them, nodding as if her answer had satisfied him. "Journalism suits Finn well. Such an inquisitive nature. I've known Stephen and his family for half my life. Good people."

"And this guy—" Emmie nudged Jason's arm. "—was my childhood bully, but he's my boyfriend now."

Marc's eyes widened. "Well, I'm sure that's an interesting story."

"She never lets me forget." A wry grin spread across Jason's face until he looked at Marc curiously. "You're Finn's godfather."

"That's right. Right there with them the day he was born. Our children even grew up together. My daughters, Amelia and Paige, used to play with Finn and Neil out on our property at an old Spanish mission that's nothing more than ruins now. Used to be called Santa Isabella Mission. Are you familiar with it?"

Emmie shook her head.

Jason answered him, "Can't say I am."

Marc nodded as if he understood. "Not surprised. It's not on any tourist map, thank God. Nothing much to see anyway, if you ask me, but you should come out to visit sometime. See the vineyard for yourself." He grinned and took another sip. "There's more where this came from, and plenty of sunshine, if any of that interests you."

"Of course," Emmie said while looking toward Jason. "But it all depends on Finn."

Marc nodded. "You've got a good heart. I can see that. He deserves the best."

"I try." Emmie glanced over at Sarah and Finn, then spotted the table near the door displaying photos of Stephen Adams at various ages throughout his life. The largest portrait stood on an easel beside the table. The man's intelligent eyes stared back through thick-rimmed glasses.

"What was he like?" Emmie asked. "Finn's dad."

Marc followed her gaze. "Stephen was like no other. Never took no for an answer and worked his ass off to build his real estate business. Never saw anyone work so hard, which probably contributed to his heart problems. That's how I came to own Isabella Mission and the vineyard. He's the one who passed me the hot tip it was for sale, and I scooped it up right away. Never regretted it for a moment."

"I wish I'd gotten the chance to meet him." Emmie turned her attention back to Marc. "Finn hasn't shared much about his family with us."

"I'm not surprised." He nodded. "Finn's a private guy, to be sure. Stephen was just like him—both a bit stubborn, if you ask me—and needed a heart operation, but kept putting it off until it was too late." He checked the time on his phone, finished his drink, then stood up while pulling a business card from his pocket. He handed it to Emmie. "I need to head out soon. Finn has my number, but here it is, anyway. Call if you want to stop by. Have you ever toured a vineyard?"

Emmie shook her head. "Never had the chance."

"There you go. Here's your chance. Lots of history at that place, in the ruins."

Emmie swallowed. *Lots of history, lots of ghosts. No thanks.* But she nodded instead. "Maybe. We'll see what Finn wants to do."

"He knows he's always welcome at Raven House. He's like a son—he *is* my godson—so he occupies a special part of my heart and family, even if we haven't seen each other in years."

Emmie read the card. "Dr. Marc Moretti", then glanced up at him. "You're a doctor?"

"A cardiac surgeon at the San Diego hospital. Didn't Finn...? Oh well, it's understandable. He's got a lot on his mind."

"You know Finn's girlfriend, Sarah, is a nurse."

"I heard." He nodded sympathetically. "Nursing is a tough

career, but I suppose it's rewarding, in a sense. I'm sure your friend would agree."

Marc's phone dinged and he paused to check his messages. "The hospital never leaves me alone. I'm very sorry. Had the day off, but I need to run—surprised I made it this long without an interruption. It was so good to meet both of you."

They stood and shook hands again. Marc's grip was warm and firm.

"Same here," Emmie said.

"Don't let my hectic schedule prevent you from stopping by the house. The vineyard isn't open to the public, but my daughter, Amelia, is usually around. Finn knows her like a sister, and she'll treat you all like family. I'm sure he could use a little wine to help get his mind off all the tragedy."

"I'm sure he'd love that," Jason answered.

Marc smiled warmly, glancing at each of them, before stepping away.

Jason's phone buzzed moments later, and he checked the screen. His pleasant smile faded. "My Uber is here."

Emmie had dreaded this moment. Jason had warned her that he could only stay for a single night—that he would need to head to the airport for a flight to Miami that evening—but she had hoped the moment would never come. "Can't you reschedule your flight somehow?"

"I can, but..." Sadness swept through his eyes. "It's my career. But I'm sure you have a ton of freelance work to do anyway, right? You'll be so busy you won't even think about me."

"Impossible."

At least he would be waiting for her when she returned home in a few days. Still, her heart ached that he wouldn't be there to enjoy the California sunshine with her. His absence would rekindle that awkward pain of being the third wheel again with just Finn and Sarah.

"Is that something you can live with?" Jason asked.

She looked at him for a long second. "Yes, of course."

He took her hand, and they walked side-by-side over to Finn and Sarah, who were engaged in a conversation with Tiffany and another couple.

Breaking Finn and Sarah away from the group, Jason tapped his phone. "Sorry for my hasty exit, but I have to go."

"Understood," Finn said.

"Just a few days this time."

"No worries," Finn said.

Jason shared a brief hug with each of them and turned Emmie away from the others to sneak a final kiss before he hurried out the door.

Emmie watched him leave with her arms folded over her chest.

Sarah leaned in and slipped her arm around Emmie's shoulders. "Finally, got my friend back all to myself."

"You think he's possessive?"

Sarah looked into her eyes. "I was kidding."

Finn stepped toward his mother, and she made room for them in the circle before introducing Emmie to the stylish couple whose smiles didn't extend up to their eyes. They seemed to study her clothes as they shook hands before jumping back into the conversation they were having before she'd arrived. The dark, tailored suit reminded Emmie that she was an outsider among the professional elite, and Tiffany almost seemed to inch sideways, coming between her and the couple as if to cut her off.

I'm embarrassing her. Emmie glanced down at her clothes. Maybe not just the clothes but *her*. The way she stood, her career, her connection to Finn. It finally made sense why Finn hadn't traveled back home since his brother's death. His parents had moved on, and his presence at the funeral was something to be tolerated.

Finn seemed to pick up on the way his mother had brushed Emmie off. His face reddened and he glanced toward the exit. "We should get going too."

"Oh?" Tiffany broke away from her conversation long enough

to give each of them a hug, pulling Finn in close as his arms hung limp at his sides. "You're going back to the house now?"

"Yes," Finn said. "I've got something to do."

She stared at him with genuine concern, although he seemed not to notice. "We'll get through this."

"Like we do everything else." Finn turned away and went outside. Sarah and Emmie followed.

4

Finn led the girls around the main house to the guesthouse in the backyard. His mother had invited them all to stay there during their visit—an old two-car garage that his family had recently converted into a one-bedroom guest home complete with a hot tub, heated floors, a pool with a patio, and a sprawling flower garden separating the two structures—and Finn had reluctantly agreed. During the tour earlier that morning, his mother had explained to the girls that, unfortunately, they hadn't managed to finish renovating the old garage until after Neil passed away, which is why he'd needed to stay in the basement.

"How convenient," Finn had mumbled under his breath.

Remembering his mother's callousness that morning only added to the growing bitterness since returning home. If only his parents had cared enough to build it *before* Neil's death, maybe he'd still be alive. The anger swelled, even as he opened the door to the guesthouse for them.

"Something's wrong," Sarah said.

"My brother." Finn took a deep breath. "Too much bad history in this place. I can't stop thinking about him, but not your fault."

Sarah moved toward him. "Don't rush it."

Finn glanced out the window toward the main house. "I've waited too long."

He went straight to his suitcase and dug through it on his knees before removing the pair of Owl Cromwell's goggles—one of the pairs he and Jason had acquired during their disturbing visit to Whisper House months earlier. The smell of the old leather strap rekindled the memories of what he'd gone through there—what he'd done—but none of that mattered now.

He'd brought the goggles along for just this purpose, and he was determined now to do what he'd been avoiding since Neil's death. To face the tragedy head on. To face his brother.

He hadn't touched the goggles since then, but there was nothing to it. Just put them on and anyone could see into the spirit world. Squeezing the straps with both hands, he carried them toward the door.

"Want us to wait here?" Emmie asked.

Finn shook his head. "Please come with."

He headed back outside with the girls at his side, and the smell of flowers and sage plants filled the air. The meticulously groomed and organized rows of roses, geraniums, Birds of Paradise, and shrubs encompassed them on both sides of the cement path that connected the two houses. Thinking about the time and money they'd spent building this little slice of paradise only fueled his anger. His parents had tended to a bunch of plants better than their own son.

Walking to the main house with butterflies in his stomach, they stepped inside, and the cool, silent air greeted them. A sprawling mess of papers covered the living room floor and kitchen table. His mother hadn't requested help with anything—not yet—but the chaos was unexpected given the importance she placed on appearance.

The girls were politely quiet.

"It's not usually like this," Finn said.

"Does she need help?" Sarah asked.

"In every way, but she won't accept it. Don't bother." Finn

wasted no time in walking through the house toward a door near the kitchen. Opening it and switching on the light, he stared down the steps. Neil was down there. The reality of the situation unnerved him a little, even after all he'd seen in recent months. He adjusted the goggle's straps a little at a time, hesitating to put them on, but then finally nodded. "I'm ready."

"You'll be fine," Emmie said.

"I just hope I can handle it." Finn smiled nervously.

Sarah stroked his back. "We'll be right here waiting for you. Don't worry about a thing."

Finn nodded and gave a nervous laugh. "If you hear me crying..."

"We understand," Emmie said. "He's your brother."

"I've got so many things I want to say to him." He ran his fingers through his hair. "But I'm not sure how far I'll get before I start crying. I won't lie. I'm really scared. This isn't like the others."

"If it's too much to handle," Sarah said while moving with Finn toward the basement door, "we can go down there with you. I know there's a lot of emotion behind all of this, so there's no shame in not wanting to go through this alone."

Finn glanced at the goggles, turning them over in his hands. "It's better this way."

"Then just say what's in your heart," Sarah said.

He nodded as his eyes watered. "I won't be angry, I know that. I'm way past angry now. I just want to talk with him one last time."

Opening the basement door, he headed down the stairs, closing the door behind himself for privacy.

At the bottom, he navigated to the far corner, to the empty, white wall where his brother had shot himself. His heart sank. His parents had painted over the stains so soon after Neil's death —only days after it happened. No sign of blood or that anything bad had ever happened in that spot and he had not been witness to any of the nightmarish scenes that the police had tried as sensitively as possible to explain to him.

His parents had failed Neil—on a massive scale—although they'd done a brilliant job of erasing the horrible tragedy, but wasn't it strange that they hadn't put anything in that spot? Nothing to cover the area except for the white paint. No pictures or boxes or old furniture or anything. They *had* pulled up all the carpeting in that back corner Neil had called his room and hadn't replaced it. The area was still as empty and cold as it had been when he'd last stood in the same spot with his mother days afterwards while she tried to justify it all as a horrible accident.

"Not an accident, Mom," he said softly in the dead air. "You made it happen."

The bitterness swelled in his chest, and he let it subside before continuing, clearing his thoughts while still gripping the goggles in both hands. He was going to apologize, even beg forgiveness that he hadn't done more to stop it.

A single row of recessed lighting lit the bare, gray cement floor where Neil's couch and chair had sat. They hadn't even used the space for storage, as if even stepping into that space might reveal the true horror of what had happened.

But there were boxes all around him. Totes and cardboard boxes stuffed full of what remained after Neil was gone. They had sent all the larger items to the dump, but his smaller possessions were untouched by the look of them.

Finn couldn't see Neil without the goggles, although somehow on a deep level, he could feel his presence. Or maybe that was just nerves. Of course, if the girls came down, they could point Neil out to him immediately. He was sure of that. But that's not how he wanted things to happen. He had dreamed of confronting his brother so many times. It was time now.

He gripped the goggles nervously in his hands and adjusted the straps again. He had only to lift them up to his eyes and see his brother for the first time since the tragedy.

His heart beat faster as he stepped toward the empty space, although he moved forward inches at a time. Maybe Neil was watching him now. The hair on the back of his neck bristled.

What was he so afraid of? It was only his brother. He should be full of joy that the goggles would allow him to see him again, to get everything off his chest, even if his words never got through to the other side, and maybe he might even come to understand why his brother had done it.

So why was he hesitating?

It'll break my heart.

Hell with that. It's already broken.

His breathing slowed until a puff of cold air swept around him and he shuddered.

Was that him?

I'll know soon enough.

He lifted the goggles, but closed his eyes as he slipped them over his head and adjusted them while facing down until he was ready.

Would Finn actually see his brother committing the act? That would be too painful for anyone to watch. Wouldn't his brother be stuck in his eternal, suicidal loop? That's what the girls always said, that the spirits became trapped in the final, traumatic moments of their life.

Dammit Neil. Why?

Finn opened his eyes.

Darkness. The obsidian stones set in the frames of the goggles revealed nothing. No suicidal ghost.

No Neil.

Neil wasn't there. Or if he was, then something wasn't working.

Twisting the strap and the stones in their frames, as if a simple adjustment might fix the problem, frustration grew in his chest.

He looked through the goggles again, but they still didn't work.

"Of course," he mumbled. How could he have forgotten? The obsidian goggles wouldn't work so far from Whisper House, at least not without evoking Cromwell's methods for energy that the man had written about in his books. And, of course, in his grief and the rush to pack his suitcase, he'd forgotten the books necessary to make it all work properly.

But there wasn't enough time to figure it out. Not during this visit, anyway.

"Well, hell." Finn ripped off the goggles and stared at them as the emotions and frustration swelled. He had tried. He really had. So, what would he do now? Would he ever get the chance to say goodbye to his brother? The question echoed in his mind as he wadded up the goggles and sent them hurling against the wall in a surge of rage.

The crack of the stone lenses hitting the wall seemed to break him out of the darkness. Turning back toward the stairs, Finn glanced around at the boxes. Many of them weren't marked, although some were open, and he could see a stack of shirts in one and books and notebooks in another, most likely left over from Neil's incomplete college days. A bowling trophy jutted from the side of an open box. Neil had bragged to him about winning it over the phone. He could still remember his elated voice so clearly in his mind.

Finn walked over and dug it out, feeling a little sentimental as he blew away the dust and set it aside to explore a little further into the belongings. There were some items that might have come from a camping trip or from a trip across the country. A metal shovel stood against the wall beside a pair of hiking boots. Neil had loved to travel as much as Finn, although his brother had tossed away that passion at some point during his descent.

Pushing aside a dirty towel and an old pair of work gloves, Finn came across some computer printouts showing an assortment of satellite images of the Isabella ruins.

Had Neil been out treasure hunting again before his death, like they'd done on Marc's property as children? Finn glanced over toward the shovel. Or maybe this had only been wishful thinking on Neil's part, a Hail Mary effort to redeem himself in the eyes of his parents. Whatever it was, Neil had failed to find any treasure of any kind in his life. The gods couldn't be bothered to even toss the poor guy a single bone. Finn set the papers down and turned to leave.

A moment later, the door at the top of the stairs opened and Sarah's voice called out, "Finn, you need to come up here."

5

Emmie glanced up toward the ceiling moments after Finn left to go to the basement.

"Something bothering you?" Sarah asked. "You've been looking a little... distracted all day."

"I saw something odd at the cemetery." She moved in a little closer to Sarah to avoid Finn overhearing. "Maybe it's nothing."

"A spirit?"

"Yes."

"A frightening one?"

"No. Someone... lingering behind." Emmie moved toward the staircase leading upstairs. "Spirits do stick around sometimes after death... to say goodbye to loved ones."

"Where are you going?" Sarah asked.

"They said Stephen died in his office." She glanced up again. "I just want to check on something."

Sarah followed her gaze. "You think he's still up there?"

"There's only one way to find out."

Glancing back toward the basement door, Sarah's expression changed as she seemed to understand what Emmie was suggesting. "We should go up there then before he comes back."

They hurried up the stairs, then treaded softly side-by-side

27

down the hallway, as if Mrs. Adams were in the next room and she might catch them if they made too much noise. Glancing inside each door along the way for any signs of Stephen's office, they narrowed their search to the last door on the left. Emmie opened it slowly.

Cool air flooded out as they peered inside. Stephen Adams lay on the floor, clasping his chest with one hand and clutching at the air with the other as if trying to reach an unseen object. His face was full of fear and panic. His eyes were like golf balls as he stared at them until he collapsed, and the looping cycle began again with him sitting upright at his desk as the early stages of the heart attack gripped him.

Between each breath of gasping air, he mumbled a string of phrases over and over while inching himself toward the door. "The price of greed, hearts must bleed," Stephen groaned as if it were an epiphany. Then a Spanish phrase, "El tesoro robado no puede ocultarse de los dioses."

She heard it clearly now, but still didn't understand its meaning. "Do you get what he's saying? Something about gods."

"I don't understand Spanish well enough," Sarah said.

Emmie grabbed a pen and paper off the desk and wrote the words down as best she could. Maybe Finn could interpret it later.

Slipping the paper into her pocket, she scanned the spirit for more clues. His hair and clothes were in disarray—Tiffany *had* mentioned earlier that Stephen had died in the morning. But his button-down plaid shirt was torn open with the buttons on the floor as if he had clawed at his chest moments earlier. The strain on Stephen's face was a mix of ghastly fear and desperation.

"Em, do you know what this means?"

She did. Stephen didn't die naturally, and her heart sank with the dread that they would need to share the revelation with Finn. He had already been through so much. How would he handle such a thing on top of everything else? "But it's clear he's having a heart attack, just like Finn said. That's a natural death, so he shouldn't be here."

Sarah turned toward her. "Poor Finn. I'm not sure how much more his heart can take."

"How are we going to tell him?" Emmie said.

The question hung in the air. Sarah stepped toward Stephen and glanced around. "There's a deep sadness in his spirit. Regret."

Emmie moved in closer to Sarah, as Stephen seemed not to notice her. The trauma had consumed the man's attention, as it sometimes did for spirits, preventing him from recognizing either the earthly or spiritual realm. Moving around to stand in front of him, she tried to catch his attention by holding her hand out and focusing on his energy. "Stephen, do you see me?"

Nothing changed. Just the same repeated phrases over and over again.

Emmie closed her eyes and watched his spirit in her mind. Maybe she could get to him that way. "Stephen," she said with strained focus, "what happened to you?"

She had encountered difficult spirits before, some of them so caught up and trapped in their trauma that nothing could get through to them. Those spirits wouldn't benefit from her help and just needed time to work it out on their own until the dark energy dissipated. Stephen had that same look in his eyes, a fixation on something just beyond his grasp. It was something precious to him, but his cryptic phrases made no sense.

"I can't get through to him." Emmie let go of his energy in her mind. "He's completely unaware of us, trapped in some other reality."

"We can't leave him like this," Sarah said.

"What can we do?"

Sarah was focusing on Stephen, too. Maybe she could get through to him through the intense emotions he'd experienced at the moment of death. At the same time, Emmie closed her eyes and tried again. This was Finn's dad, after all, and it was worth putting everything she had into communicating with him. She strained her mind to reach into his spirit and called out again, a little louder this time. "Stephen, can you tell us what happened?"

Emmie couldn't help but notice that there was an intensity about Stephen's spirit that reminded her of Finn. Finn had inherited that relentless mind from his father, no doubt, and Stephen's stubborn single-mindedness wouldn't break anytime soon, if Finn's behavior were a clue. She continued pushing forward in her mind, trying to draw his spirit closer, but the reality of the situation soon became clear. This wasn't something they would be able to solve with brute force.

Sarah seemed to come to the same conclusion, backing away while letting out a heavy sigh. "I feel Stephen is consumed with pain. I'm not sure there's anything we can do right now."

The chill in the air seemed to grow colder even as Emmie's face warmed under the strain of trying to communicate with Stephen's spirit. Opening her eyes again, Emmie glanced around the office. There were so many things left in disarray, untouched since Stephen's death. A dry erase board with hastily scribbled notes. Scattered papers and folders nearly obscuring the computer's keyboard. Nobody had gone in to clean the room yet, and there was also a strange smell of coffee in the air. A ceramic mug lay on its side beside the desk on a smaller table. Traces of coffee left a stain on the papers and carpet below. Had Stephen knocked it over during his struggle?

Tiffany hadn't had the strength to enter the room again after the coroner had removed the body. The pain must have prevented her from going back inside. So much grief in that house. Their son Neil had died in the basement and now Stephen upstairs in the office. How long could a woman like Tiffany survive in a house surrounded by so much tragedy?

Emmie's heart ached thinking about it. "Finn should know about this. Right away."

"I'll get him." Sarah nodded solemnly then left the room.

6

Emmie stood alone with Stephen's ghost, scrutinizing every moment of the man's final moments, searching for clues as to what happened. The heartbreaking tragedy had just started another loop when Finn and Sarah walked into the room.

"What's going on?" Finn asked.

Sarah's eyes filled with tears and her voice cracked, "Oh, Finn."

Emmie stepped toward him, trying to form just the right words. How could she tell him such a thing without breaking his heart? It wasn't fair that he had to face another tragedy on top of all the others. "Your dad..."

Finn glanced around the room, his face a mix of confusion and shock. "What about him?"

"He's here," Sarah whispered.

"What do you mean, he's here? He died of a heart attack. Isn't that natural? You said spirits move on if they die naturally."

"Yes." Emmie stared into his eyes. "According to everything we've learned so far, that's true."

"So, what are you implying, Em? That my mom killed him? Or he committed suicide? That's ridiculous. I saw the death certificate."

"We're not saying that, Finn," Sarah said. "But he's stuck here, and we don't know why."

Finn seemed to take a long time to process everything she'd said, and he stepped back from Sarah, just a little, taking a deep breath before speaking again. "So, if that's true... how could this have happened?"

Emmie carefully chose her words. "Did your mom mention anything about him in recent days? That he was acting strangely or anything like that?"

Finn's expressions shifted from frustration to sadness to annoyance in a matter of moments. "I hadn't talked to my mom in months before this happened. Either of them."

"Do you know if he had any enemies?"

Finn narrowed his eyes at Emmie, as if trying to make sense of what she was asking. "Enemies? He wasn't a criminal, if that's what you're wondering."

"I'm not suggesting that, but maybe he upset the wrong person?"

Finn let out an exasperated sigh. "I don't know. But none of that makes sense, anyway, right? He died of a heart attack."

"Okay, I'm sorry," Emmie said. "We'll work this out."

Finn cringed and stared at the floor, where Stephen's spirit still played out the scene of his death. "Does it look like something... violent happened to him?"

"No," Emmie said softly, "nothing like that."

"It *does* look like a heart attack," Sarah said, "from what I can see, but he keeps repeating something in Spanish."

"Spanish?"

"Does your dad speak Spanish?" Emmie asked.

"A little."

"And he also keeps repeating something in English. Something about greed. The price of greed. Hearts must bleed."

Emmie took out the paper with Stephen's words from her pocket and handed it to Finn. "I don't know what it says."

Finn's expression changed as he read the paper. His eyes

widened as a revelation seemed to come over him. "I do. The treasure."

"From the Isabella Mission?" Sarah asked.

"You know about that?" he asked her.

Emmie spoke up, "Marc talked about it a little, at the funeral reception."

Finn looked at the note again. "Why would my dad say this? He never believed in any of that superstitious stuff. He was a diehard skeptic, just like me before I met you."

"Maybe that was on his mind when he died?"

Finn ran his fingers through his hair and took in long, drawn out breaths while staring into the space where his father had died, as if trying to see what only the girls could. Squeezing the paper in his hand, he seemed to calm a bit before continuing, pressing his eyes together then opening them again slowly. "Are there any signs of... a struggle?"

Emmie and Sarah both watched Stephen again.

"I only see that he's clutching at his heart and collapsing," Sarah said. "It all fits what you told me, Finn."

"Then I don't get it," Finn said. "If he's still here, then they're wrong."

"Was your dad involved in finding the treasure?"

"Never," Finn said. "Why would he be?"

"But he keeps talking about it..." Sarah said.

"He'd never say something like that," Finn said. "But those words have a connection to the treasure's curse."

"Is that common knowledge?" Emmie asked. "The curse?"

"Everyone who grew up in this area knows about it."

Finn looked into the space where his father's spirit lay dying on the floor. His face was growing pale and mercifully, he couldn't see the heart-wrenching scene playing out only feet away. Shifting toward his dad's spirit with a curious stare, he shivered when his father's spirit came close to passing through him. He lurched back. "I need to leave."

"We all do," Sarah said.

After stepping out into the hallway, Emmie closed the door behind them as Finn headed downstairs. Stopping in the kitchen, they gathered around Finn, where he was leaning against the granite countertop with a dazed look on his face. Sarah moved in to comfort him, and he didn't pull away.

"That's all he said?" Finn asked them. "Did he say anything else?"

"That's all," Emmie said, "We tried talking with him, but we couldn't get through. Something's traumatized him."

"I don't believe in curses," he said. "Not this one, anyway. Even after seeing so much stuff related to it over the last year. You don't know all the stories, all the nonsense that's circulated about that place."

"Do you know what your father might have meant with those words?"

"I'm not sure," Finn said, "but the stories they told us about the ruins, that place where I used to dig treasure for fun as a kid, there was always plenty of talk of a curse from centuries ago. Something about an Aztec priest cursing anyone who touched the treasure. But... there is no treasure. Or if there was, then it's long gone. Believe me."

"I do. But who would know more information about this? I mean, the details of it, and anything that's happened in the area lately related to the treasure?" Emmie asked. "Marc? It's on his property, right?"

"Of course he would know." Finn nodded. "But if you're suggesting that a curse killed my dad, that sounds even more ridiculous than my mom killing him. Dad never had anything to do with the treasure or had any interest in the stories. I'm pretty sure he would have mocked anyone who even suggested it might be true."

"Then why would his spirit say those things?"

"I don't know." Finn shook his head. "But I'd rather not ask Marc about it. He would probably tease me even more than my dad."

"Then who else could we talk to?" Sarah asked.

Finn looked up sharply, but his face looked as if he had just eaten something rotten. "There is someone. Not someone *I* ever want to see again, but I wonder if Mrs. Blackstone is still alive."

"Who's Mrs. Blackstone?" Emmie asked.

"She was Amelia and Paige's nanny growing up. She used to watch us all, keep us in line like a Nazi."

"Marc mentioned something like that."

"He mentioned Mrs. Blackstone?"

"Not her, but that you got into trouble once in a while."

"He said that, huh?" Finn looked at her curiously. "What else did he say?"

"Not much else." Sarah smiled warmly. "No shocking revelations. Nothing we don't already know."

"God knows, I wasn't the easiest kid to deal with. Marc was always good at steering my incessant energy toward something with the least possibility for disaster."

"He said you used to dig for treasure with his daughters."

"I did. Many, many hours of back-breaking digging."

"Did you ever find anything?" Sarah asked.

"Nothing of value."

"Do you think this woman would talk to us?" Emmie asked. "... if she's still alive."

Finn scoffed. "A woman that cranky couldn't still be alive. Someone would have pushed her over a cliff by now." Finn seemed to ponder the thought. "But if she is still alive, you'd probably make her day if you asked her about the curse. She was obsessed with all that stuff, the curses and the ancient traditions. I was a bit afraid of her, actually, when I was young. She was one of those mean women. I guess maybe it was just the way she looked. A permanent scowl. A real pain in the ass."

"Dare I ask if you wouldn't mind trying to contact her again?" Emmie asked. "You seem to have all the contact info here."

Finn glanced down with a defeated stare. "I'd rather not, but given the circumstances..."

They gathered in the living room, huddling on a large couch with Finn in the center. He took out his phone and started flipping through websites. The house was uncomfortably quiet while Emmie and Sarah waited for him to find the information. The air conditioning had switched off and there was nothing to fill the silence except the clicking of his phone and their breathing.

Finn finally spoke up after a long pause. "Even if she is still alive—and I'm hoping she isn't, quite honestly—you won't enjoy her company."

"If she can tell us more about the origins of the curse and the truth," Emmie said, "then that's all I care about."

"Annabelle Blackstone," Finn said, cracking a grin for the first time that day as he continued searching the Internet. "Impossible to forget her first name. All the kids teased her about it. Belle sounds so... sweet, but the way she screeched at the kids to stay away from the ruins, they nicknamed her Hells Belle. You'll see what I mean. Her nose is a little crooked, maybe broken at some point, and she couldn't smile if her life depended on it. Nothing subtle about sweet little Belle. She was always jabbing her boney finger toward us like it was a dagger." Finn mocked her by emphasizing each word with a sharp jab of his finger. "You stay away!"

"She's not violent, though, right?" Sarah asked.

Finn shook his head. "Nothing like that. I'm sure she had good intentions... somewhere in that black heart of hers."

"How old was she when you knew her?"

"In her 80s, I'm guessing. That's why I'm thinking—praying—that she's passed on."

Sarah elbowed him sharply. "Don't wish for someone's death. Ever."

Finn's eyes widened at her reaction and nursed the ribs where she'd struck him. "Just praying for her peaceful passage."

Sarah scowled.

Finn pointed to her face with a wry grin. "Yes, that's exactly how Mrs. Blackstone looked. If you only knew..."

"Oh wow," Emmie interrupted. "Then she would be in her 90s. Probably not so scary now?"

Finn scoffed as he continued swiping through websites. "My experiences refute the possibility that a woman like that could ever grow less scary. But... we shall see." His focus narrowed until he stopped on one page and gasped as if he had seen a ghost. "Oh, dear God. Here she is. Still alive. Annabelle Blackstone, 23 East Dale Street."

"Far from here?" Emmie asked.

"Not far."

"Will you be okay if we go there now?" Sarah asked.

Finn shrugged. "Not okay, but what choice do I have? She *is* the expert on all the ruins and treasure and all the curse stuff. Guaranteed, if she can still open that shrill beak of hers."

"What makes her the expert?" Emmie asked, while standing up with the others.

Finn stepped toward the door after slipping his phone into his pocket. "She's a direct descendent of the Aztec priest who placed the curse."

7

Emmie hadn't seen Finn that anxious in months. He hadn't said a word since they'd left the house, and from the back seat, she watched him clutch the steering wheel while making sharp corners through narrow, rolling San Diego streets until finally lifting his hand briefly to gesture ahead.

"That's the place," he said.

"You can wait in the car, if you'd like." Emmie gave a wry grin, attempting to lighten the mood. "We got this."

Finn rolled his eyes and shrugged. "I'm not afraid, but don't expect some sweet old lady to answer the door. Mrs. Blackstone was a bit... abrasive, I guess."

"I can handle difficult people," Sarah said from the passenger seat.

Finn smiled warmly at her. "You're still with me, I see."

"Exactly my point."

Parking on the street beside a row of palm trees and Spanish-style homes with clay-tile roofs and stucco exteriors, he turned off the engine and pointed to Mrs. Blackstone's house. It was a small beige rambler with a simple wooden fence lining the yard. The landscaping looked as if no one had tended to it in decades, with overgrown shrubs reaching up to the windows and a layer of dirt made clear in the beaming sunshine. Despite its neglect, there was a certain charm in the way the owner had let the original style of the home shine through, standing out from the other newer and renovated homes further up the block.

"Maybe," Finn said while turning toward them, "she won't even remember me. But either way, we'll keep this short. Just get the information we need and get out of there. Okay?"

Sarah touched his arm. "Was it really *that* bad?"

Finn looked at her for a long moment. "Yes."

Gathering at the wooden gate, Finn pushed it open and led them up the sidewalk to the front door. The window blinds were closed, with no sign that the old woman was even home.

"Maybe we should have called," Emmie whispered.

"She kept to herself, mostly," Finn said. "So probably home."

Several dream catchers dangled on the woman's front porch and a set of bamboo chimes clicked gently in the breeze. There were some more Spanish influenced items nearby, some of them reminiscent of Day of the Dead celebration.

Finn rang the doorbell and stepped back, but seemed to put on a brave face for them as he spoke under his breath. "I guess your childhood traumas are the hardest ones to overcome. Funny how she can still get under my skin after all these years."

"Then this is therapeutic," Sarah said. "You'll laugh on the way out, I bet."

"I'll take that bet."

Emmie glanced around for a video doorbell or other surveillance equipment, but there were no signs of technology anywhere. And no signs of someone coming to the door either. After the silence lingered for two minutes, Finn knocked again.

"Just as well," Finn said, seemingly relieved.

Then a noise came from inside. The rustling of footsteps against old wood creaked just inside the door. A moment later, the door opened, but instead of the cranky old woman Finn had described, a tall, vibrant woman in a pink and white kitchen apron stood in front of them. She stood hunched forward, her long gray hair pulled back into a ponytail. She *did* have a crooked nose, like Finn had mentioned, but nothing like the old hag Emmie had imagined.

The woman's eyes were watering and red as she brushed her cheek with the back of her hand. "Sorry, I didn't hear you. I was cooking and the onions..." She looked at Emmie, then Sarah, then settled on Finn. "Do I know you?"

"Mrs. Blackstone?" Finn asked. "Finn Adams. Do you remember me?"

She squinted at him and leaned forward before her face lit up. "I do! Good heavens, what are you doing here, young Finn? Come in!" She moved aside and gestured for them to step inside. "I didn't recognize you. You know, I don't have my glasses on and those awful onions."

Emmie glanced at Finn suspiciously. Was this the evil witch Finn had warned them about? He shrugged as they stepped inside, but the tension remained on his face.

"I hope we're not bothering you," Emmie said.

"Not at all." Mrs. Blackstone turned back and grabbed Finn's arm, leaning in toward him with a somber face. "I heard about your dad. And Neil took us all by surprise. I'm so sorry. So tragic, and both so young."

The smell of seafood filled the air but also the smell of old books, which lined the floor-to-ceiling bookcases in a small reading room near the front of the house. The antique furniture filling every room was faded and dark, contrasted with colorful pottery, bright artwork and an earthy decor straight out of the 1970s.

Mrs. Blackstone took off her apron and tossed it aside sharply, revealing a soft, flowery dress. The woman's harsh stare and dark eyes came through for a moment as she seemed to scrutinize each of them. But it faded quickly as she gestured to the living room.

"Please have a seat." Mrs. Blackstone stepped over to a small desk with an outdated and probably non-operational rotary phone, grabbed her glasses and slipped them on.

The word *angular* came to mind while observing Mrs. Blackstone. She had long arms and broad shoulders, with sharp, assertive movements as if she wasn't afraid to take charge of the situation. Her narrow eyes commanded respect.

Emmie sat down on the couch beside Sarah and Finn sat opposite her, while Mrs. Blackstone dropped into an oversized, worn leather recliner. Judging by the assortment of TV remotes, magazines and a foot massager at the base of the chair, she spent many hours sitting in it. Making herself comfortable, she didn't lean back but instead sat upright and listened intently, clasping her fingers together as a wave of essential tremors shook her hands involuntarily during the conversation.

"Did you stop by to tell me about your father?" Mrs. Blackstone asked Finn. "Dr. Moretti left a message on my phone. I'm so sorry for your loss."

"It's something else." Finn glanced down. "We were on our way to the ruins..."

The old woman lost her smile and the hint of a scowl formed. Was her true personality—the cruel figure Finn had dreaded so much—slipping through? "Why would you go back up there again? You kids just can't seem to leave that place alone. Remember what I told you? All the stories?"

"Oh, I remember."

"I hope you're not thinking of digging for treasure again. Just because your godfather owns that land doesn't mean it's a giant sandbox to play in. Is that what you're planning?"

"No, nothing like that."

She scoffed. "I suspect you already went up there and scoured every corner of that property. What did you find? You're more likely to find a grave than a treasure."

Finn nodded. "I need your advice, that's all. You were always so knowledgeable about the ruins. I wanted to take my friends there and show them where I grew up."

"It's better to leave it alone, don't you think? It was far from an ideal place for a child to grow up, but that wasn't my decision. All I could do was try to steer you away from the worst parts of it." She looked at each of them. "You all know about the curse by now?"

The woman's stare was intimidating. Emmie dared to shake her head. "Only some rumors."

"It's real. Look at the gravestones that line the old cemetery next to it. They stretch back hundreds of years. People buried a long line of cursed souls there, along with plenty of newer ones. At least Marc purchased the property and promptly fenced it off to keep more misguided souls from losing everything in that place. Things seemed to have cooled down a bit. He understands the draw the treasure has on people, even if he doesn't believe the worst of it." She nodded with a firm expression. "At least he's gotten it under control. But there is *no reason* you need to go back there. None at all."

While Mrs. Blackstone's gaze turned back to Finn, Emmie glanced around the living room. A group of paintings against the wall behind the old woman caught her attention. One folk-style painting of a landscape with a coarse texture beneath the paint focused on dark colors and shades of gray, but the shapes and details came through on an almost subliminal level. Buried within the hills and fields, there were structures—the ruins? The designs were more abstract than anything she'd seen before, yet there was a clear play of light and darkness as if the artist had tried to capture the moment of greatest contrast between the final moment of a brilliant sunset and the murky haze of darkness as the night swallowed the landscape.

Another painting, housed in a horizontal frame, caught her eye longer than the others. Something within the artwork disturbed her on a deeper level, although it seemed the painting was composed of nothing more than a few grand strokes of the brush on a black canvas. But the longer she stared, the more the forms seemed to come to life, like a shadow emerging from a fog.

"It draws you in," Mrs. Blackstone said.

Emmie looked back at the woman, who was staring at her with a curious expression. The woman's eyes held a "knowing" that caught Emmie off guard.

"The ruins," the old woman continued. "There's a lot of history behind that place. How much has Finn told you about it?"

Sarah looked at Finn before answering. "A little."

Finn sat silently with his arms over his chest, watching Mrs. Blackstone with overt contempt.

"It's just an old Spanish mission, of course," the woman said, "on the surface, but a couple of hundred years ago it was a much different place."

"Here she goes," Finn cut in.

Sarah frowned at him.

Mrs. Blackstone continued, "Driven by the rumors of the vast horde of gold, the outlaws from the north, mostly failed gold rush miners and crop businessmen, took over the mission and slaughtered many of the missionaries and churchmen in their pursuit of the treasure. Additionally, they killed many locals who refused to cooperate and held countless families hostage, threatening to burn the town to the ground unless they revealed the treasure's location. After ransacking the village and killing many innocent people, it took an act of God to bring it all to an end. An earthquake brought it all crumbling down in a single night. Most of the outlaws were crushed inside the mission where they had set up residence. The place was never the same after that, and the churchmen who survived the ordeal reiterated that the curse the Aztecs had placed on the treasure was to blame, although they made some changes to the exact wording. No longer brought down by the Aztec gods, the curse now became the will of the Christian God, and that curse, originating from my ancestors, is why the treasure should never be recovered."

"Nobody ever found it?" Emmie asked.

Mrs. Blackstone gave a slight shake of her head. "No."

Finn scoffed. "Because it doesn't exist. There's no proof it ever existed."

Mrs. Blackstone looked at Finn. "Please tell me that after all I've told you about the Santa Isabella Mission, that you aren't *truly* planning to take these lovely two ladies to a place so full of tragedy? Better to leave it alone as I told Marc so many, many times. But I know he only sees the historical value—none of my *opinions* seem to make a difference to him—so he just let the children play wherever they wanted. It saddens me to think of what would happen if someone got hurt as a result of his negligence, to end up just another tragic tale in its long history." She looked at Finn.

"I'm not a kid anymore," he said.

"Of course not," Mrs. Blackstone said. "You know, I was only trying to protect you. I know you don't appreciate it."

"I *do* appreciate it," Finn said with a hint of strained impatience in his voice. "But we just wanted to explore and have fun. We were just kids, you know? All the talk of treasure… we knew it wasn't real, but it's every person's dream, right? To dig for buried treasure?"

"The treasure *is* real," Mrs. Blackstone said. "It may not still be there—it's possible it was moved—but it exists. And my ancestors are watching over it—protecting it—to this day and forever if necessary."

"Are there any records of the men who arrived here with the treasure? Historical evidence that they passed through here?"

Mrs. Blackstone opened her mouth to answer, but Finn cut her off. "It's not a curse driving people to this place. Greed is to blame for all the deaths you're about to reference. Sure, I've heard the stories, but there's nothing that can't be explained through sheer human nature. Take the California gold rush. That's a perfect example of what I'm talking about. Lots of death followed the initial discovery—murder, robberies, mine collapses, disease—even though nobody cursed the gold they found. Money always brings out the worst in people. It's the same thing here. The stories of buried gold attracted the worst of the worst, and they did what humans always do—kill. There's no point in blaming their evil actions on a curse. No, it all stems from simple, raw human nature."

"Yes," Mrs. Blackstone said with a smug grin. "Greed is the great deadly sin of our times, but not greater than the curse that sits at the heart of the ruins."

"Are you sure that's where the treasure is?" Finn asked. "Do you know the exact location?"

"I wouldn't tell you, or anyone, if I did." Mrs. Blackstone pressed her lips together for a moment. "Hernán Cortés's men hid the gold well, but my ancestors made sure the Spaniards left without it, and they will never allow it to leave. Not without a great sacrifice. So many have paid the price already, even before seeing a glint of gold. It's still there, in the place. I know that because I can feel it." She looked at Emmie and Sarah. "And I think your friends can also feel it, can't you?"

Emmie's eyes widened as the woman seemed to peer through her.

"No need to pretend, young lady," Mrs. Blackstone said in a stern voice. "Not here. Not with me. I can see the fire in your eyes. You've seen things, and I have too."

"She hasn't seen anything," Finn said. "We came here to learn more of the curse and the history of the ruins, for the sake of my friends. They wanted to know what happened."

"It's just as I told you." Mrs. Blackstone leaned toward Sarah. "Do you feel its darkness calling to you? Has the treasure filled your dreams? Don't let it pull you in like the others. The catacombs beneath the ruins are stacked with the dead for a reason. So many of its permanent guests went there for the same reason —to find the source—because they also were drawn in like insects to the fire."

"If it's so dangerous," Finn said, "why did I see you go to the ruins so many times alone? I believe in ghosts. God knows, I do. But all the stories... they were just meant to scare us."

Mrs. Blackstone tilted her head as if in deep thought. "It's true I meant to scare you, but that fear is necessary, in this case. The ruins are a sacred place, and I went down there as much as possible in my younger days to connect with my ancestors."

"You can see them? Your ancestors?" Emmie asked.

Mrs. Blackstone stared at her with piercing brown eyes. "I can hear them. And I feel their longing and desperation to end the cycle of death. So much sorrow lies within that place."

"So how *does* it end?" Sarah asked.

"The treasure's curse always ends in death. Always. There are no exceptions."

"It can't go on forever. How would someone go about breaking the curse?"

"When the treasure is returned to my people, or the gods are satisfied. I see neither case ever happening because the tormented souls cannot let go." Mrs. Blackstone leaned back in her seat as if the conversation had come to an end. "So, what is the *real* reason you came here to see me, Finn? I know you were frightened of me as a child, but it was necessary for me to do my job. I kept you and the girls away from the most treacherous areas, didn't I? So, I succeeded. What did you *really* come here to ask me? I can see the question in your eyes."

Finn looked at her for a moment, then leaned forward with one hand clasped around the other. "I *do* have another question for you. Did my dad talk about the ruins and the curse before he died?"

"He did." She sat back in her seat. "So many questions when he arrived, and like a child, he listened with wide eyes and an open mind as I answered each one."

8

"So, you're the one who filled his head with all that nonsense about curses." Finn's face reddened.

Mrs. Blackstone stared at him curiously. "Stephen wanted to know more about the Mission. He was determined to know everything about it, so I reluctantly gave him a tour of the cave system. He deserved to know the complete truth about what happened."

"I thought Marc sealed up the cave's entrance," Sarah said.

"Oh, he did," Mrs. Blackstone said. "A big metal door to keep out the curious. But there is another way inside, although not as convenient. Stephen didn't object, and he insisted on being allowed to explore the area to the fullest. I obliged, if only to protect him from the spirits who would have done him harm."

"You failed," Finn mumbled as his face tightened.

"I don't know what you mean."

Emmie stood. It was better to end the conversation now before things escalated. "Thank you so much for your help."

Sarah stood a moment later and turned toward the door, gesturing at Finn to do the same.

He let out a sigh as he followed her, and her guidance seemed to diffuse whatever anger had welled up inside of him. "Finn, it's not her fault."

"My fault?" Mrs. Blackstone asked. "Did something happen?"

"Nothing happened," Finn snapped at her. "We've heard enough."

"Did you see Stephen?" Mrs. Blackstone asked, her question pointed at Emmie. "In a vision?"

Emmie shook her head. "Nothing like that."

"You did." A pained expression swept over Mrs. Blackstone's face. "I'm so sorry. Stephen had so many questions. What could I do? I was only trying to steer him in the right direction, away from danger, away from the ruins, but he was so determined."

"Relentless," Finn said.

"Yes." Mrs. Blackstone nodded. "Stephen was driven."

"Did he say why he was drawn to the ruins?" Emmie asked on the way out.

"He didn't," Mrs. Blackstone said. "So many are drawn by its dark energy, but Stephen... he wasn't one to believe in such things. But for those who visit the ruins, the lure of hidden treasure—the dream, it's like a mirage in the desert—soon begins to gnaw at the back of one's mind, as it did for so many before him."

Finn scoffed as Sarah led him toward the door. He opened his mouth to say something on the way out, but the words came out as an exasperated sigh.

Emmie hurried ahead and opened the door before turning back toward Mrs. Blackstone. The old woman looked defeated, her face angled down and her shoulders hunched forward as they hurried away.

"I never meant to upset you," Mrs. Blackstone said softly. "Or anyone."

"Thank you again," Emmie said. "It's been a difficult time for everyone."

It was dark by the time they arrived back at Finn's house. They found Tiffany in the dining room, surrounded by several open boxes as she sorted through stacks of paper strewn across the table and floor.

Finn stepped toward her. "I can help."

Tiffany waved him away. "I've got this, for now."

Examining the nearest box, he shuffled through a pile of papers. "You can't do this all by yourself."

"It's under control. Marc and Amelia offered to stop by on Thursday to help me sort through all the bills and accounts. Your father handled everything, I'm afraid, which leaves me a bit overwhelmed."

Finn nodded, moving around to the other side of the table beside his mother. "I can stay longer, if you want."

"Not necessary. I know plenty of accountants. Where did you go today?"

Finn seemed distracted by something he'd found in one of the boxes, so Emmie answered, "We stopped to see an old woman Finn used to know."

Tiffany looked at her curiously, then turned to Finn. "Who?"

"Mrs. Blackstone," Finn said without making eye contact.

Tiffany's eyes widened. "What on earth for?"

Finn flipped through a few more papers, gave up, then closed the box and pushed it aside. His gaze stopped on an extra cellphone beside his mother. Picking it up without asking, the lock screen switched on to reveal a photo of Tiffany and Stephen, leaning in against each other with the top of their heads almost touching. Finn silently stared at the photo.

Tiffany watched him without blinking, then spoke a little louder. "Why did you go to see Mrs. Blackstone?"

Finn switched off the screen but held the phone. "I wanted to know more about the ruins and the curse. It's fascinating, don't you think?"

Tiffany shook her head almost imperceptibly. "I don't understand why anyone would find that place interesting."

"Have you ever been out there?" Sarah asked.

Tiffany leaned back in her chair. "Marc took us a few times. I suppose it's interesting on a certain level, for historians maybe, or the superstitious, but I expect some developer will drop an apartment complex on the land one of these days. And that'll be the end to any talk of a curse."

"So, you and your husband never believed in it?" Emmie asked.

"Heavens no."

"Mom," Finn asked, "is this Dad's phone?"

"Yes."

He held it with a strange curiosity. "What's the passcode?"

Tiffany looked at him skeptically. "What for?"

"There's a ton of unanswered messages. Have you gone through any of these?"

"I haven't had time." Tiffany sank forward. "I suppose Amelia will help me take care of all that. But... if you'd like to do it, the passcode is the month and year of your father's birthday. Do you remember it?"

"I do." Finn typed it in, and the screen unlocked. "Dad never was good at security."

"You can have your father's phone, if you need it."

Finn stared at the home screen solemnly. "I already have a phone, Mom. I'll go through the messages tonight and answer as many of them as I can."

"Thank you." Tiffany leaned toward him. "You're all I have in this world now, Finn. Do you know that?"

Finn glanced at Emmie and Sarah, then gave his mother a brief hug. "You'll be okay."

Tiffany waved her hands over the papers on the table. "Are you sure about that?"

"Positive."

She straightened in her seat as if ready to continue her battle through the paperwork, then looked up at Emmie and Sarah. "Sorry, you must be tired. We can talk tomorrow."

"Sure." Finn headed toward the back door with his face buried in the phone, flipping through a series of screens and typing something.

They headed outside a moment later, making the short walk to the guesthouse. The caws of a raven broke the soothing quiet of the night. The cool breeze rustled the branches in the trees along the edge of the property, and something—someone—whispered Emmie's name in the wind that swept around them. Staring into the darkness, she didn't sense any spirits beyond the house, but couldn't shake the feeling that someone was aware of her presence.

Inside the guesthouse, they gathered around the small kitchen table where Tiffany had placed a note explaining she'd left pizza in the refrigerator. Finn was still focused on the phone in his hands, although he took time to dig out the pizza.

Taking a seat at the table beside Sarah, he ate the pizza and gestured to the phone. "This will help."

"The pizza?"

"The phone."

"How?"

"The GPS data. I can see where he went before he died. That might help explain what he was thinking before his heart attack."

Sarah stood and stepped over to a pile of boxes in the corner. Someone had labeled one of them as Christmas decorations. "What are these doing in here?"

Finn glanced over at them. "My parents have too much stuff."

She opened one, then pulled out a thick, gray photo album. "Doesn't look like Christmas decorations."

"I'm not surprised."

Sarah carried it over to the table and opened it. The photos were laid out four per page and showed a young Finn standing beside a blonde girl with her hair tucked beneath a baseball cap. Both were dressed as if they'd intended to go hiking, although the background showed lush green trees and sprawling grass.

Finn had his arm around her shoulders as she leaned in toward him with a wide grin.

"Who's this?" Sarah nudged Finn.

He looked at the photo then to Sarah. "Amelia, Marc's daughter."

Sarah scrutinized her. "She's pretty."

Finn scoffed. "Don't tell me you're jealous."

"Why would I be jealous?"

"You have that look in your eyes."

"Do I?" Sarah flipped to the next page, but the photos of them together only continued. Not only Finn and Amelia now, but Neil and another girl.

Finn looked away. "The other girl is Paige. Amelia's sister. Neil had a crush on her."

"So, you and Amelia were...?" Sarah asked Finn, not looking up from the photos.

"We were a team, the four of us, and we spent a lot of time together back then. Lots of fun and laughs and some bad times. But... we were kids. Nothing to worry about."

"I'm not worried."

"Good." Finn turned his attention back to the phone.

Sarah gestured to a photo of Neil. "He was handsome."

Without looking over, Finn nodded. "Neil was a great guy, despite his flaws." His eyes seemed to water. "When I tell you that the ruins were our playground, I really mean it. We spent a *lot* of time out there. Every summer for years. I don't regret a minute of it."

Sarah moved to the next page. One of the photos showed all four friends standing together, arm in arm. Amelia, Finn, Neil, and Paige.

Emmie leaned closer to get a better look and Sarah slid the photo album over, turning it toward her. The background showed a glimpse of the ruins, as Finn had described it. A wall of stones leading to a doorway stood directly behind them, although the environment was out of focus.

Finn let out a heavy sigh while staring at the phone and settled into his seat. "That's just what I was afraid of."

"What did you find?" Emmie asked him.

Finn took his time answering, running his hands through his hair and leaning back with an expression of disdain. "Of course... Belle must have filled my dad's head with all kinds of superstitious BS, because he drove out to the ruins only a few hours before he died."

"We need to see this place," Emmie said.

"Sure," Finn said. "We can go there tomorrow. No problem."

"What do you think he was looking for out there? If Belle did convince him the curse was real, then why would he have gone out there?"

"The treasure?" Sarah asked.

Finn scoffed. "My dad would never have bothered to go looking for it. Never."

"Then why?"

Finn focused on the phone again, working through something while forming a curious expression. "Well, this is odd. He went to the ruins, yes, but he didn't go straight home afterwards."

"Where did he go then?"

"To Marc's house."

9

Marc's estate wasn't more than ten miles from Finn's parents' house, although it took them almost thirty minutes to get there through the heavy traffic along the edge of San Diego and out across the winding roads overlooking the Pacific Ocean. Palm trees lined the area, along with Spanish-style homes with vast properties stretching tens of acres for each estate.

Turning onto a narrow road, Finn gestured to the land. "This all belongs to Marc's family."

Emmie's eyes widened. "Your dad had wealthy friends."

"He had a way with words, that's for sure. His expertise in real estate investing gave him an advantage when schmoozing with the upper-class."

She marveled at the vast field of grapes that seemed to stretch as far as they could see in every direction. The vineyard's flowering vines hung on the weathered rows of trellises, radiating the soft morning dew of each bright green plant. There were teams of Hispanic workers tending to the vines on foot, and some moved on ATVs, towing carts full of equipment behind them.

Finn had called Marc before they'd arrived, and judging by

the light-hearted tone in Finn's voice, their unexpected visit wouldn't be a problem.

Marc opened the door with arms open wide as if to embrace them all at once. "So good to see you!"

"Sorry for the short notice, Marc," Finn said.

"No problem. Not a problem at all." He gestured for them to step inside when a black cat slipped between their feet and darted across the lawn.

Sarah scrambled to catch the cat, but Marc waved it away. "Nevermind him," Marc said. "Pluto has a mind all his own. He'll come scratching at the door when he's ready to come back."

The formal suit and tie Marc had worn at the funeral were gone, replaced with khaki pants and a light blue polo shirt. No doubt, his version of "dressing down."

Stepping aside and making a wide gesture, he guided them through the front door.

Classical music came from every direction, filling the air with a Mozart concerto that Emmie hadn't heard since college when she'd taken a music history class.

"I would have prepared food..." Marc said.

Finn shook his head. "We were driving by on our way to the beach, and I wanted to show them the vineyards."

A dog barked from another room.

Marc seemed unconcerned with the noise, but Finn turned toward it. "I thought Scrubs passed away?"

"She did, I'm afraid. Got another dog, a rescue Pitbull named Lenore. I usually let her run free through the house, although I keep her locked up in my office when we have guests."

Stepping through the living room, the elegant Spanish architecture and warm colors welcomed them inside. Terracotta tiles lined the floor and exposed wooden beams crisscrossed the ceiling. Sunlight filtered in through wrought iron grilles that adorned the windows, casting broken patterns of light and shadows across the room. A massive fireplace took center stage, its intricate tile work depicting scenes of a Spanish mission.

But a stuffed raven perched on the mantel over the fireplace caught Emmie off guard. Its sleek black feathers were ruffled just enough to give the illusion of life, and a sparkle of light reflected off its beady glass eyes as if her presence might break its fixated stare at any moment.

Passing into the kitchen without a pause, wine-themed decorations of various designs surrounded them on every side, made from used corks and bottles, framed paintings, faux vines running down the sides of cabinets, and wood plaques. Both the formal dining area off to the left and the casual dining area displayed variations on the same theme, with each room focusing on a homage to either Californian, French, or Spanish vineyards.

"You came at a bad time, though, I'm afraid," Marc said. "I'm on call, so don't be surprised if I have to leave for the hospital. A cardiac surgeon is always on call."

Finn turned to Emmie and Sarah. "He works at the top hospital in San Diego."

Reaching the kitchen, Marc turned back to Finn. "I thought I might never see you again."

"I always knew I'd be back again someday."

"I wish it was under better circumstances," Marc said. "You know, my home is your home."

Finn nodded warmly. "I appreciate that. Thank you."

"I mean it. And your friends are welcome here anytime too. I'm happy to show them around Raven House Vineyards. There's so much of Finn's history here." He grinned at Sarah. "Did he tell you any of it?"

"A little," Sarah said. "He mentioned something about treasure hunting."

"Oh, the treasure." Marc scoffed. "Those tales never seem to die. But of course, there is no treasure, or someone would've found it by now. I'm guessing the truth is it never existed or someone before my time hauled it away. Believe me, if I knew where it was, I would've scavenged it long ago." He laughed.

Walking them over to a bar against one wall, he opened a wine refrigerator and gestured to several bottles. "What kind would you like? Amontillado? Merlot? Chardonnay? Just name your favorite. I have no preference."

Emmie scanned the names on the bottles and stopped on one. "What's that Pinot Noir Reserve?"

"Only the best Pinot that Raven House ever produced. You won't regret it." He pulled the bottle off the rack and poured a glass for each of them before they could object, then poured himself a glass of Perrier water as they sipped the wine. Emmie basked in the fruity flavors as the wine soothed her throat on the way down.

The classical music seemed to come from everywhere, and the fruity smell of wine filled the air. There was nothing to do but relax and enjoy the moment. After taking a few sips, she even forgot why they'd stopped by.

Several deep, foreboding chimes from an ornate gothic grandfather clock snapped her back to reality. The towering clock with three spires along the top stood against the dining room wall, chiming ten times before it allowed them to return to their conversation. The pendulum swung hypnotically beneath the antique face with a series of brass weights hanging within the shadows of the glass cabinet.

Lenore's muffled barking from the next room seemed to agitate Marc. He grabbed the bottle of wine by the neck and gestured toward the side patio door. "We should go outside. Lenore won't stop until you're gone, and it's such a nice day..."

None of them objected as he led them outside where they each took a seat at a table overlooking the vineyard.

There were dozens more workers in the field on this side of the house. Emmie gestured toward them. "What do you do with all the wine?"

"You think I drink it myself?" Marc laughed and grinned while patting his stomach. "Wish I could. But it's not mine. Not anymore. After my wife died, I hired another company to do all the work, although I keep a percentage of the profits and stash away a few cases of the finest Reserve wines each year in my cellar. That suits me well."

"Finn," Emmie said in a mocking, harsh voice, "why didn't you ever tell us about this place?"

"It used to be Finn's second home before he took off to explore the world. His sisters—" Marc laughed. "My daughters, Amelia and Paige, got along so well when they were kids. I often joked to Stephen that my godfather status might change to father-in-law someday." He turned to Finn.

Finn glanced at Sarah, who gave a quick grin before looking away.

"Have you spoken with them lately? Social media?" Marc continued.

"Not since Neil died," Finn said.

Marc nodded solemnly. "Everything seems to have stopped after Neil passed away. We've got a lot to talk about. But I know you said on the phone you had some questions?"

Finn's smile faded. "It's about my dad. I think Mrs. Blackstone was feeding him some nonsense before he died, and I'm wondering if he came out here or said anything to you about it."

Marc nodded and met Finn's gaze. "He did. The poor guy stopped by the morning he passed away. He didn't look well, I'm afraid. You know, his heart problems were getting worse, and he didn't have time to schedule an appointment to see me in the office."

"You were his doctor?" Sarah asked.

"Heart specialist," Marc answered with a smile. "We went to college together—University of California, along with Tiffany and my late wife. We all met there, but I went on to medical school, and he pursued a business degree. He was one of my first patients after setting up my practice here, and we shared a lot of the same interests. Golf, sailing, and wine... I was even the best man at their wedding. Yes, we've shared a lot of ups and downs.

But after Neil passed away, Stephen was never the same—maybe it contributed to his heart problems. He was a wonderful man."

Finn gave a faint smile tinged with sadness. "He didn't mention anything about Mrs. Blackstone?"

"Nothing." Marc shook his head. "He hadn't brought up her name in years. Why do you ask?"

"It's probably nothing." Finn's expression showed that he seemed a little embarrassed to even bring up the subject.

"Did you talk with Stephen before he passed? I know he hoped to reconcile with you someday."

"No reconciliation." Finn glanced at Emmie, seemingly looking for a way to answer Marc's question without mentioning ghosts or the phone's GPS data that had led them there. "I—"

"We found a note from her in his office," Emmie jumped in. "It said something about a curse."

Marc scoffed. "Ah, the evil curse. Mrs. Blackstone doesn't let anyone forget the Mission's history, does she? She's got a point though, and she knows better than anyone what happened here hundreds of years ago. Something awful did happen here back then, but that woman would have you believe there's an alien spaceship buried beneath the old Mission if you listened to her long enough. What did the note say?"

Emmie opened her mouth to answer, but Finn cut her off.

"I tore it up," Finn said. "Got a little pissed off after reading it..."

"You've always had a bit of a temper," Marc said.

Finn glanced down. "I'm working on it. But it was clear that she was trying to scare him, like she always does. I'm wondering if that might have contributed to his heart attack."

Marc smirked. "The curse?"

"The added stress."

Marc seemed to consider it. "Stephen wasn't one to believe in things like that, but... Mrs. Blackstone does have a way with words. Who knows what she told him... But I guess that *does* explain his frazzled appearance when he stopped by here that morning."

Finn frowned. "Mrs. Blackstone got him worked up about something."

Marc sipped his water while staring out at the vineyard. "Last time I saw Stephen, he was a nervous wreck and wouldn't stop asking me to go with him to the ruins. So prone to anxiety—had a weak heart, you know—but I talked him down. So much fear in his eyes, like something was out to get him."

"Why did he want to go there?" Sarah asked.

"He never said exactly. But my impression was that he'd gotten the itch to look for the treasure—everyone considers its existence at one time or another—and I assumed something, or someone, had finally lit that fire with him. Never said anything about the curse to me, anyway, but he wouldn't let it go until I finally had to back away and let him have his treasure hunt. He went off alone, and that was the last time I saw him alive."

"So he didn't mention anything about Mrs. Blackstone or the curse?" Finn asked.

Marc shook his head. "He knew how I felt about her crazy theories, so I guess he kept it to himself. If only he'd confided his concerns with me that morning. He was a good man, my closest friend, and I'll miss him dearly." Marc held out his glass and made a toast. They clinked their glasses together and drank.

A noise came from inside the house, and Marc glanced toward the patio door. "And I believe Amelia has arrived."

Only moments later, the door opened and a young, blonde-haired woman with a bright smile stepped out onto the patio. Her violet dress flowed over her healthy body.

"Amelia," Finn's smile widened.

She glanced at each of them with radiant, welcoming eyes before rushing toward Finn.

He practically jumped out of his chair to hug her as Sarah took another sip of wine and smiled, watching them embrace.

"Sorry," she said. "I couldn't make it to the funeral. Did you get my flowers?"

"Mom put them beside the coffin, then took them to the house."

"So sorry to hear about your dad." She watched him, even as her eyes watered a bit.

Finn nodded solemnly and glanced down.

The silence lingered for a long moment before she looked him up and down. "So, where have you been? I thought I might never see you again."

"Living in Minnesota now. I never planned to come out here again."

"Why not?"

"Too much..." He closed his mouth.

She nodded. "I get it. How long are you staying?"

"Not long. A few days." He turned toward Sarah. "This is Sarah, my girlfriend."

"Oh, nice to meet you, Sarah." Amelia extended her hand. "You're so beautiful."

"And you." Sarah shook her hand. "I love your dress."

Amelia glanced down at it, then turned to Finn. "A far cry from what I used to wear. Right, Finn?"

"I'm not sure I've ever seen you wear a dress before." Finn looked around. "Where's Paige, by the way?"

Marc stepped over. "Paige is off traveling the world with a gentleman named Liam. Do you know the young man?"

Finn shook his head. "Someone she met at work?"

"She quit her museum technician job at the Natural History Museum shortly after meeting him. Maybe not the best decision she's ever made, but she always was one to travel. Such an adventurous soul. I suppose she'll be back when she's ready." He turned to Amelia. "Amelia, maybe take them out to the ruins. Show them around."

Amelia turned to Finn and grinned. "Glad to! Got your shovel ready? Remember all the time we spent in that place?"

"How can I forget?" Finn said. "Treasure hunting is fun, but such a waste of time."

Amelia turned to Emmie and Sarah. "Would you like to see the ruins? We can go there now if you'd like."

"Yes, absolutely."

Marc's phone rang a moment later. He checked his text messages in front of them while putting down his glass of water suddenly with an irritated expression. "I'm afraid I can't go with you. They need me at the hospital. Got to keep those hearts pumping."

"I understand," Sarah said.

"She does," Finn added. "Sarah's a nurse."

Marc's face seemed to approve. "Emmie mentioned that at the reception. Amelia is working toward her nursing degree, so you'll have a lot to talk about, I'm sure. Nursing is such a difficult job—so much admiration for all the nurses I work with. I keep talking about retiring one of these days, but they're a bit short-staffed at the moment." He flipped through his messages before switching off his phone. "They just keep calling and calling... The incessant sound of beating hearts fills my ears all day and my dreams at night."

"Dad, you'd die of boredom if you stayed home all the time," Amelia said. "You can't retire."

"You're probably right." He grinned. "I asked the Director at the hospital when I might hang up my scrubs—an older woman with the eye of a vulture—and she squawked at me like the Raven in that poem by Edgar Allan Poe, you know. '*Nevermore. Nevermore.*' It's a bit gloomy there sometimes." Marc looked at Amelia as he started to leave and gestured to the guests. "Give them anything they need."

"I got this, Dad," Amelia said.

Marc went into the house without glancing back.

Amelia touched her hands together and seemed to bubble at the idea of showing them around. "So, we're off to the ruins."

10

There was a spirit nearby. Emmie was sure of it. Probably more than one. The sense that someone was watching her seemed to come from every direction.

The feelings grew stronger after she climbed into the rental car with Finn and Sarah.

"Do you feel that?" Emmie asked over Sarah's shoulder from the back seat.

Sarah turned back. "I do."

Finn gave a concerned glance as he followed Amelia's SUV out along a paved road past the vineyards. "If you see any spirits, please keep it to yourself this time. This place holds a lot of fond memories, and I'd like to keep it that way."

Emmie grinned. "Don't like the idea that you might have accidentally played tag with ghosts?"

"We didn't play tag." Finn smirked. "But... no."

Sarah turned to him. "We're bound to encounter something —someone—considering its past. So, your dad *never* came here with you?"

"Never," Finn said. "Just the kids. I'm inclined to think he dropped Neil and me off here to keep us out of his hair for the day, knowing that all the digging for the treasure would wear us out. Neil always dreamed of finding it one day, but nobody *really* believed any of that stuff when I grew up—not the treasure or the curse or any tortured spirits haunting the place."

"I guess we're about to find out," Emmie said.

The paved road ended, and they continued toward the ruins over a winding gravel road through sparse groups of trees and rocky terrain toward the edge of the desert. Beyond the hills and trees, the landscape seemed to extend to the horizon with no end in sight.

To the right, the ocean wasn't more than a mile away and the smell of saltwater hung in the air, although they couldn't see it from where they stood.

After the ruins came into view, Emmie expected to see a host of spirits waiting for them. But... nothing. The ruins lived up to their name. Barely a single structure stood on the property, except for the face of a building with a single doorway. All the other buildings had crumbled long ago, leaving just the foundations behind—piles of stones like an ancient Roman structure. Grass and trees surrounded the structures, which nestled along the side of a hill facing the ocean, and the hint of a cliff jutted up through the earth just beyond. Piles of stones and rubble that had once been walls and ceilings lay abandoned at the base of each structure, many of them still holding together despite the destruction. The skill and craftsmanship of the original builders had helped to preserve it all for so many years, with rows and columns of stone still displaying the grandeur of what the mission looked like hundreds of years earlier. A single massive stone wall stood with a window opening centered near the top. It was the tallest structure among the ruins, coming to a peak at the center with sloping sides where the roof had attached to it. The other structures rose only to eye level, at the most.

After Finn stopped the car, Emmie stepped out and let the breeze rustle her hair as she scanned the area. "I thought there'd be more to see here."

"Nope," Finn said. "This is it. From what I know about the

place, most of it collapsed during an earthquake a hundred years ago. Whatever was left got carted away for salvage or picked apart by thieves."

Sarah's face was turning pale again.

Emmie walked beside her and spoke softly, "Want to leave?"

Sarah shook her head. "Nothing I can't handle."

They hurried a bit to catch up with Amelia, who had already reached the edge of the ruins. The nearest structure was a lone wall only a few feet high, held up by a pile of crumbled stones on both sides. Judging by the angles and design, Emmie concluded they were approaching the base of the mission. The Spanish architecture was clear everywhere despite the destruction. Whoever had constructed the place had used a stucco-type mortar to fill the space between the stones. The surfaces were cracked and crumbling, but their skill had endured, and the care they'd taken showed they'd intended the place to last.

"Not much left to see here," Amelia said, gesturing to the remnants of a wall. "I always tell visitors that there's not much to look at but if you use your imagination and squint... If only the walls could talk, right?"

Emmie glanced at Sarah. Her friend was probably thinking the same thing. *If only it were that simple.*

Finn answered Amelia while stepping a little closer. "If only the stones could tell us where the treasure is buried."

Amelia laughed and grinned at Finn. "Wouldn't that be nice?"

"Where did the name Raven House come from?" Sarah asked. "The name of a previous owner?"

Amelia extended her grin. "No. The previous owner's name was Milton Conroy, but he officially coined the name because of all the ravens in the area, although he might have adopted it from the Spanish locals, who seem to hold a lot of reverence for this place. Everyone calls it that now, so it rubbed off on us when we bought the house. Dad didn't feel like ruffling any feathers, if you pardon my pun."

Sarah seemed satisfied with her answer and stared at another structure ahead.

Continuing their tour, Amelia led them further inside the compound to a crumbling area that stretched out hundreds of feet in every direction. Someone had taken the time to clear paths between the buildings, judging by the natural flow of the debris as it had cascaded over everything.

They skirted around a few more walls and arrived at what looked like the shallow stone stairs to what would have been a grand doorway. The outline of what it had been long ago was clear, although inside the separations between the rooms blurred within a mix of grass and moss and dirt.

"This is where you used to play Finn?" Sarah asked.

Finn's face lit up. "We used our imaginations a lot back then."

"It was always a lovely time with you," Amelia said, brushing her hand across a line of stones just inside the doorway. "We were so full of adventure back then, weren't we?"

Finn nodded and glanced toward the girls. "Amelia's dad bought the metal detectors. I just couldn't get enough of the idea that somewhere in this mess was a pile of gold. Funny how we always came up a little short."

"A lot short," Amelia added.

He laughed. "But that's every kid's dream, right? To find buried treasure? I suppose adults have the same dream."

"All a waste of time," Amelia said. "We never found a damn thing, if you don't count the occasional rattlesnake, spiders, and a few rusty nails. But we still had a blast."

"I miss it." Finn pointed to a hill overlooking a group of smaller structures where the land rippled as it faced the ocean. "Neil and Paige used to run to the highest point and hang out for hours. You can see everything from up there."

"I'd like to think they just sat and talked." Amelia gave a cheeky grin.

Finn glanced toward the ocean. "They were very close."

"Who knows what might have happened..." Amelia looked at Finn, then at Sarah before looking away. "I'll never forget it."

Sarah moved in closer beside Finn as they walked along, putting her arm under his as if helping him navigate the rugged terrain.

Amelia balanced herself over a floor of loose stones and entered a massive, raised area opposite the tallest wall on the other end of the compound. After waiting for the others to reach her, she gestured at the area with an air of reverence. "This is where they held mass. The native people gathered here to worship and were undoubtedly forced to convert to Catholicism. Everyone the missionaries encountered had to go through it—to save their souls—whether they liked it or not."

"The cruelty is astounding," Finn said.

"That's how things were back then," Sarah said.

Amelia moved across the open area and stood along the edge. "They *must* have had some gold here at one time, taken from the Aztecs or the locals or whoever, but it all disappeared. That's about all I know. All the talk of a curse came later, but I think someone just made that up to keep people from ransacking the place after the earthquake. Apparently, it didn't work, but it's amazing how superstitions can so easily become the stuff of legends."

Finn stepped up to where the priest would have stood during mass. "We used to pretend to hold mass here, just the four of us."

"And then we took turns making a confession," Amelia added with a grin.

He looked at her curiously, then silently broke into a wide smile.

Emmie studied the ruins for any clues to what might have happened there, but the looters, weather, and time had swept away all of that. "Is there a map of this place or what did you use to search for the treasure?"

"There's no map," Finn answered while turning to face

Amelia. "Wasn't Paige looking into that? She was into all that history stuff, right?"

"There's only so much information available about the place online, so she hit a roadblock right away, but she pushed it as far as she could drawing from all available sources. Maybe she'll publish a book one day."

"Was Belle one of them?" Finn asked.

"Unlikely," Amelia said. "You know Paige. She keeps herself grounded. Doesn't let herself get caught up in superstitions."

"Do you have her number? I'd like to stay in touch."

Amelia stepped back toward them, shaking her head. "I'm afraid she's been traveling a lot lately to remote locations. I don't even remember the names of the places anymore, overseas somewhere. She used to send text messages and emails to keep me updated, but her phone doesn't work at her current location. Probably out in the jungle somewhere."

Finn's eyes widened. "It's hard to picture Paige ever trekking through a jungle. She didn't seem the adventurous Indiana Jones-type girl. More likely to find her hiding away under a shady tree with a good book than trying to live it. A lot like me, really. She'd choose books over boots any day."

"She's changed a lot over the years. You'd be surprised."

Amelia then led them toward the side of the largest hill beyond the ruins to a cave covered with two large metal doors sealed shut with a chain strung through both handles. "My dad had to seal off the cave after a group of vandals came through and damaged the area. He found them camping there one afternoon. They were setting fires and marking up the walls with graffiti and who knows what else. But sealing it up has kept them out." Amelia kicked her shoe against the metal door and a hollow clang rang out.

"Can I take the girls inside?" Finn asked. "I'd love to show them the place."

Finn turned toward Sarah, his face full of sincere concern. "You okay with that?"

"Depends." She gave a curious look.

"On what?"

"On what's down there."

"The catacombs," Amelia said.

"Catacombs?" Emmie's eyes widened.

"Didn't Finn mention it?"

Emmie threw Finn a sharp stare. "No, he didn't."

"Does that scare you?" Amelia asked Sarah with a gentle smile.

"Not so much *scare* me." Sarah stared at the doors, seemingly building her emotional defenses for what might lie ahead. "Let's go."

"Great!" Amelia unlocked the padlock, pulled aside the chains and swept open the doors. "No electricity though. You'll need to use your phones to get around since I didn't bring flashlights."

Each of them switched their phones into flashlight mode and stepped down into the cool, musty air. The darkness echoed every sound, and the walls were riddled with graffiti. Kicking aside a few pieces of trash, Amelia descended along the sloping, shallow stone staircase.

Emmie struggled to keep from falling, grabbing at Finn's shirt along the way a few times as her shoes were far from ideal for hiking and there were no handrails to hang onto.

After reaching the bottom, the narrow walls opened further into a web of natural caves that looked no more inviting than the bottom of the ocean. Someone had altered the walls and floors long ago, judging by the tool marks, creating a more accessible and practical environment for visitors.

Emmie sensed the presence of many spirits within the darkness. No need for meditation. The energy was palpable as they continued forward, like a rising tide of dark energy, and she expected the worst at every turn. Her body tensed as the cool air chilled her, and she shivered a few times, although the others didn't seem to notice.

Amelia stopped where the cave branched off in two directions. She gestured to the opening on the left. "That's the way to the catacombs."

"How much further?" Sarah asked.

"Another hundred feet or so."

"Where does the other one go?" Emmie asked.

"The throne room," Finn said. "At least, that's what we called it back then. Just a big empty room with some sort of altar near the front. And then a few smaller rooms beyond that, as if someone might have lived down here or held ceremonies for the dead."

Emmie stared into the darkness. "How far does it go?"

"Who knows?" Amelia said. "It's uncharted and very dangerous. My dad and I went in as far as we could, but... nothing."

Finn watched Sarah carefully for a moment. "Want to go back?"

She seemed to contemplate the limits of her strength, but shook her head. "I want to stay with you."

They continued toward the catacombs, but only a moment later Sarah collapsed against Finn.

"Sarah!" Finn clutched her arm to keep her from falling while lowering her to the ground with great care. Her face was pale, and her eyes rolled up into the back of her head while letting out an almost inaudible gasp.

At the same time, from the corner of Emmie's eyes, the shadows were moving. The pressure of bad energy surrounded them and filled her mind. This was not a place to take lightly, and they needed to leave. "Get her outside."

Finn lifted Sarah to her feet with Emmie's help, and together they hurried back toward the exit.

A flurry of sounds erupted behind them, although neither Finn nor Amelia seemed to notice. Booming sounds, like the winds of a hurricane rushed past them, mixed with the agonized voices of a hundred souls crying in unison from the fires of hell.

Sarah must have felt the flood of pain before Emmie had heard them.

"I'm so sorry," Amelia repeated again and again as they raced to get Sarah to the surface.

Stumbling up the stairs with Emmie on one side and Finn on the other, Finn said nothing as he cradled Sarah's head against his chest. The light streaming down through the open door revealed that Sarah wasn't just pale; she was turning blue.

"I'll call 911," Amelia said.

Finn nodded, although Sarah let out a choking breath while shaking her head.

"No," Sarah pleaded.

Amelia stopped short of dialing and looked to each of them for direction with a panicked expression. "What should I do?"

"Wait." Emmie held up her hand.

Moving Sarah outside, her normal skin tone slowly returned, although she coughed for a minute as if she'd nearly drowned in the cave's darkness.

Trying to calm Amelia, Emmie offered an explanation. "She's claustrophobic."

Amelia was trembling, watching Sarah recover. "I'm sorry."

"It's not... your fault," Sarah said in a hoarse voice. "I'll be fine."

"We'll take her home." Finn didn't wait long before leading Sarah toward the car.

"Yes, of course." Amelia stared apologetically.

Walking on her own for most of the way back to the car, Sarah took deep breaths and remained silent until they'd shut the car doors and Finn had started to back out. "I couldn't breathe."

"There were spirits in there," Emmie said. "A legion of them. Did they attack you?"

Sarah shook her head. "Worse than that."

"Worse how?"

"Something tried to... keep me there."

The words hung in the air between them. At the same time, Emmie caught sight of something moving back toward the ruins. A single shadow appeared near the entrance to the cave. The form shrank within the darkness, disappearing like a mirage as quickly as it had appeared. But even within that glimpse of a spirit trudging forward through a captive existence, the sight of it caught her off guard.

Emmie gasped. "We're not alone."

Finn glanced at her in the rearview mirror, then back toward the ruins. "What do you mean? They're following us?"

"No. They can't leave."

"You saw them?" Finn asked.

"One of them. Yes. And I'm sure we'll find plenty more."

Sarah turned back toward Emmie, her face now almost normal. "Something happened here. Something horrible."

11

Emmie checked on Sarah after they'd arrived back at Finn's home. Her friend had lost all trace of whatever debilitating energy had affected her in the ruins and had even recovered with a renewed push to search Stephen's office again.

"There's more to this," Sarah insisted as they approached the front door. "A lot more."

"We'll take another look." Finn nodded while leading them inside the house.

They found his mother in the dining room. She had started sorting through a stack of boxes, and there were small piles of paper covering every available space. The chandelier above the dining table was on, illuminating the room in an elegant glow of twinkling crystal, but she seemed to feign the light, her hair frazzled, her shoulders hunched forward over the pile of papers in front of her.

Emmie stayed by the door with Sarah as Finn approached her.

"You okay?" Finn asked.

Tiffany turned toward them with a polite smile, then stood. Seeing her in sweatpants and an oversized T-shirt was a stark contrast to the formal dress she had donned during the funeral.

"Hope we're not bothering you," Finn said as he stepped over and gave her a hug. "You don't have to do everything alone, you know."

"There's so much to do." She gestured to the boxes.

Finn picked up a few of the letters, scanned them, then put them back down. "Are these all bills?"

"And taxes. I need to go through everything before handing it off to the accountant. It can't wait." Tiffany looked at Emmie and Sarah with a tilt of her head. "Where did you go today?"

Finn answered, "To see Marc and Amelia in the ruins."

Tiffany's expression lightened before turning her gaze back toward the piles of papers. "I can't seem to find the will. I'll need to update it."

Finn stepped closer and put his hand on her back as he glanced at the ceiling. "Wasn't it in the safe?"

She turned to him with a puzzled look. "What safe? We don't have one."

He gestured toward the ceiling. "There's one in Dad's office."

She tilted her head and seemed to think about it for a moment before answering, "Oh, that one belonged to Neil. I think your dad was cleaning it out or something."

Finn looked incredulously toward the stairs. "Really? Neil? Why would he have a safe? He didn't have any money... or anything of value, really."

Tiffany shrugged. "I'm not sure." Her attention shifted back to the papers in front of her. "Things are a mess, you know. Your dad wasn't very organized."

Finn gently laid his hand on his mother's arm as he looked back toward the girls. "We'll get through this. Do you know the combination for it?"

She shook her head and didn't look up. "It's there somewhere."

Finn gestured to Emmie and Sarah before leading them silently up the stairs. They stopped outside Stephen's office door and Finn turned toward them with a pained expression. "Not sure I want to go in there again."

Sarah took his hand. "I know this isn't easy for you."

"At least I can't see him." Finn took a deep breath then opened the door.

Everything was the same inside. Stephen was in the same place, repeating the same lines over and over with the same intensity and heartbreaking desperation on his face.

Finn turned his gaze away from where Stephen stood, instead keeping his eyes on the girls. "Has anything changed?"

"Unfortunately, no." Emmie closed the door behind them.

Finn sighed, averting his gaze from where Stephen stood, then stepped over to the safe and sat at his father's desk, while staring at the small safe with suspicion and curiosity as if it held some great secret to Neil's life. It was a digital safe with a keypad, and Finn wasted no time in trying to figure it out. "It looks like my dad was messing with this recently, but if it's Neil's... I can't imagine what he could have put in it."

"Everyone has important papers."

Finn scoffed. "Neil was just like my dad, in that sense. Not that organized or careful. No idea where he got the money to even buy this thing."

Finn dug through the desk drawers. "The combination's got to be around here somewhere."

Emmie and Sarah helped look for it, but only a minute later, Sarah tapped her finger on Finn's shoulder. "What year was Neil born?"

He looked at her curiously. "Two thousand-one."

She nodded and grinned. "Then it's right in front of your face. Hidden in plain sight. Do you see it?"

Finn glanced around the room. "Where?"

Emmie spotted it and gazed into Sarah's eyes as they shared a knowing grin. "I see it now."

Finn seemed to pick up on their inside knowledge and folded his arms over his chest. "Are you going to tell me?"

Sarah finally pointed toward the dry erase board, and Finn followed her gaze. There was an eight-digit number mixed in with all the other notes that someone had scribbled almost incoherently.

His eyes widened as the significance sunk in. "Oh."

"It's a mix of your birth year and his, but backwards," Sarah said softly.

Finn's eyes watered, although he turned away from them back toward the safe. In silence, he typed in the number and the small light on the safe lit up green and clicked softly. Pausing to swallow before opening the safe, Emmie and Sarah moved in behind him.

There were no piles of gold or cash, but plenty of papers. Lots and lots of papers and thick notebooks stuffed with loose pages. Digging everything out, Finn laid it all on the desk, studying each piece with intense curiosity. He stopped on one notebook and flipped through it. "What the hell is *this* doing in here? This is in Paige's handwriting. Looks like the notes for the book she was going to write. Why would Neil have this?" He turned toward the girls as if they might have the answer.

"He was keeping it for her while she traveled?" Sarah offered.

"For two years? I mean, maybe this is an old copy, but... wouldn't she have asked to get it back by now? And why would she have given it to *him*? Neil wasn't exactly Mr. Reliable."

Skimming through several pages together, it was clear that the papers and the notebook contained a detailed draft for a book, with the subject matter focusing on the Spanish explorer Cortés and his conquest of the Aztec people. It went on to describe a treasure and how it came to the mission two centuries later, with a group of churchmen mortifying the flesh and laying curses on the treasure. The notebook included a portion written in Spanish, as well as her transcription of the churchmen's letters.

With the sun setting on the ancient stones and the whispers of forgotten tragedies, I am compelled to reveal a solemn secret—a curse that has plagued those who lust for abundant riches. Take caution of the silent guardians, whose watchful eyes see beyond human limits, and fear their wrath. Listen to the whispers carried on the breeze of those who erred in judgment before you. To uncover concealed truths, look beyond what your eyes can see and rely on the heart.

Within the sacred walls where faith and history converge, a hand deemed worthy may stumble upon a key to unveil ancient enigma's cloak's embrace. However, be careful, as this treasure carries a curse that has caused untold deaths and immense suffering.

Beneath the branches, where weary spirits find rest, lies a key to the past and a dangerous pledge of untold wealth tainted by suffering. Let the whispers of the wind guide your heart to revere our sacred resting place, where history and fortune come together in a foreboding harmony, and take refuge knowing that you are not as them, writhing within the eternal clutches of unfathomable and inescapable sin.

The souls of those who entered but did not leave unscathed lie beneath the twisting roots, for their souls intertwine with history without end. Heed the ancient whispers to unlock the tribulation's dangerous secrets and break the curse that has plagued the foolish for centuries.

May the ancient spirits lead your journey, and may

our shared heritage be a cautionary tale as you seek the coveted treasure.

Finn flipped impatiently to the end of the notebook, and several photos dropped out. Picking them off the floor, he placed them on the desk again. They showed Paige standing next to a young man who appeared quite comfortable at her side, his arm draped around her.

"Boyfriend?" Sarah asked.

"I don't know him." Finn checked the photos against the page in the notebook where he had found them and spotted the name Liam.

Another photo showed Liam standing beside Neil, both of them seemingly proud to pose with the ruins in the background. Finn stared a little longer at that photo before going to the next one, which showed more of Paige and Liam standing in various places around the ruins as if they were taking vacation pictures.

"I'll go through all of this tonight." Finn gathered up the papers and stuffed the photos back where he'd found them before standing up. "I want to know everything about it. Dad was obviously stuck on it for some reason before he passed—the whole curse thing." He glanced back toward the door. "Mom has to know something about it. Maybe it's not the best time to talk about stuff like this, but I know I won't be able to sleep unless I hear what she has to say."

Emmie turned toward Stephen's spirit and watched him repeat the cryptic lines again. If only they could get through to him on some level. His spirit would remain that way, maybe indefinitely, unless they discovered the cause of his fixation.

Leaving the safe open, Finn took everything and put his arm around Sarah as he stepped toward the door.

"Maybe we should wait until morning to talk with her," Sarah said.

Finn glanced over toward where Emmie had been staring. "No, I have to ask her right now."

12

Finn waited until Emmie and Sarah had gone to the guesthouse before approaching his mother, who was still sorting through papers at the dining room table.

Standing beside her, she looked up at him with a tired stare. "Did you find what you were looking for?"

Finn shrugged. "We opened Neil's safe."

She seemed to snap out of her thoughts and locked onto his gaze before glancing down at the items that Finn was holding. "What was in there?"

"No bars of gold," Finn said with a bittersweet smile. "But we did find a lot of Paige's papers—her notebook—along with some photos of Neil and some other guy." Finn picked the photo of Neil and Liam out of the papers and set it on the table in front of his mother. "Who is this Liam guy?"

"Oh..." Tiffany tilted her head and sighed as if reminiscing about some long-forgotten memory. "He was friends with Neil, and Paige's boyfriend. Neil probably liked him as much as Paige did."

"How come I don't know about him?"

"You were off at college by then. He stopped by the house every so often, but he kept busy with traveling. He's running around with Paige now, if I remember correctly. Marc said they were vacationing overseas."

"Do you know where they're at?"

"Marc has all the details. But I think he said they were traveling in some remote area of Europe, off the grid."

Finn stared a little closer at the photo. Paige's expression showed so much joy while standing beside Neil and a pang of sadness swept through him. She was Neil's girl, wasn't she? That's how he had imagined it, the four of them sharing their lives together, getting married, having kids. It had all seemed so clear back then. The emotions flooded back with more intensity than he had expected, and he turned away from his mother, fearing she might see his eyes watering. "As long as she's happy."

His mother nodded. "I suppose Paige likes it like that. She always wanted to travel the world, you know. They're like two peas in a pod."

Finn set Paige's notebook in front of his mother. Shaking away his emotions, he centered his attention on what he'd found in the safe. "I wonder why Paige would leave this behind? There's even a stash of her travel notes."

"I'm sure she has more than one copy."

"So then, why would Neil have kept it in his safe?"

His mother shrugged. "Maybe she forgot about it... or gave it to him for safekeeping while she was away?"

"Did she ever ask about them? Or stop by to pick them up... after Neil died?"

His mother winced as if Finn had stuck a needle in her arm. The forbidden subject of suicide had rattled his mother. "Not yet. I suppose she'll come by someday when she gets back."

"Do you have any idea why he might have been holding it for her? Why didn't she just give it to Marc?"

His mother let out an exasperated sigh and frowned. "I don't have an answer for that. Paige and Neil were good friends, so I wouldn't be surprised if there are more things still packed away in the basement that once belonged to her. You know that. It's just like how you and Amelia always paired up. Neil and Paige were so very close. They shared a lot, and I actually had high hopes that someday..." Now it was his mother's turn to get emotional. Her voice trailed off and she turned away from him.

Finn nodded knowingly. "They would've made a great couple."

His mother looked up at him with red, watering eyes. "But the past is the past. Liam's a wonderful guy. You'll meet him someday, I'm sure, and he earned her love and respect, and mine too, so that's that. I wish them both the best." She picked up the photos and the notebook Finn had set in front of her and placed them in his hands.

Finn swallowed. "I've always wondered something."

His mother narrowed her eyes as if she could sense the uncharted pain Finn was about to pass to her.

"Why didn't you do more to help Neil?" he asked.

He flinched as a flash of anger filled his mother's face, but it quickly dissolved into remorse as she seemed to surrender to his audacity. "We all knew he wasn't well, especially not in his final days. We did try to get him the help he needed. I know you don't believe that."

"It wasn't enough."

"No, obviously not."

"What he needed was a mom and dad that cared enough to take him in off the streets."

"We did that."

"But you treated him like a dog."

Her mouth dropped open. "That's not true. He was a *drug addict*. What were we supposed to do? He refused to go to rehab or do anything we asked of him. We tried to help, but he was... he was just acting so strangely. We could barely hold a conversation with him, much less get him to meet with the people who could truly get him some proper care."

"You were trying to get rid of him."

She raised her voice. "That's not fair! We were right there, holding his hand through every step of the process to get sober, except for the final step. That was his choice not to walk through that rehab door. He wouldn't listen! He kept denying he was on drugs, but it was clear. I could see it in his behavior."

Finn's heart pounded, and he clamped his teeth together to keep from saying anything he might regret. He pictured Neil sitting alone in the basement taking drugs, although Finn had never actually seen his brother light a cigarette, much less a crack pipe. After taking a deep breath, he asked, "What sort of behavior?"

"Stealing, staying out all night and sleeping all day. He had nightmares a lot." His mother spoke softer now. "He was hallucinating and paranoid. We saw that in his eyes when he first asked to move back into the basement, and we just thought it would somehow get better, but then he started acting even more strangely, all focused on... strange things."

"What sort of strange things?"

"He painted on the walls."

"Painted what?"

"Horrible things. Devil worship things, like occult symbols. After he moved back in, we realized he was worse than we thought."

"What do you mean, devil worship?"

"Maybe not devil, I don't know, but all that black magic stuff. Sometimes he wouldn't leave the basement for anything. Made me leave food at the top of the stairs and then hurry back down like an..." She paused and met Finn's gaze for a moment before continuing. "And when he did leave, he just came back with more stuff like that. After Neil was gone, I told your dad to get rid of everything."

Finn remembered the darkened stains on the walls beneath the paint. "Those are Neil's symbols beneath the paint in the basement?"

His mother looked at him curiously. "You went down there?"

"I had to."

"Your dad tried to paint over them after Neil's... accident. I never went down there again after that. I never will."

"Why didn't you tell me about all this before?"

His mother looked irritated while trying to hold back tears. "Don't you think we tried? But you were never in any mood to listen to us after all of that happened and we were too exhausted to fight with you anymore. What was the point? We didn't know what to do. And where were *you* through all of this?"

Finn glanced down. "I encouraged him to get treatment a few times. Even offered to pay for it, but he refused. I guess... I didn't know how bad it was until it was too late."

"Well, neither did we," she said softly.

"I thought dad painted over it because of the blood."

His mother nodded solemnly. "There was a lot of blood. It was the most awful nightmare, yes." A tear streamed down her cheek. "The worst day of my life, but all those occult symbols and crosses and evil... like he had joined forces with the devil himself. It was all too much."

Finn held the revelation in his mind, turning it over and examining the truth from every direction. "So that's why."

Tiffany nodded as tears streamed down her face. "That's the truth."

"I'm so sorry." He leaned forward and embraced his mother, holding her as tightly as he could until she finally backed away to wipe the tears from her face.

Finn stepped back and looked at the photo of Neil and Liam again. "Something's not right with all of this. I have to talk to Liam somehow, even if he is traveling with Paige off the grid. Do you know his number? Or email? Or *anything?*"

"His last name is Carver. I remember Paige mentioned moving in with him somewhere north of San Diego. Carlsbad, I think."

"That helps."

"Marc would know more."

Finn nodded. "I'm sure I can find his information based on that."

His mother reached out and clutched his hand. "I wish your father was here to see us finally talking about what happened."

Finn glanced toward his father's upstairs office. "I'm sure he knows."

His mother's expression changed to confusion and concern. "You don't think Liam had anything to do with Neil taking drugs, do you? I've always wondered about that. Or this had something to do with Paige? Neil was so close to her. I always thought that he just couldn't deal with letting her go to another man. Do you think he was jealous? Is that what drove him to all that devil stuff? The heartache?"

A million questions swirled through Finn's head. He was too tired to sort it all out. Backing away from his mother with the items, he met her gaze for a final moment that evening. "Tomorrow, I'm going to find out."

13

Sarah found herself standing at the side of her bed. The lights were off, and the room was still. She was dreaming, of course. There was no other explanation because she was staring down at her own sleeping body. Her head was turned to the side, snoring softly against the pillow, and she was curled up like an infant beneath the blankets beside Finn—her face looked so angelic in the dim light.

She had experienced something similar one time before as a child while on a camping trip with a friend. At first, she'd thought she was sleepwalking, as something had drawn her consciousness away in the dead of the night, after she'd gone to sleep. She had wandered into the forest then, seemingly driven toward a spirit calling to her just beyond the edge of the trees, but she had "awakened" after glancing down at her body. She'd had no body. Just an ethereal form—like *them*—and it had terrified her so much that she'd snapped backwards in an instant, dropping into her sleeping self with a jolt that sent her heart racing.

But that experience had been a fluke, right? Taking in her surroundings, she wasn't so sure.

Her "dream" was so real, and she was fully awake. Was this a form of sleepwalking? But was it even possible to sleepwalk outside your body? This was a psychic's version of lucid dreaming, like an out-of-body experience. But what had triggered it?

Before she could finish her thoughts, something powerful jarred her senses. A horrible scream from someone in the distance. An emotional cry for help resonated through her like so many other spirits she'd encountered recently, but this one was somehow different. It was calling to her on a deeper level, pulling at her heart and mind so much that it had drawn her awareness out of her body unconsciously. The cry was full of raw, emotional energy, a guttural desperation from someone suffering on a level she had never faced before.

Moving through the dim light toward the door to outside, she spotted Emmie sleeping on the couch nearby. Her friend stirred and turned away as if sensing a shift in temperature and covered her face as if she had sensed some of the same disturbance.

The need to get outside grew stronger. Arriving at the door, she moved to open it, but instead felt no resistance as her fingers slipped through it and then her arm, followed by her whole body. Stepping outside into the cool darkness, it was not the night sky that she expected. Instead of stars and moon or clouds, everything seemed to stretch forever in every direction. This was not reality, she reminded herself. Only a dream. This was the twilight zone in every sense of the word. Glancing back, even the guesthouse and the door that she had just passed through were now gone. The backyard and the Adams' house had disappeared as if the world had swallowed it up.

The voice of the spirit called to her again in the distance. But within the suffocating emptiness, she spotted the source at the edge of the horizon. It stood within a flickering orange flame that seemed to connect with her soul. There was a need to get there as quickly as possible, an urgent plea for help, but she also held an unease about what lay ahead. Still, she had to act.

Moving forward through the darkness as the flames

surrounding the figure grew brighter, she slowed to consider the dangers. If she continued, would she be cut off from her body? And how far had she already gone, as distance seemed irrelevant in that space?

Taking the time to focus closer on the figure, she saw they weren't alone. Dozens of formless figures appeared around them, rising and falling within the flames, and their anger and frustration swept through her. The churning shapes reminded her of the illustrations in religious books she had seen, lost souls burning in the flames of hell, screaming and gnashing their teeth.

But the singular soul, the spirit who had drawn her from sleep, rose above the others and stood out in an unexpected way. Their murky figure looked nothing like the others. And it wasn't trapped within the flames, but stood beyond it, instead begging for help in a way that stirred all her senses. Lost in that place, but not damned. Not yet.

I can help this one.

The shadowy form moved toward her, twisted and flailing. Its disfigured frame seemed at the edge of collapse, although somehow it held itself upright and called out with such longing. She could hear the pounding of its heart as it struggled to draw her closer, begging that its voice be heard and that she find a way to set it free.

"Who are you?" Sarah called out.

The shifting form lurched forward, then sank back before its cries intensified.

"Help me." Its shifting mass of shadows grew and shrank with each wave of emotion.

The flames swelled into a wall between them as they grew closer, although the spirit was still far beyond her reach. The searing heat prevented her from moving closer. What would happen if she tried to step through the flames? This was only a vision, wasn't it? But dream or not, she instinctively knew the rules of this reality. Stepping over the line would unite them... forever.

A cold wave of desperate energy swept through her, and she shivered. The twisting spirit was trying to communicate between gasps of breath that erupted from its throat in guttural groans of pain. So much heartache in those sounds.

"What happened to you?" Sarah felt safe within its presence, but still approached cautiously.

The cold came again, this time like icy hands tugging her forward, although she resisted. The spirit cried out again and again as its form shifted from one muddy shape to another, sometimes appearing as a man, then a woman, then a feeble child. What was its true identity? It was human—she could feel that with certainty—but its appearance changed with every moment. Staring at its outline, she caught a glimpse of something white over its head. White and red. Bloody bandages?

Despite the frazzled communication, she understood that there was still hope for this soul, that it wasn't yet doomed to burn forever in that place. There was still a chance for rescue. But if she didn't do something soon, it would follow the same fate as the others around them. It would join the field of flames.

"Help me," the spirit cried again, the only clear words to come through.

But the flames rose between them like a veil, a harsh red and orange wall. Sarah backed away. It wasn't possible to move in any closer without endangering her life. If she attempted to rescue the spirit, she would only become more fuel for the flames. She would need to find another way.

Focusing as hard as she could, she tried pulling at the spirit with all her strength, like Emmie could do so well, but that only exhausted her. Instead of connecting with the spirit, a flurry of chills swept through her again and took her breath away, even in that altered reality without a body. Somehow, she knew that time was running out.

This was nothing she had ever faced before. The darkened dimension loomed in every direction and might have the power to hold her there forever if she didn't back out soon. She had no option but to retreat.

But moving back, she found that a thin stream of the spirit's energy had somehow made it through the flames and latched onto her. Its icy grip seized her, then slipped away. Its feeble attempt wasn't enough to pull it free, but it had passed along a mental image, a brief vision that flashed through her mind and flooded her senses. A whirlwind of colors and pain—so much pain—took her breath away on a scale she'd never experienced before. The spirit's trauma had become her own for that moment, and it flashed through her soul like lightning.

Another jolt of energy came through, this time like a bony hand had reached into her spirit, and it didn't let go. It had locked onto the depths of her soul and was pulling her down toward the flames as it tried to free itself, just like a drowning victim's desperate attempt to rise above the water's surface even as the rescuer sank beneath the waves.

"No!" she pleaded. "Let me go."

Her panic flared as she railed against the spirit with all her strength. What would it take for her to wake up? She focused on the guesthouse, her bed, her body, Emmie and Finn. *Any* connection with reality would do. She *had* to wake up now. Grasping at everything she loved, every cherished memory to snap her out of this nightmare, she found nothing to hang onto.

"Help me!" Sarah screamed into the flames between them.

But the shifting spirit had seemingly pierced her soul and was now about to drag her into that damned place.

"Let me go or I can't help you," she screamed.

She focused everything on Emmie. If she could connect with her friend... "Wake up, wake up, Em! Wake me up!"

A sharp pain filled Sarah's ethereal body and her senses numbed where the spirit had pierced her. It was draining her energy, weakening her resolve to resist.

Is this how I die? she asked herself. *Dragged to hell in my sleep?*

Sarah screamed with every ounce of her soul.

Something snapped.

"Sarah!" Emmie's voice came from somewhere far away. "Sarah, wake up!"

Another crack broke something between her spirit and her captor. And then, as if a link in a chain had snapped between them, she surged backward at incredible speed from the flames and the tormented spirits. A moment later, she was back in her own body.

Her eyes sprang open, and she gasped. Emmie's horrified face stared down at her. Finn stood beside her with the same expression.

"Wake up, Sarah!" Finn said in a panic. "You're having a nightmare."

The reality of what had happened rushed in as Sarah sat up and embraced Finn, who was trembling almost as much as she was.

"It was just a bad dream," Emmie said.

"Not this time." Sarah shook her head and cried.

14

Sarah waited until morning to talk about her dream. She had managed to fall asleep sometime during the night, although the sights, sounds and emotions of her vision had shaken her as much as if she had encountered a real spirit. Finn had gone out of his way to help calm her down in the darkness, holding her tightly until his warmth seemed to melt away the distress.

Still trying to make sense of her vision the next morning, she kept quiet until Emmie pulled her aside, her face full of concern. "Would you like to talk about last night?"

Sarah put on a brave face and replayed the entire dream for her friend, sharing every disturbing detail whether she believed it was important or not.

Emmie listened attentively and took Sarah's hand at one point. "Maybe it was just a reaction to what you experienced at the ruins?"

Sarah shook her head. "I don't think so. It was so... vivid."

Emmie nodded slowly. "There's a lot of activity around that place. Lots of trauma."

Sarah glanced back toward Finn, who was busy working on his laptop at the kitchen table. "I feel like I should do something about what I saw, at least check it out, but I know Finn's already got enough to deal with on this trip."

Emmie spoke softly. "Agreed. Maybe it's better to keep this between us."

Joining Finn at the table, their presence seemed to break him from whatever he was focused on. He sat back in his chair and clasped his hands together behind his head. "A little good news. I found the address where Paige and Liam had rented an apartment in San Diego. I already contacted the landlord and arranged to stop by this morning."

"What did you say was the reason for our visit?" Emmie asked.

"Just said we're old friends." Finn closed his laptop and stood up. "Trying to get in touch with Paige."

"Maybe they think you're stalking her," Sarah said.

Finn shrugged. "Maybe they do. And I suppose I am, in a way."

"Okay, stalker," Emmie stepped toward the door. "The girls are ready."

Finn leaned in and gently cupped his hand against Sarah's cheek. You okay?"

Sarah nodded, despite the lingering emotional weight of the previous night's dream. "Nothing I can't handle."

"That's my girl."

~

They wasted no time in getting back onto the main highway leading toward downtown San Diego. Finn seemed to know where he was going, but Emmie asked anyway. "Where exactly are we going?"

"An apartment in Old Town. Apparently, all that wealth from Marc's vineyard hasn't trickled down yet to his girls."

"Shouldn't we talk to Marc about the notes we found in Neil's safe?" Sarah asked.

Finn shook his head adamantly. "Better to leave him out of it, since we aren't sure of anything at this point. Why get him all worried?"

They arrived at the apartment forty-five minutes later after getting stuck in heavy traffic. It was a small, beige, two-story building lodged on the side of a hill with no view in any direction. It looked like all the others along that street. A simple place to live for those just starting out in life or those who had given up. A layer of dirt, like thick dust, covered everything and there were graffiti markings along some of the light poles and on the backs of street signs.

Making their way inside after the landlady buzzed them in through the main door, they met the woman in the hallway. She stood with her arms folded over her chest, a curious look on her face as Finn started the conversation maybe a little too abruptly.

"Does Paige Moretti live here?"

She looked him up and down before speaking in a hoarse and low voice. "How much does she owe you?"

"Excuse me?" Finn tilted his head.

"You don't need to beat around the bush with me. Seems like they owe everybody money. Or did you come here to score a lid?"

"Nothing like that."

She sniffed the air in front of Finn. "I know what went on in there. I'm not stupid."

"She doesn't owe us any money," Finn said.

"Then who are you?"

"An old friend."

"I see." She looked at each of them suspiciously. "You said on the phone you had some questions."

"I did." Finn peeked over the woman's shoulder. "Have you seen Paige lately?"

She shifted to the side while closing the door a little. "What's this about? Are you the police?"

"No," he said. "Nothing like that."

"Then what business is it of yours?"

Finn's face turned a shade of red. It was clear he was getting a little flustered by the woman's resistance to his questioning.

Emmie stepped forward and nudged Finn back a bit. He was coming on too strong. His background as a journalist wasn't serving them well at that moment. If only Jason were here with them. She could use his help, his smooth voice. "We're just concerned about our friends." Pointing out Liam in the photo, Emmie continued, "We lost contact with Liam and Paige some time ago and we're trying to find them."

The woman stared at Emmie for a long moment. "They owe me *three hundred* for the broken window."

Finn dug out his wallet and counted off three hundred in twenty-dollar bills before handing them to the woman.

Accepting the cash with a satisfied grin, her expression softened. "They haven't been here in ages, but that doesn't stop folks like you from bothering me." She said *folks like you* with an expression of disgust.

"But she still lives here, right?"

"They rent the place, that's all I know."

"She gives you a check every month?"

The woman furrowed her brows. "What does it matter? She and her boyfriend missed rent a couple of times early on, but then her dad started paying. Money is money. I don't care where it comes from."

"Obviously," Finn mumbled.

Emmie spoke over him. "So, her boyfriend lives here too? Liam?"

"I haven't seen either of them for a long time. Not since someone broke into their apartment." The woman shifted and let out an exasperated sigh. "Her dad said they went off traveling together, to get away from it all, you know..."

"Do you have any idea where they might have gone?"

"Don't know. Don't care. None of my business. But when they get back, I plan to have a nice long talk with them about all of this nonsense since they left. It seems they owed money to everyone in San Diego. I gave them the benefit of the doubt, even after doing a background check on both of them—drugs, theft... you name it—but I still let them move in because the tea leaves said I should."

"Tea leaves?" Finn asked.

"My fortune," the woman said with a smirk. "Nothing *you'd* know anything about. It's the way the universe *really* works. I get a psychic reading every week from Liam's mother at a shop on Upton Street. That's how I ran into them. Fate, I guess. She owns the place, and he works there too, reading palms. Doesn't matter though, because I only listened to his mother for advice. She's the *real* one, in my opinion, although my friends had success using him."

"What's the name of the business?" Sarah asked in her gentle voice.

"The place is called Mystic Rhythms," the woman said. "Do you know that Madame Calista got my fortune right every time? Every... single... time. Do you believe in all that stuff?"

Emmie glanced at Sarah. "I suppose we do."

The landlady seemed to perk up at the talk of palm reading. "Well, Madame Calista is the real deal, I can tell you. I don't fall for all that psychic nonsense most of the time, but they've got something *real* going on in that place. She's got such a heartfelt way with words—it's like she looks straight into my soul. If you go there, tell them Gladys sent you. Be sure to get your palms read and listen *carefully* to everything she says because it's the honest-to-God truth. You'll be amazed."

Finn stared at her for a moment before responding, "You mentioned that someone broke into their apartment around the same time they left town. Do the police know who did it?"

The woman nodded. "Some lowlife named Tony DeLuca. One of Liam's *friends*, I heard. And another guy named Damon Williams, the one who broke into the apartment through the window you just paid for. Liam associates with some real losers, I'm telling you."

"Do you know *why* he broke in?" Sarah asked.

The woman seemed to ponder the question. "I heard they tried to steal something valuable, some old antique or relic, but I guess it doesn't matter anyway."

"Why not?" Finn asked.

She answered with a wry grin. "Because they're both dead."

15

Finn still had a ton of questions to ask, but the woman cut them off after receiving a phone call and shut the door.

Returning to the car, they immediately continued their conversation. The revelation about Liam being psychic had caught them off guard. And the name Damon Williams echoed through Finn's mind.

"We could have talked to the neighbors too," Finn said to Emmie in the back seat a moment after he'd started the car. The agitation was clear on his face. "Who is Damon Williams, what did he take, and why is he dead?"

"And what about the mail?" Emmie asked. "Who's been picking up the mail?"

"I doubt the post office would give up any info like that," Emmie said. "I'm guessing Paige's mail is forwarded to Marc—we'll ask him later—but didn't you see the way she was looking at us? I know she thought we were druggies or something."

"We gave up too quickly." Finn buried his face in his phone and started scrolling and clicking through a barrage of websites.

"We have to visit Liam's mom." Sarah turned back to Emmie. "Do you think she's a real psychic?"

"Hard to say," Emmie said. "There are a lot of frauds out there."

"I'm looking for the address now." Finn was silent for a few seconds, then turned his screen toward them. "Here it is."

His screen showed the Mystic Rhythms website, with the storefront prominently displayed. It was far from a glamorous location. The faded sign across the only window offered "Genuine Psychic Readings" with images of tarot cards and astrological signs painted on the wall and door.

Emmie leaned in a little closer to Finn. "Paige is from a rich family, right? So, psychic or not, why would she get caught up with a fortuneteller? Especially from a place like that?"

"It's not like her." Finn shook his head. "She's smart. Either the guy is incredibly good-looking or incredibly charming. Paige isn't the type of person to get caught up in some cheap parlor act. She's all about sticking to the facts, like me—into science, researching and all that. But she did hit it off with my brother, so I guess she had a soft spot for the dark horse."

"Knowing her interest in the ruins, would she have sought out a psychic?"

"I'll add that to my list of questions," Finn said.

"Didn't Tiffany say that Liam was a friend of Neil's?" Sarah asked.

"I've never heard of the guy," Finn said. "But Neil hung around with all sorts of riffraff in his final years. Wouldn't surprise me at all if Paige had met the guy through Neil."

"So, I guess there is only one way to find out."

"Time to get our palms read." Finn straightened in his seat and started off down the road using the GPS to direct them.

Mystic Rhythms was only a short drive away. The location was in a rundown area with a strip club nearby and a homeless encampment in a nearby vacant parking lot.

Finn didn't bother to call ahead. Better to just walk in unannounced.

Opening the front door, a gentle puff of smoke rose and

escaped into the air, along with the scent of incense and other aromas. It was the same type of burning candles Emmie's parents had used at home while growing up. This was a place bent on putting on a good show.

The darkened establishment obscured the woman at first, who appeared after a few seconds sitting in the back corner. She was helping another customer at a small table with a candle between them and soothing music coming from every direction.

The door jingled when they walked inside. The silence seemed to close in around them as if they'd fallen prey to a scam artist—maybe not so far from the truth—and the woman didn't seem to notice them at first.

After several seconds of standing ignored near the door, Sarah whispered to Emmie with a smirk, "I guess we came at a busy time?"

"I'll be right with you." The woman stared over at them finally, then turned back to her client.

"No rush," Sarah said.

A vast assortment of objects surrounded them. There was a set of crystals and dozens of candles—only some of them lit—beside a line of figurines representing various deities from around the world. Some of them looked authentic, but many of the objects looked as if someone had picked them up as souvenirs from a tourist shop. A shelf of books gave the place more credibility, covering topics like astrology, tarot reading, energy healing, dream interpretation, and spiritual philosophy. A variety of dimmed hanging lights helped set the dark atmosphere, along with beads and colorful tapestries on the walls, which no doubt were there to give the clients confidence that this woman knew what she was doing.

They only had to wait a few minutes before the woman stood up and followed her client to the front door. On his way out, he passed them with his face down as if he were ashamed to be seen there.

The woman had a bright pleasant face, and she greeted them

with open arms that jingled with amulets and bracelets. She held out her arms as if she were going to hug them, but then made wide gestures to the chairs at the small table where the previous customer had just vacated.

"We'd like a psychic reading," Finn said.

"Yes, certainly," she said. "I'm Madame Calista. Please, have a seat." She pushed a laminated card across the table toward them listing the prices for her services. "What sort of reading would you like?"

The list was short—fifty dollars for a thirty-minute session—but she had the usual variety: palm reading, astrology, tarot cards, dream interpretations, tea leaves, fortune telling, and psychic counseling.

Finn picked up the card as if to consider his options, but didn't waste any time. "We're friends of Paige Moretti. Do you know her?"

The woman's smile faltered for a moment as she scrutinized them. "Yes, my son's fiancée."

"Liam's *fiancée*?" Finn repeated.

"You know Liam? If you do, you know they're engaged."

"Since when?" Finn asked.

"You don't know my son." The woman leaned back. "I can see that. But he and Paige got engaged a couple of years ago. What's this about? I take it you're not here for a psychic reading, then?"

Emmie looked at Finn, and he pointed at the list of services. "Yes, we are. I'd like you to read my palm. We can talk while you're doing the reading."

The woman stared at him for a moment, then extended her hand. "Sure, if that's what you want."

He put his hand in hers, and she used her thumbs to trace the lines over his palm. He glanced at Sarah with a deadpan expression, and she smirked.

"Is this a family business?" Emmie asked.

"Long line of psychics in my family. The Carvers go back

generations. It was a bit more crowded if you'd stopped by a few years ago. But my husband died, and Liam's sister passed away recently." She glanced around the darkened tables. "We had every table full of customers back then, when it was truly a family business. Liam's specialty is palm reading, if you don't already know."

Finn looked at her curiously. "What's yours?"

"I'm good at it too," she said, "but I specialize in fortune-telling using tea leaves. Would you like to add that to your visit?"

Finn shook his head. "I'll stick with the palm reading."

The woman rubbed the skin of his palm in every direction, holding one hand beneath his palm with the other on top. She observed the lines, running her middle finger down each one slowly and thoughtfully as if she were deciphering some great mystery. "You've been through a lot."

He gave a single laugh. "You have no idea."

"I *do* have an idea." She continued without elaborating.

"Have you seen Liam lately?" Emmie asked.

The woman answered without looking up. "Not lately. He doesn't come around much anymore, as all children do at this stage of their lives, I suppose. It's only natural for children to leave home and see the world when they become an adult. He's spending his time with Paige now. She's such a wonderful person. How do you know her?"

"I grew up with her," Finn said.

"Then you'll be happy to know that she complements my son perfectly. She's so full of adventure and he's got so much passion. They're both in love with life. The look in their eyes when they talk about each other... Do you know they're out creating the memories of a lifetime right now? I wish *I* had found such love when I was young."

"We spoke with their landlord earlier," Finn said. "She has a different opinion of them."

Madame Calista looked up sharply. "What does *she* know?

He's a good boy—he could charm anyone into seeing things his way—and she's a good girl."

"So, you've spoken with Liam and Paige recently?" Finn asked.

"It's been a while, but my Liam was never one to check in with me often. I give him the space he needs, you know."

"When was the last time you heard from him?"

The woman paused to consider it, then continued with a furrowed brow. "Got a text from them only a few weeks back, I think. Said they were going off the grid for a while, but I don't blame them for living the dream, do you? He ran into some good money with his investments recently, so he's no doubt out spending some of it. Good for him. Better that they see the world while they're young. Don't you think?"

"I guess that makes sense." Finn tapped the laminated card on the table. "Do you know someone named Damon Williams? He was caught breaking into their apartment a while back."

The woman frowned. "He was a troublemaker. I told Liam to avoid that one."

"So, you knew him?" Emmie asked.

"I knew *of* him." Madame Calista slowed and squeezed Finn's hand a bit. "What does it matter? He's dead."

"We heard," Finn said.

"Good riddance." The woman rubbed her thumbs over the lines in his palm again and again. "Nobody steals from my son. He got what he deserved."

"How did he die?" Sarah asked.

The woman glanced at her. "From what I heard, he bled to death on broken glass after trying to escape out the window."

"What did he try to steal?" Finn asked.

She looked up into Finn's eyes for a long moment. "Why don't you ask the police? It was never returned."

"The landlord said it was some sort of antique or relic."

"My son owns a lot of things," she said. "Are you worried

about your friend? Is that what this is about? My son is a gentleman, I can assure you, and a skilled psychic."

"It's not that," Finn said. "I just wanted to talk with her again while I'm visiting the area."

"She's in good hands." The woman focused a little closer on Finn's palm. "And you are too, although I see by the lines here that you've encountered a lot of distress lately."

"That's an understatement," Finn said.

"And you have a deep Life Line."

"Is that good or bad?"

"That's up to you. Your Heart Line suggests you are very passionate."

Finn glanced over out of the corner of his eye and winked at Sarah. "You hear that?"

Sarah rolled her eyes.

Madame Calista continued through each line of his palm, giving her interpretation of his relationships, financials, and health issues, but paused on one line with a curious look. "Your Head Line shows that you are very analytical. Too much, in fact. Better to follow your heart on matters in the future." The nail of her thumb followed one line slowly until it ended, and she frowned. "Your Fate Line…"

A silence hung between them for a moment until Finn spoke up, "What's wrong?"

She stared at his palm. "It's wise that you don't want to know your future—better that way."

"That bad?" Finn asked.

Gently curling his fingers into a ball, she released his hand and met his gaze. "The future is what you make of it. I will stop there for today."

Finn glanced at Sarah and leaned back in his seat.

Emmie glanced around the little shop. Faded and frayed tapestries hung on the walls, their mystical symbols barely discernible in the dim light. A velvet curtain partially concealed a corner where a crystal ball sat on a cracked pedestal. Another psychic station sat empty across the room. The place where Liam had worked? Beyond the woman's golden bracelets, there was no sign of affluence in the Carver family. "Liam invested a lot in the stock market?"

She shook her head. "Not a lot, until recently. But whatever he's doing, it's working. And if it wasn't for Liam's money coming in, I wouldn't know what to do."

"Are you sure he got the money from investments?" Finn asked. "Maybe from another source?"

The woman grimaced and narrowed her eyes at him. "Liam is the epitome of honesty. He always had an eye for a good investment, and if you're concerned about his relationship with your friend Paige, I guarantee he'll treat her like a princess."

The room went quiet for a minute as Madame Calista completed her reading and began to write her notes on a chart for him.

Before she could present her findings, Finn spoke up, "You said Liam texted you recently. Mind if I get his phone number?"

She stopped the reading and leaned back in her chair with disdain. "I suspect your friend Paige will have that information… *if* you really are friends with her. This psychic counseling session has ended. That will be $50, please. Cash only."

16

Emmie was feeling a little nostalgic in the driver's seat as she drove them home, as Finn had insisted on sitting in the backseat alone to research something on his phone, just like old times. But even with Sarah in the passenger seat, they hardly spoke a word until they'd reached the guest house to give him the quiet he needed to focus.

This was important. Everything they had discovered up to that point seemed to connect back to either Finn's family or his childhood friends. And it was clear that something was tragically wrong.

The sun had reached the edge of the horizon and the cool night desert air had already drifted in by the time they got home, but instead of going back to the main house with his mother, Finn followed the girls to the guesthouse and gathered with them around the small kitchen table. He switched from using his phone to his laptop, and Emmie caught sight of his computer screen a few times. He'd been looking up information about the Aztec culture and the history of 16th-century Cortés.

Holding back a slew of questions, it was better to leave him alone when he got on a kick like that. Better to just let him focus and digest the information before prodding him. It would eventually come out, anyway, so she kept herself busy in the meantime.

Sarah didn't seem content to wait, and she slid in beside him while looking at his screen. "What do you think, Finn? Do you think Madame Calista can truly read palms?"

He glanced up and spoke for the first time in half an hour. "I see no evidence. There's a lot of superstition and fear in this area, and I'm starting to remember what caused me to be so skeptical in the first place. The curse, Madame Calista, Belle... It's no wonder I turned out the way I did, surrounded by all that."

"So how is a curse any different from the black magic we've already encountered?" Sarah asked. "You believe in that don't you?"

"Of course."

"So how is it different?"

"It's not... verified."

"So, you don't believe anything until you experience or see it?" Emmie asked.

"I suppose not," Finn said. "What can I say? You knew I was a skeptic when you met me. That's just my nature."

Sarah gestured to his laptop. "Did you find anything?"

Finn straightened, as if he'd been waiting for her to ask that exact question, and turned his screen toward her, showing a black-and-white photo of someone's barely legible handwritten text. "Just following all the threads back, seeing if anything connects. I *did* discover a little history of the Santa Isabella Mission. Apparently in 1801, Father Antonio Velasco, a revered clergyman known for his compassion and wisdom, along with three Spanish officers, Captain Ramirez, Lieutenant Morales, and Sergeant Fernandez, arrived at the mission carrying *some* sort of treasure."

"So, Mrs. Blackstone was right." Emmie smirked at him.

"Maybe in *principle*," Finn admitted, then continued paraphrasing from the text on his screen. "The men said it was part of the loot that Cortés plundered from the Aztec centuries earlier. They talked about how it had made its way up through the remote regions of Mexico over the years, and how each generation had fallen victim to the curse, including their own families. The soldiers believed that the sacred grounds of the mission could purify the cursed wealth, and even redeem all the souls who had died in its wake.

"But in 1804, a mysterious fire swept through the mission and left the place in ruins, killing those who had brought the treasure there, along with dozens of villagers and churchmen. Fearing the treasure might once again fall into the wrong hands, the survivors buried it somewhere near the mission grounds, vowing to never reveal its location and praying that it's dark legacy might never again see the light of day."

"*Now* do you believe it?" Sarah asked.

Finn leaned back in his seat. "I admit this is interesting. Most people in the area don't believe that any part of the treasure lore is true, but now I'm thinking there's a chance."

"Okay, then," Sarah said. "I think we're all thinking the same thing at this point."

"What thing?" Finn asked.

"That Liam probably found *something*, whether it was the Cortés treasure or something else of value, and he sold it and gave some of the money to his mother, then used the rest to fund a years-long vacation with Paige."

"We might be on the same frequency, but I'll still need some proof."

Sarah turned to Emmie. "Everything I felt at the ruins... Do you think that by removing the treasure that Liam somehow invoked the curse? Do you think Liam and Paige are in danger?"

Finn scoffed. "Enough with the curse stuff. As I said, when you mix human greed with a legend like Cortés and throw in a series of circumstantial deaths, then you have the ingredients for a curse. It's just like the curse of the Hope Diamond. Are you familiar with that?"

Both Emmie and Sarah nodded.

"There you have the mystery of a diamond with traces of boron in the stone, which gives it the blue colorization, and a flurry of unexplained deaths seemed to follow anyone who owned it. But any object like that ignites the worst in people—greed—and any unexpected death even remotely linked to the owners of the stone was believed to validate the curse's existence. The superstition fuels the fear, which fuels the belief that the curse is real. It's the same thing here with the Cortés treasure." He took a deep breath. "Now, what you said about my dad... and what he said in his office... that I can't explain."

Sarah moved in by his side. "We need to find them—to find out what they did, if anything—and fix this so your dad can move on."

Emmie rubbed her forehead. It was getting late, and they seemed to be no closer to solving Stephen's cryptic situation. "Was Paige... prone to believe the stories?"

Finn shook his head. "She's like me. Skeptical. I don't know this Liam guy, but Paige isn't stupid. She wouldn't take off with just anyone, especially someone she didn't trust. But she *did* have an appetite for adventure of all things historical and mysterious, things like that. Liam might have enticed her to go with him with the promise of seeing the world."

"I don't buy Madame Calista's *investments* explanation," Emmie said.

"We can only take her word at face value," Finn said. "I'm sure that's what she believes, but without any proof of the treasure..."

"So, you believe her?"

"Not particularly, but I have no reason not to believe her."

"No reason," Emmie said, "except the treasure."

Finn mirrored Emmie's exasperation. "I see no connection

between any of what might be the case with Liam and Paige with what you said about my dad's spirit. My dad wasn't interested in the treasure, and it makes no sense why he'd say all those things."

"So, you don't think he would have gone searching for the treasure, even for the nostalgia of it?" Emmie asked.

Finn adamantly shook his head. "He wouldn't have wasted his time. Even for that."

"We have to track down Liam and Paige," Sarah said. "Soon."

Finn tapped his fingernails against his laptop as if his brain had struck on some grand idea. "If we knew exactly what treasure Cortés might have hidden at the ruins, then we might be able to—"

He stopped talking and focused again on his laptop, typing and scrolling through a dozen websites.

Emmie and Sarah stepped away after he tuned them out. No sense in distracting him. Let him do his thing.

Twenty minutes later, he came back to them.

"I heard there was gold." Finn's sudden words startled them. "But anytime someone talks about treasure, they picture a chest full of gold and jewelry. I'm not sure this was in the same ballpark as pirate treasure. Cortés stole a lot of gold, yes, but there would no doubt be lots of religious artifacts from the Aztec people. I'm thinking it would be more like this."

He turned his laptop screen toward them so they could see a picture of a 16th-century Aztec gold bracelet. The design and intricately sculpted panels covering the item were unique and stunning, showing faces and figures linked together as if to tell a story. Emmie peered at the graphics over Sarah's shoulder.

"If Liam found anything," Finn continued, "and that's a big if, I doubt he would have made any of those transactions in public. He would have taken it to an underground collector."

"Like who?"

"There's a market full of rich, unscrupulous characters."

"So how do we contact them?" Emmie asked.

"We can't," Finn said. "It's underground."

"Not even you?" Emmie prodded him with a smirk.

"Not even me."

"So what do we do?"

"Not we," Finn said with a growing grin. "But you know him."

"Jason?" Sarah and Emmie said at the same time.

17

They had Jason on the phone in minutes. Before they even had a chance to explain, he profusely apologized for not calling more often.

"I'm so sorry, Em, but my clients are keeping me very busy most of the time, much more than I'd expected. How is Finn holding up?"

Emmie glanced over at Finn. He didn't seem to be listening, so she put the phone on speaker. "Ask him yourself."

"Finn?" Jason asked. "How are you holding up, buddy?"

Finn's expression lightened. "As well as can be expected."

"We'll talk soon."

"Listen," Emmie cut in, "we need a little help out here."

"Sure, whatever you need."

"You seem to know a lot of shady people."

The line was silent for a moment. "Is that a question?"

Emmie laughed. "Don't deny it. But that's a good thing in this case. We need you to look into the type of objects that might be found in a treasure from the sixteenth century, from a horde of Aztec treasures that Cortés plundered during his conquests. We think someone might have uncovered a treasure here and sold the items recently, within the last couple of years.

They wouldn't have been sold in the usual channels but through the underground market. You have your pulse on that stuff, don't you?"

"Not that specific type of property, but I'm aware of it."

"I'll take that as a yes."

"Why the sudden interest in Aztec treasure?"

"It's not just the treasure—not really the treasure at all—but all the baggage that might have come with its removal."

"Stolen?"

"Worse. We think it's cursed."

"I see. You believe in that stuff?"

"You don't?"

"Not really."

Emmie scoffed. "You and Finn are so alike."

Another pause on the line. "Thank you?"

"Anyway," Emmie continued, "if we can find any evidence that someone sold it, then we're fairly certain that a guy here actually did find it."

"And triggered the curse."

"That's it."

"This guy…"

"You wouldn't know him." The line seemed to go silent for a long time. "Hello?"

"Sorry," Jason said. "I'm looking now. There's a… place I go to browse for stuff like that."

"You don't have to give us an answer tonight."

Jason seemed not to hear her, but instead continued, "When would this person have sold it?"

"Within the last couple of years."

Jason mumbled as he seemed to read through various descriptions and subject lines. "That's a large window of time, but…"

"I'm guessing they'd have been very expensive—"

"Found something." Jason cut her off. "There's one piece that fits the description, and oh boy, it's a doozy. Sixteenth century

Aztec art. Two pounds of solid gold with the face of an Aztec god. Freaky as all hell. Just the sort of thing to chill your blood. Finn would love it. Someone named *GraveRobber2112* sold it almost 2 years ago for a ridiculously low price, assuming the thing is real. In the description they talk about their bad luck with it, as the purchaser and his family died in a boating accident days after receiving it. But take the description with a grain of salt as people always try to hype up their property like this to give it an air of mystery. It helps to boost the value, you know."

"Any clue to its location?" Emmie asked.

"Definitely not. People don't post that stuff out in the open. After the buyer is verified by the seller through an underground third-party service, then the transaction takes place in secrecy. Probably got paid in cryptocurrency too. No way to get that information."

"Any way to connect that with the Cortés treasure hidden near San Diego?"

"Unlikely, but if you had a photo of what you're looking for..."

"We don't."

"Okay, I understand," Jason said. "Let me do more digging and I'll get back to you."

They ended the call.

Finn leaned back in his chair and cupped his fingers behind his head. He met Emmie's gaze, but his stare was distant as his brain was no doubt churning through everything Jason had said.

Emmie folded her arms over her chest. "So now I want to know more about this thing Jason found."

"We can't assume that it's from the Isabella ruins treasure," Finn said. "Plenty of Aztec treasure circulating in the underground markets, but I will admit that what Liam's mother said about coming into a stash of money certainly stoked my interest. It's possible he found *something* of value in the ruins. Maybe not gold or silver, like everyone thinks, but something of value to underground collectors. If he'd sold some priceless items connected to Aztec gods or something of that nature, it might have attracted a buyer."

"And the curse."

"I suppose I *do* believe in curses," Finn said, "on a theoretical level. I've seen enough of the occult in the last year to thoroughly convince me of all that stuff, but I'm not sure that we're on the right track with this. Liam could have gotten this windfall from anywhere. Investing, like his mother said, or maybe just a big gambling win that he managed to keep quiet. I know my dad talked of the curse, but what if there's another explanation? Something more plausible. Maybe it's just that Mrs. Blackstone or someone brainwashed him into believing he was cursed."

"For what purpose?" Sarah asked.

Finn leaned back in his chair as frustration grew on his face. "I still think Mrs. Blackstone is hiding something. She *does* have a vested interest in keeping everyone away from there."

"You're suggesting she knows where the treasure is and wants it for herself?" Sarah asked. "I didn't get that impression from her at all."

"Not out of greed," Finn clarified, "but to win the favor of her ancestors. Maybe she sees herself as some sort of sacred guardian over it."

"She sure made an impression on you."

"PTSD."

"But listen," Emmie said. "If anyone found the treasure, there'd be signs of their activity at the ruins, right?"

"Unless they dug somewhere deep inside the cave," Finn said.

"Either way," Emmie said, "we need to go back there and find where they were digging. Even if there's nothing left of the treasure, they would have left *something* behind. Any ties to Liam or Paige or Mrs. Blackstone... or even your dad would confirm something bigger is at play here."

"Let me tell you," Finn scoffed. "Lots of people have been out there digging for the treasure over the years, at least hundreds of people, including me. There are holes under every rock and plant, and plenty of vandalism too."

"So, what do you recommend?"

Finn seemed to consider it. "Paige's notes. We found those maps of the ruins in her notebook. Maybe that's what Liam used to lead him to the treasure, if he found it. I'll go through the safe again tonight and try to narrow it down."

"If we all go back there..." Sarah said. "Someone might spot the car from the road."

"You can drop me off at the ruins." Emmie turned to Finn. "You can take Sarah over to Marc's house again and keep them busy while I look around."

"The cave entrance is locked, remember?" Sarah said.

"I know the combination," Finn said. "I watched Amelia dial the lock when she let us in. But you won't know where to look inside, anyway. It's like a maze down there, and it can be treacherous."

"Then *you* go to the ruins. Sarah and I will keep Marc and Amelia busy with a few glasses of wine—" She grinned. "—and we'll pick you up on the way out."

Finn frowned while looking at each of them. "Yeah, you're right. You better go to the ruins, and I'll take Sarah to the house. It won't take long to go through Paige's notes and compare them to satellite maps of the area. Then I'll send you the directions."

Sarah moved in closer to Emmie and spoke softly. "What about the nightmares?"

"You think your dream last night is connected to the ruins?" Finn asked.

"I'm sure of it."

Finn nodded slowly, then more assuredly. "My dad was on to something big, and I won't stop until I know what it is."

18

Emmie climbed out of the car and stood at the edge of the ruins. There was no sign of anyone else around, spirits or living.

Sarah's face was already full of concern as she rolled down the passenger window. "Just call if you need help."

Emmie nodded, putting on a brave face for her friend. "Nothing we haven't faced before, right?"

"It's not that," Sarah said. "I'm just not sure of this whole curse thing."

Finn leaned over from the driver's seat, holding a curious stare as if trying to connect with her psychic sense. "See anything yet?"

Emmie glanced around again and sensed a multitude of spirits nearby. "Not yet. But they know I'm here."

"Don't let them get in your way," Sarah said. "Focus on the treasure. If Liam or Paige are connected to this, then we can start working to make it right."

"You have the combination to the door," Finn said, "and the map I drew. I know it's not the best to go on, but I haven't been here for years."

"It'll work," Emmie said.

"Just send one of us a text message when you want to get picked up. We'll make an excuse to leave."

Emmie checked her phone's reception. Two bars. Enough to send a message. "I'm not worried, but if I type in all caps, you better hurry."

Sarah gave a reassuring smile and a small wave before rolling up the window. The rental car kicked up a bit of dust as Finn took off down the road, back toward Raven House.

Emmie turned toward the ruins. She was alone now. But she had an immediate sense that spirits were all around her, and they were acutely aware of her presence.

Were they hiding? "Don't be shy," Emmie said into the wind as she started walking toward the mission. "We've got a lot to talk about."

Following the road up toward the ruins, it didn't take long before she stood beside a rock formation that must have been a wall at one time. Pulling out her phone, she checked through the satellite maps and the notes that Finn had sent to her on where Liam might have left behind signs that he'd found the treasure.

Spirits were closer than she thought. Within moments of passing over the Mission's threshold, she spotted them darting within the shadows. They eluded her, hunkering down behind the fallen structures with their faces obscured within the wispy manifestations that they had become. None of them dared to step out into the light, but that was okay... for now. She wasn't there to solve their problems right now, but they could help answer a lot of questions if they cooperated. It was important to focus on Liam and anything that might connect him to the treasure or the curse he might have stirred up.

Moving through the property to the first location Finn had identified, she scaled a small hill, then stepped past sections of the ruins that she had only seen from a distance. If Liam had removed a large amount of treasure from any area on the property, there would be fresh damage—he couldn't have concealed all the evidence. Moving from one corner of the main structure to the other, with the spirits still cowering in the shadows on every side, she headed toward the highest point to get a better view. There were signs of vandals every so often—graffiti and garbage—along with misaligned paths that had no doubt shifted during an earthquake.

But she continued moving through the rubble, paying special attention to any areas where the earth dropped into what looked like a hole, where someone might have chipped away at the earth in search of a valuable treasure. But those were the areas where any amateur treasure hunter might have looked first. They would have searched behind every pile of stones, beneath the mission's floor, following every fringe theory, no matter how implausible.

The story *was* exciting, on a deep level. Who didn't dream of finding hidden treasure? But the greedy and the curious must have scoured every inch of the property and no stone had remained unturned. She had to see the place in a different light, to search with an open mind and follow her intuition.

Let the spirits reveal the location.

They would no doubt start to push back if she got too close. They would defend their treasure, or what was left of it, with all their anger and wrath, as their souls had become entwined in the eternal history of the place.

She glanced around. So why weren't they trying to drive her away? The location where the Adams brothers and the Moretti sisters had so enthusiastically hunted for treasure was just ahead, but still no signs of resistance from any spirits. Following the map and notes on her phone, she circled around to a flat stretch of land sprinkled with a few live oak trees just beyond the ruins where hundreds of stones were laid out in rows. Many of them were nothing more than crumbled piles of rubble, but some of them were still upright. She had seen that layout so many times in her life. A cemetery. Even back then, Finn had been drawn to the cemetery, if not searching for signs of the afterlife, then he had been searching for hidden treasure.

Examining the closest ones, she spotted some of the writing

etched into the stones. Some of the dates were still visible, 1884. But except for the occasional date, the names had long weathered away with time. No way to identify them anymore.

But some of the gravesites were showing deep pock marks. More evidence of amateur hunters, as someone had overturned a massive stone and left a deep scar in the earth. The grass had long settled in over the upturned soil, and she hoped Finn's posse had nothing to do with that. No—impossible to believe he'd cross the line and dig up graves.

Continuing past a row of simple, gray headstones, she scanned the area for any signs of recent disturbances. The grass and dirt had worked to heal whatever damage vandals had done in past years. Nothing to show that anyone had explored the area recently.

A massive and ancient oak tree stood in the middle of the cemetery, like a mighty guardian stretching out its arms to shelter the sleeping residents below. It seemed to call to her, and she approached with a bit of curiosity after spotting a bare patch of earth near the base. A closer look revealed that someone had stripped away the bark and carved their initials deep into the wood. 'FA + AM.'

Emmie grinned. Finn Adams plus Amelia Moretti?

"Ha! You sly dog." Emmie touched her fingers over the letters and pictured Finn standing in the same location, carving out the letters with a pocketknife. Or maybe Amelia had done it? Either way, its discovery might provoke a bit of jealousy in Sarah, even if Finn had created it as a teenager. It was better that she not bring it up.

Moving past the tree and further from the Mission, she came to another tree not too far away with the same patch of bark stripped away. Another set of initials. This one read: 'NA + PM.'

Neil Adams plus Paige Moretti.

Emmie's heart warmed at the romantic gesture between the two brothers who had fallen in love with two sisters. Emmie squatted down and ran her fingers over the letter 'N.'

Neil.

Her fingertips seemed to tingle as she moved them through the grooves in the wood. Neil had carved this one. The image appeared clearly in her mind. Paige had stood beside him with her face full of joy.

Standing and turning back toward the center of the Mission, she caught a view of the sprawling vineyard over the landscape behind it. From where she stood, she could see over the top of the rows to Marc's house far off in the distance. The lush green landscape soothed her, but there was work to do and they didn't have much time.

Still, she couldn't help but take a moment to watch a group of workers moving among the rows of grapes. They were working methodically from vine to vine, with some kind of machine assisting them.

But not too far away, yet still within the vineyard, stood a blonde woman in a white shirt and jeans wandering aimlessly between the rows. The other workers further away seemed to pay no attention to her, and she slipped effortlessly between the walls of grapes as though she were...

A ghost.

The other spirits had avoided her, but this one seemed lost. Emmie hurried toward her. Crossing through the ruins as fast as she could, she arrived at the edge of the vineyard within minutes and charged into the first open row while straining to peer over the top every few seconds to catch her bearings. Weaving between the rows was difficult, but the vines were young and hadn't filled in the gaps between the wooden and wire scaffolding. The chaotic vines scratched against her skin and clothes as she pushed through toward the woman.

Closing in to within several yards of the woman, Emmie called out carefully to avoid being heard by the other workers. "Hello."

Glimpsing the top of the woman's head before losing her a few times, Emmie tried to focus on her spirit, to pull her closer while continuing the pursuit without the benefit of closing her eyes. The woman's spirit was clear in her mind, but hard to pinpoint. She was driven by a powerful desire to find something or someone. The treasure? Only confronting her would answer that question.

"What's your name?" Emmie said out loud and mentally, in the hopes the woman would stop moving away. Even so, the woman seemed so distracted, so determined. Was this also another soul like Stephen, trapped within the ruin's curse?

Glimpsing the back of the woman's head through the vines, Emmie called out again. "Who are you?"

She was only a few yards away now.

Rushing through a twisted clump of vines, she stumbled and recovered before turning sharply to face the woman. Only a few feet between them. An open wound in the woman's skull had drenched the top and front of her hair with a trail of blood that flowed down her face and chest. Struggling to wipe the blood from her eyes, the woman glanced in every direction with fear and longing.

The woman let out an emotional, panicked cry. "Oh, where is he?"

Emmie worked to hold the woman's attention before recognizing her.

Paige.

19

Finn spotted Amelia as soon as he pulled into Marc's driveway. She was outside near the back of the house at the edge of the vineyard talking with a man in a plaid shirt and straw hat. Her long blonde hair flowed over the shoulders of her fashionable khaki jumpsuit, and her ankle boots gave her a touch of rugged elegance as she glanced toward her visitors with a radiant smile. Finn parked the car, but even from that distance, there was a glimmer in her eye that seemed to transport him back to when they had played in the fields so many years earlier.

Sarah seemed to pick up on his distraction. "She's pretty, isn't she?"

"I suppose so." Finn glanced away and shut off the car.

"She's awfully happy to see you."

"Look," Finn said, "you don't have anything to worry about."

"Don't I?"

"No."

"That makes me feel better."

"What do you want me to say?"

"Say whatever you want."

"Please..." Finn said softly as he reached over and held Sarah's hand. "You're my angel."

She looked into his eyes. "Am I? You should remember that I can see your aura. You had the same bright colors when you were with her yesterday at the ruins."

He had forgotten that it was impossible to hide his feelings from an empath. "What bright colors am I?"

Sarah seemed to study his outline. "Reds and blues. There's a lot going on in that head of yours right now."

"She's just an old friend."

She narrowed her eyes at him and nodded. "I believe you."

Stepping out of the car, Amelia had already started toward them. Her smile seemed to radiate in the cool, California sunshine. A window at the side of the house was open and classical music gently filled the air. Something from Mozart? A plow moved along one row in the vineyard followed by two workers, who started and stopped every few seconds as if to test the fruits of their labor.

Finn swept his arm around Sarah's waist and pulled her closer. She would need a little extra assurance that he wasn't about to run off with an old flame—wasn't even *thinking* about it, which was the truth. She could see his aura, yes, but thank God she couldn't read his mind.

Finn waited until Amelia had almost reached them before speaking. "Sorry for the short notice."

Amelia made a wide gesture as if to embrace them both at the same time. "No worries. I'm so happy you could stop by again."

Breaking away from Sarah a moment before Amelia embraced him, he couldn't help but feel the joy of reuniting with his old friend. A wave of sadness passed through him until he retreated to Sarah's side a few seconds later. Amelia was only trying to comfort him, but he could feel Sarah's stare burning a hole in his back and there was no need to make it more awkward than it had to be.

Amelia then hugged Sarah, pulling away with an expression of concern. "Are you feeling better?"

Sarah seemed confused for a moment before nodding. "Oh, yes, at the ruins. Probably just a bit of nausea."

Finn spotted Marc's car in the driveway and gestured to it. "Good. Marc's home."

Amelia laughed. "That's a mirage. He carpooled today. His friend picked him up and he won't be back until late. Such is the life of a doctor." Amelia glanced back at their car. "Where's your other friend?"

"Emmie wanted to sit on the beach and meditate."

"Hope she brought a jacket." Amelia glanced down at Sarah's clothes. "Think it's chilly here? It's colder than a morgue down by the ocean this time of year, especially with this wind."

"It was below freezing in Minnesota when we left," Finn said. "This is paradise."

"Paradise," Amelia repeated. "Then why'd you leave?"

Finn laughed and looked out across the vineyard. "Yeah, why did I leave?"

Amelia smiled at Sarah. "Looks like you found the best kind of treasure in Minnesota, anyway."

Finn looked at Sarah, and she looked at him. He hoped his colors were better now. "I did."

Instead of heading into the house, Amelia led them over toward where she had stood talking with the man in the cowboy hat. He had gone out into the field with the other workers. She stopped and watched them for a few seconds as if scrutinizing their work.

"Did we come at a bad time?" Finn asked.

"Not at all. I find it helps to stay in their peripheral vision. You know what I mean?"

"Sure," Finn said. "Keep the workers on their toes. So... that guy with the hat. Is he the one in charge?"

Amelia scoffed. "*I'm* the one in charge."

"Well, I know that, but I mean the one running the vineyard. Marc said—"

"I know what he said, but I'm the boss." Amelia slipped her

thumbs beneath imaginary suspenders and stuck out her chest. "Dad put me in charge. I can handle it just fine."

Finn looked at her curiously. "But... weren't you busy with medical school or something like that?"

"I was," Amelia corrected him. "Dad seems to forget that I put my nursing degree on hold after Mom died. He needed my help, but it's actually empowering to run a place of this size. I kind of like it."

Finn nodded slowly. "I suppose that suits you."

"What are you saying?" Amelia turned to Sarah. "Is he like that with you too?"

"Only since I met him."

"Like what?" Finn asked.

"You're a bit... old-fashioned, Finn." Amelia grinned. "Hate to break it to you."

Finn frowned. "Didn't mean it like that. I know you're more than capable of running this place on your own. It's just that I thought you had other aspirations."

"I did. I'll finish my degree eventually. Doing this now, and maybe do the other thing later."

Sarah seemed to look at Amelia with a bit of admiration.

A sudden gust of wind through the trees shifted their focus to the fields around them. The rows of grapes were in the early stages of growth. There was nothing to harvest at this time, yet Finn longed to run out into the fields as he had done as a child and sneak a handful of grapes. The memories flooded back as the silence lingered between them.

"I suppose you'd like some wine?" Amelia said finally.

He cracked a smile. "Not necessary."

"Wine is always necessary. Let's go inside and warm up with a glass." Amelia glanced at the workers again.

"Not sure how much time we have."

Amelia seemed to scrutinize Finn. "You could never handle much."

"You weren't much better." Finn smirked. "But your dad never poured more than half a glass anyway."

Amelia laughed. "He didn't want you to get drunk."

"I wasn't going to get drunk."

"Sometimes you got a little... tipsy."

"I suppose I learned to appreciate how to drink wine from all the bottles I sampled here."

Amelia scoffed. "Sampled."

"I never got carried away."

She narrowed her eyes with a slight grin. "Not *too* much."

"Not like your dad, anyway." Finn turned to Sarah. "Marc would go through a bottle, and it barely fazed him, but he has a laugh like you wouldn't believe."

Amelia looked across the vineyard. "It's a crazy world out there. Either laugh or let it break you."

"So, Paige decided to pull up anchor and sail the seven seas?"

"Last I heard, she was hiking with Liam in Europe—something like that. You know how much she wanted to get out and see the world. So of course, when Liam gave her the opportunity, she jumped at it."

"So, this Liam guy is rich?"

Amelia shrugged. "Not rich, but enough cash to make it happen. Doesn't take a lot of money to travel the world if you manage it well."

"I suppose not. So where did she meet him?"

"You worried about Paige? That's so sweet of you, but she can handle herself quite well, if you remember."

"Not worried about her so much," Finn said. "Just curious."

"I think they shared a few college classes together." Amelia continued and stepped toward the house as they followed along. "It all happened so fast. One month she was talking about where she would go next to get her doctorate degree in New York, and the next month she couldn't stop talking about exploring the world with Liam."

"Not rich..." Finn said. "So, he's handsome?"

Amelia rolled her eyes. "Hardly. But I guess she saw something in him. He *is* charming... in a way."

"Can't wait to meet him."

Amelia paused and glanced over at a group of workers who had camped out beneath a tree at the edge of the property beside a sprawling grassy mound of earth that bubbled from the ground for hundreds of feet beside the vineyard. Watching the men with narrowed eyes, she continued, "But... it's her life. She never listens to me anyway."

"I miss her," Finn said.

Amelia seemed not to notice, instead frowning at the workers with increasing agitation. "They aren't supposed to take their break over there. They know better."

"Something buried under there?" Sarah asked.

Amelia seemed amused. "I hope not."

"It's their wine cellar," Finn answered.

Sarah nodded.

"I just don't like cleaning up after their mess." Amelia gestured toward a garage in the other direction. "We gave them a break area with picnic tables, bathrooms, everything, but they still do what they want." Inching toward the workers as if she might storm over there and shoo them away, she let out an exasperated sigh instead. "My dad stores all his best wines in there. I think it used to be part of the mission as well, from what I heard, a place where the missionaries stored all their food and supplies and plenty of wine. It's the perfect spot for a wine cellar, but we've had a few break-ins recently, so my dad had to install better security. Of course, we suspect one of the workers got a little too curious when we weren't around, but he's concerned that someone will break in again and steal it all."

"Did they take anything?" Finn asked.

"I don't think so," Amelia said. "Just an attempted break-in."

"Sorry to hear that," Finn said. He turned to Sarah. "We used to sneak in there once in a while and hide from her dad. Couldn't touch the wine, but we were always on the lookout for hidden doorways or lost relics."

"Never found anything of real value." Amelia turned to Finn. "God knows we tried."

Sarah moved forward. "Did Paige ever take Liam up there?"

Amelia scoffed. "She brought every boyfriend up there at one point. It's practically a rite of passage for anyone in this family or friends of the family to take their dates to the ruins. Don't blame them at all. The ruins *are* a bit romantic, especially if you climb to the top of the hill. You can see the ocean and the breeze just—"

Finn's phone pinged. "Sorry." Checking his screen, Emmie's name appeared. Without reading her message, he slipped his phone into his pocket and looked at Sarah. "We should head out."

Amelia seemed surprised. "So soon?"

"I promised Emmie I'd give her a tour of the city this afternoon."

"Probably just as well." Amelia glanced back again toward the workers at the back of her property. Her face contorted into a deep frown. "I've got to keep things moving..."

They all embraced.

Amelia smiled at Sarah, then caught Finn's eye. "Give me a heads-up next time and I'll prepare some food. Maybe tomorrow?"

"It's a date." Finn immediately realized his mistake. A glance from the corner of his eye confirmed it. Sarah was glaring at him.

Amelia walked with them around the side of the house toward their car and stopped at the end of the driveway. "See you tomorrow, Finn Adams... and my new friend Sarah."

Sarah smiled, although it was clearly forced. "Later."

As soon as Amelia hurried away, Sarah jabbed him with her elbow and whispered, "A date with whom?"

"I know it came out wrong," Finn said apologetically while getting back into the rental car.

The look on Sarah's face didn't change, but they had something more important to deal with. Before Finn drove away, he pulled out his phone and checked Emmie's text message: *Hurry back, if you can.*

Finn showed the message to Sarah.

Her irritation seemed to melt away. "Let's go."

Finn didn't hesitate. Starting the car and heading back down the road toward the ruins, his mind wandered for a moment as both of them had gone silent. Emmie wouldn't have sent the text unless something had gone wrong.

A flood of memories rushed in from his time at the ruins with Neil, Amelia, and Paige. Some of them he had forgotten until stepping back onto that land, but something else—something dark—stirred uneasy feelings in his chest. Fragments of his childhood flashed through his mind—some that he'd much rather forget—and the unexpected pain threatened to drive his thoughts into a dark corner... until he glanced over at Sarah.

Sarah met his gaze and seemed to sense his conflict. Reaching over and touching the back of his shoulder, she glanced ahead, and her eyes widened as she pointed ahead and yelled, "Finn, look out!"

He looked back to the road just in time to see Emmie rushing toward them, waving her arms frantically. His heart seemed to stop as he slammed his foot against the brakes, and the car veered a little too far in her direction.

Sarah screamed as the front edge of the car came within a couple of feet of hitting her. But when they finally stopped, Emmie was safe.

Both Finn and Sarah jumped out in a panic. Sarah called Emmie's name a few times, but Emmie seemed distracted by something off in the field and brushed off their concerns for her safety.

"Paige." Emmie's eyes were full of fear and sadness.

"What wrong?" Sarah said with outstretched arms.

"Paige," she repeated. "She's dead."

20

Finn's reaction took her by surprise. He stiffened and stared as if he had lost all sense of reality. Stepping back, he shook his head and looked away. "There's no way."

Emmie pointed to where she had seen Paige's spirit, but now the girl was gone. "She was over there."

"You saw somebody else." Finn shook his head.

Emmie stared at the tense muscles on his face, taking a moment to consider his feelings. First his brother, then his father, now his childhood friend. No wonder he wasn't accepting her words. She spoke gently, "It was her, but we need to—"

He slumped, then bent forward, dropping his hands to his knees. "She can't be here."

"I know it's difficult to accept," Emmie said.

"Are you sure, Em?" Sarah asked. "Paige is out traveling with that Liam guy."

Emmie focused on Paige's spirit in her mind again. Finn's denial was normal, she guessed, just the first stage in the grieving process, and the pain in his eyes would also fade with time. She only wished she could do something more to help him through it. At least Sarah would be there to comfort him. "I'm sure. It's not easy, I know, but we should talk with her before she wanders away."

Sarah seemed to prop up Finn as they moved forward side by side and turned to Emmie. "Where did you see her?"

Emmie pointed out toward the endless rows of vines. "Over there. Moving between—and through—the rows."

"I won't lie," Finn said while moving slowly forward. "I'm not sure I can handle much more of this. I hope to God you're wrong this time."

Emmie swallowed. "Me too." Searching the field again, Emmie caught a glimpse of Paige through the vines, not far from where she'd stood earlier. Emmie hurried forward. "She's back."

Finn seemed to snap upright again and hurried along with Sarah beside him.

Emmie led the way toward the edge of the vineyard, but Paige seemed to elude them, moving between the rows as if lost. Reaching the spot where Paige had stood only moments earlier, the girl was gone.

"I see her." Sarah raced ahead to a row several yards away, then veered to the right and gestured for them to follow.

The trellises and sprawling vines prevented them from moving between the rows easily. Finding Paige's spirit reminded her of chasing after a friend's dog through a cornfield as a child, with the cornstalks whipping against her face. They had to keep their heads down to avoid the workers from seeing them, but Paige wasn't making it easy for them either.

It took them a few more minutes to reach Paige and Sarah arrived first, standing before the girl as if to cut her off while wasting no time trying to communicate with her. "Paige?"

Paige was even more heartbreaking to witness up close. The full extent of the young woman's injuries hadn't been visible from a distance, but at least Finn was spared the ghastly site of his friends' tragedy. Blood poured down Paige's face from a fresh wound that would never heal, leaving trails over her T-shirt and cargo pants. One missing sneaker revealed a bare foot as she limped forward. Her face was full of confusion and longing and her gaze passed through them without stopping.

"Is she here?" Finn spoke softly.

"She's here," Sarah answered. "Paige, can you hear us? What happened to you?"

Paige pivoted to her left, then back to her right as if unsure which way to go.

The look in Paige's eyes showed no connection to the world of the living. Emmie moved up and stood in front of Paige, but the girl's stare passed straight through her. It would take more than simple questions to break her from her trauma. Emmie closed her eyes halfway, keeping an eye on the girl's spirit, while also holding the unsettled energy in her mind, and whispered, "Paige, where are you going?"

"He's around here somewhere." Paige turned suddenly as if to hurry away, but Emmie strained to keep the girl in place.

"*Who* is around here?"

"Liam told me he would come back for me." Paige winced as if a sharp pain had swept through her from top to bottom. "Oh, this is bad. Where is he?"

Despite the blood smeared over the front of Paige's shirt, she seemed unaware of what had happened. Emmie gestured at it. "Who did this to you?"

Paige met Emmie's gaze for the first time, but seemed to grow even more confused at the question. "Do you know where I can find Liam? I'm afraid he's lost."

"Did he hurt you?"

Paige tilted her head. "Hurt me?"

Emmie gestured to her shirt again, but it made no difference. "You're bleeding."

"Am I?" Paige moved a few feet off to the side as if to peer around an imaginary corner, then hurried through a row of vines. "Where is he?"

"Paige," Emmie called out, keeping her voice down to avoid

attracting attention from the workers in the distance. "Stay with us."

"Where is she going?" Sarah asked.

"Please, find out what happened," Finn pleaded.

"We will." Sarah followed Emmie as they pushed beneath the trellis now separating them from Paige and came out on the other side to discover she had disappeared again.

After Finn slipped through, he moved in front of them and stared into their eyes with resolve. "That Liam guy did this, didn't he?"

"We don't know yet." Emmie looked in every direction, but Paige was gone. Closing her eyes, she still sensed that the girl was nearby although moving away.

"Is she leading us somewhere?" Sarah asked.

"I'm not sure."

"Don't lose her," Finn said.

"She's not making it easy," Emmie said.

"Paige!" Finn called out without regard for stealth.

"Finn," Emmie said sharply, "keep your voice down."

"Don't let her go without telling us who did this to her." Finn seemed to temper his anger but searched their faces for clues. "Ask her who did it."

"She doesn't know she's dead." Emmie rushed ahead, following the energy within her mind's eye.

Sarah spoke in a calm voice. "We won't let her get away."

Pushing through several more rows and peering over the tops of the vines every few seconds, it was clear that Paige had somehow slipped away from them.

"Do you see her?" Sarah asked.

Emmie hesitated, gesturing straight ahead. Paige's energy had dissipated in Emmie's mind. "Somewhere there, I think."

"I know he did it," Finn said, his eyes watering and full of pain. "I know that Liam POS did it and I'm going to find him and…"

"Not until we get answers, Finn. We have to get answers first before we can bring her justice."

A man's commanding voice called out from across the vineyard. "You're trespassing!"

Finn turned his head suddenly then ducked down. "I think he saw me. Not a big deal, but it's better that Marc doesn't know we're snooping around here."

"We'll have to come back," Sarah said.

Emmie glanced over the tops of the vines for a moment. A group of three men were now rushing toward them. Her heart beat faster. "I think you're right. Run."

Nobody argued. They scrambled through the broken soil toward the car.

"You're trespassing!" The low, menacing voice called out again.

Breaking out of the field, they arrived at the car moments later and climbed inside. As soon as everyone shut their door, Finn sped off down the road while mumbling a string of curses under his breath.

Emmie kept her head down in the back seat and didn't dare to even glance back for fear someone might identify her, but the trees and terrain had already come between them. Still, the pounding in her heart didn't slow until they had made a few turns on their way back to Marc's house. Even then, her mind still reeled from everything she had seen.

"What did she look like?" Finn asked.

Emmie knew what he meant. *How did she die?* She paused to consider her words carefully. "Paige's wounds... they showed trauma. She was murdered. A curse didn't do that."

Finn winced and grumbled. "That Liam guy. I knew that punk had something to do with this. If he *is* on the run, I'll find him."

Sarah spoke up, turning toward Emmie from the passenger seat. "Where was Paige heading before we lost her?"

"Good question," Emmie said. "I got turned around in all those vines."

"The house," Finn said. "You were both moving toward Marc's house."

21

They arrived at the guest house a short time later and gathered at the kitchen table. Finn immediately dug into the cupboards and pulled out a bottle of rum, pouring three drinks without glancing at them.

"A little thirsty?" Emmie tried to lighten the mood a bit.

He glanced over and his expression softened for a moment. "Aren't you?"

"Of course," Emmie said. "It's been a long day."

Sarah stood and stepped toward him, but he waved her away while carrying all three drinks to the table. "I've got this."

After distributing the drinks, he gulped his drink down in a single move.

Emmie laughed cautiously. "I thought you didn't like to get drunk."

"I don't." Finn's expression softened again and a faint grin appeared for a moment before it slipped away. "But I'm not sure I can sleep unless I do. I just can't get over how off-the-rails everything's gone." He looked into Emmie's eyes. "What *exactly* did Paige say?"

Emmie swallowed. "She wanted to know if I could help her find Liam, that he was lost."

"Lost..." Finn stepped to the counter and poured himself another glass. "So, she doesn't remember that he brutally killed her."

Emmie shook her head. "We don't know for sure it was him yet."

Finn's gaze dropped to the floor without a response.

"If Paige died near the ruins," Sarah said, "her body would also be nearby."

Finn looked at her, his eyes full of sorrow. "How am I going to tell Marc and Amelia?" He cringed. "They think she's traveling overseas with that guy. I know he did it."

"We have no proof... yet. The authorities will need evidence."

"We have to recover her body," Finn said softly.

"Yes."

Finn nodded. "I know what happened. It doesn't take a genius to know that sleaze bag must have found the treasure, killed her, and then run off with it. Probably halfway around the world by now, but I'll find him."

Emmie could see the resolve in Finn's eyes.

"Paige must have helped him locate it." Sarah looked at Finn.

"I doubt she knew where it was," Finn said.

"But didn't you say she knew all about that stuff? He was probably taking advantage of her the whole time to get to it."

"He must have come across some new information and used her knowledge to get to it."

"Maybe Neil or your dad left something behind in the safe?"

Finn looked at her for a long moment. "I'll look through it again tonight."

"And we'll go back to the ruins tomorrow and search the area again," Sarah said.

Finn took his time with the second drink, turning the glass in his hands with a contemplative stare. "Neil was *so* sure he'd be the one to find the treasure. He even took the time to calculate how much it might be worth—in the tens of millions—and how he would spend the money. If Liam actually found it, then I'm sure he's long gone. I know Marc and Amelia aren't thinking straight right now, but eventually they'll *have* to know something is wrong. It's just too bad that they didn't suspect something earlier. Unfortunately, Paige has always been so adventurous, so going off the grid like this isn't out of the ordinary for her."

"We could bring it up to them tomorrow," Emmie said. "Tactfully tell them about our suspicions."

Finn frowned. "Based on what?"

"The papers we found in Neil's safe."

Finn shrugged. "That doesn't connect anything to a crime. You're right that we need real evidence to get anyone's attention."

Emmie considered everything that Stephen's spirit had communicated. "I don't get the feeling that your dad has anything more to say to us. I'm afraid he's caught in a loop."

Finn sank a bit in his seat. "So, it's up to Neil then."

Emmie and Sarah both shifted toward him but stayed back. Finn was right. It was better to give him some space. "It seems so."

"I just hope he has the answers."

Sarah moved closer to Finn. "We'll do our best to communicate with him."

He nodded. "I was prepared to face this when I came here, with the goggles from Whisper House, but now... I wish I could just somehow tell him goodbye." Finn looked at them, his eyes full of pain. "I can't do it tonight. Too much on my mind. Give me some time. Can it wait until morning?"

"Absolutely," Sarah said. "Whatever you need."

Finn's expression softened at her response. "Mom will be there all morning. She might even come down while we're talking with him, so I think I should stay upstairs and keep her busy while you both go down. I won't see anything anyway, and if you do get through to Neil—if he's not a broken record like my dad—I'll try to break away and... pass along some..." His eyes watered.

"We will." Sarah embraced him.

Emmie glanced out the window toward the main house. The setting sun cast a long shadow over the still, dark windows. "Tomorrow."

22

Sarah moved within a field of flames that whipped around her like demons preparing her for the fires of hell. The searing intensity threatened to consume her soul, and she charged ahead through the seemingly endless inferno.

The strange cry filled the air. But now it sounded more like a... boy? She wasn't sure. It was garbled, muffled, difficult to discern within the murky atmosphere, and it seemed to come from somewhere just beyond her vision, somewhere within the blinding flames. But she could feel their panic and pain as if it were her own. A blinding torment beyond any patient she had ever assisted.

Sarah charged ahead without hesitation. This was the same place and the same spirit as the previous night, and she knew what to do, but her strange new reality seemed to hold no direction. No up, down, left, or right. Just straight ahead toward the boy's voice that pleaded desperately from within the flames.

"Where are you?" Sarah yelled.

"Help me!" the voice replied.

Sarah turned her head to locate the source, but nothing in that space seemed to follow reality. "I don't see you."

"Help me, please!"

The urgency swelled in her chest and sent her heart racing. She had to get to him before the fire consumed them both. If only Emmie was with her, she might be able to locate the boy faster, but she was alone in that sweltering heat between utter darkness and blinding flames.

Straining her mind for an answer only drew a blank. The answers to any question seemed out of reach in that place and even unimportant as her emotions had flared with the alarming thought that this boy would die without her help. But how would she get to him? The self-doubt and fear crept in like a demon whispering softly, nudging up beside her, threatening to throw her off track. Pushing the thoughts away, she refused to listen. The boy needed her and the fires that danced between them wouldn't stop her from rescuing him.

The fires moved in waves across the landscape as the strange sense that she had been there before filled her mind. There was soil beneath her feet, charred earth covered with a layer of smoke that oozed from its pores, but there were also structures within the flames. Rows of weathered gravestones and monuments that stretched in every direction with blackened, dead trees rising above them, stretching toward an eternal darkness like witch's fingers. The stench of death filled Sarah's nose, and she tasted it on the air as she gasped for breath.

Despite the confusion, it was clear that something had called her to that nightmarish place. Was she asleep? It seemed so real.

Following the sound of the child's voice through the cemetery, an icy chill spread through her like nothing she'd ever felt before. Another presence lurked somewhere nearby. A dark evil that permeated the area. Was this the one holding the child captive? A growing dread spilled into the pit of her stomach. She felt its eyes on her. The unseen entity was aware of her presence, and she could sense its resolve to keep her from reaching the child.

The child's heartbreak and pain became her own, and she raced ahead, trying to stay focused on what she had to do. But to find them, she had to keep her senses wide open, and the raw sting of emotions and flames stabbed her with every step.

Still, the area seemed so familiar. Stone structures surrounded the cemetery, and their forms teased her like a distant memory. The construction guided her on an intuitive level as she passed through rows of gravestones, burnt flowers, and weathered stone monuments. And beyond the dim, abandoned structures lay blackened fields that held a strange allure. Was this a place she had once visited... in another dream?

The child was close now. Although she didn't see them, she could sense their presence. At least she was on the right track with the older, larger, and more ornate gravestones leading her out of the cemetery.

Beyond the last gravestone, a single house came into view. It resembled something from the 18th century, painted white with an arched doorway and black shuttered windows. A simple wooden fence lined the property with no gate blocking the walkway to the front door, and on either side of its entrance stood two statues of angels with their wings spread apart as if guarding it from intruders. Judging by its darkened interior and ragged appearance, it had sat empty for a long time.

The angels held no comfort as Sarah approached the door, and they stared down at her with accusing eyes. They may as well have been demons, and they only reminded her of the gravity of the situation and the stakes for trying to rescue the child.

Glancing back, everything she had passed through—the flames, the cemetery, the field—all of it had darkened now, as if swallowed by a thick veil. She could only go forward, but how would she get the child out of there?

"Hello?" Sarah called out, somehow expecting the child to answer.

No reply.

But the dark entity was approaching, watching her from a distance. Had she given away her location by calling out?

Hurrying through the gate, the eyes of the angels seemed to follow her across the dark path that led to the front door. Before she turned the handle, she paused to whisper this time. "Are you here?"

"I'm here," the child replied, although the voice was still muffled as if he was hiding behind something... or beneath something?

The ground trembled. A minor earthquake? Then it happened again a few seconds later... and again. Not an earthquake, but... footsteps?

All her senses bristled as she opened the door and called out. "Where are you?"

"Please help me!" the child cried, his voice echoing through the walls of the house.

Stepping inside, she contemplated her next move while leaving the door open behind her.

"I need help." The child's weak voice was even more muffled now.

"Tell me where you are," Sarah said.

"I'm right here," they replied. "Can't you see me? Please take me out of here!"

The emotions grew stronger with every step inside—so heartfelt and vulnerable. Sarah struggled to keep from breaking into tears as she moved blindly through the house, checking behind every door and piece of old furniture.

"Keep talking," Sarah said. "I need to hear your voice."

"It won't let me out." The child's cry was coming from somewhere within the walls, either beneath the floorboards or high in the attic. When she looked up, the sound came from below. When she looked at the floor, the sound came from above.

"You have to come out," Sarah said. "I can save you."

"Yes," the boy pleaded. "Please save me. I'm dying."

Sarah shook her head in the darkness. "I won't let you die."

The house shook again, rattling the walls. The dark entity was closer than ever, maybe just outside the house, and she had a sickening sense that it could kill her, despite her psychic abilities. In that place, if she died, she would never wake up.

She swallowed and spoke under her breath, "I can do this."

Finding the last room empty, she took one final charge through the house, calling out to the child as she headed for the front door. "I can't find you!"

"Don't go! They're going to kill me!" The child's voice faded as the dark presence seemed to envelop every bit of light around them.

"I won't let them hurt you," Sarah said.

"Get me out of here!"

The child's cries ended abruptly.

Silence filled the darkness as shadows moved in through the windows ahead of her. Sarah had been through enough moments like this to know that even a vision or a dream could harm her, but there seemed to be no way out. Fear and panic swelled in her chest, but she knew it was too late to get back to safety in time wherever that was. The dark entity had surrounded her and the strange new reality was suffocating her.

Closing her eyes and focusing on Emmie, there seemed to be a ray of light in her mind that connected them, a frail cord that she clutched and pulled at with all her strength.

The darkness pressed down on her as if sensing her attempt to escape.

"Em," Sarah cried, "wake me up." She pulled at her friend again, but she hadn't the strength or the ability to connect with someone's spirit from such a long distance.

Only a moment later, the connection broke, and at the same time, Sarah snapped her eyes open.

She awoke in Finn's arms.

Brushing aside the hair that clung to her sweaty face, he leaned back in the darkness. The panic on his face was clear. "Oh, thank God."

Emmie knocked on the door. "Everything okay in there?"

"Come in, Em," Finn said. "She just had a nightmare."

Emmie entered, her wide eyes focused on Sarah. "Another one?"

"Yes," Sarah said.

The girls stared at each other knowingly for a long moment before Finn interrupted the silence.

"Is someone going to tell me what's going on?" he asked.

Sarah took a deep breath. "We have to talk."

23

Sarah told Finn everything about her vision. Everything she could remember, anyway. The images were still so vivid in her mind, yet there were so many questions about the identity of the child and what happened to him.

She watched Finn's reaction, ready to cut the conversation short if the added mystery spirit became too much for him in his time of mourning. "There's something evil about this place. About the ruins, and maybe it's connected with Stephen and Neil, but the dark history is affecting me in a way I've never felt before. There's just so much bad energy. So much... suffering." She turned to Emmie. "In my vision... I think it's a child."

"Why didn't you say something about this before?" Finn asked.

"We were going to tell you," Emmie apologized. "We just didn't want to add to your stress."

Sarah continued, "There's a spirit trying to connect with me from that place. It desperately wants my help."

Finn looked into Sarah's eyes. "A lot of people died there over the years. I'm sure lots of spirits will try to get your attention."

"But this one is different." Sarah sat up in bed a little more.

Finn paused then shook his head. "Remember what

happened when we visited the ruins? I think it's better if you let this one go."

Sarah glanced at Emmie before continuing, "But I can help them."

"Sarah," Emmie said. "I think Finn's got a point. The spirits in that place really affected you. Lots of spirits out there need our help. We don't have to save the world."

"I get that," Sarah said. "Not trying to save the world. Just this one."

Finn rubbed his eyes. "That spirit you saw in your dream. How do you know it's at the ruins?"

"It has to be there," she said. "All the same structures, even though they're gone now. The same hills, the same cemetery, the same layout. All of it was just as it had been long ago, except fires burned everywhere."

Finn seemed to think about it for a moment. "The place did burn down in the 1800s after an earthquake. I'm not doubting what you saw, just concerned about what all of this is doing to you."

"You don't need to worry." Sarah sat up straight. "I'll let you know if I can't handle it."

Emmie stepped closer to Sarah. "I wonder if any other psychics in the area are experiencing the same thing. I mean, think about it. If all these spirits have been crying out for so many years, wouldn't other psychics have reacted to it? We can't be alone in this."

"Maybe there aren't any other psychics in the area. Not like us anyway."

"Lots of people *claim* to be psychics in the San Diego area," Finn said.

"What about Liam's family?" Sarah asked. "His mom and their business."

"She claimed to be a palm reader," Emmie said. "Nothing like us. And that's my whole point. It seems we're the only ones who can see what's happening, that something awful happened to

Paige." Emmie touched Finn's arm. "The nightmare Sarah had again last night seemed to focus on the same theme, that the ruins are somehow a hotbed for psychic activity."

Sarah nodded. "I'm picking up their cries for help like it's a distress signal and I'm the radio antenna."

Finn looked at Sarah. "Did you pick anything up from Paige?"

Sarah solemnly shook her head. "Not from her. This was a different spirit, a different energy. When Paige was standing in front of me out near the vineyards, her energy was so lost and confused, but not... terrifying." Sarah looked at her hands and let out a nervous laugh. "I'm still trembling."

Finn cupped his hands over hers. "I can take you home."

Sarah shook her head again. "Not necessary. I want to stay. Your dad needs us... Paige needs us. We have work to do."

"But it's targeting you," Finn said.

"It's calling for help from anyone." Sarah squeezed Finn's hands. "Not the same thing."

"The problem," Emmie said, "is that nobody knows yet that Paige is dead. Marc and Amelia will be devastated when they find out, and Stephen is somehow connected as well."

"We can't leave until we find closure for them all," Sarah said.

Finn and Sarah looked into each other's eyes as if trying to read the other's mind.

"You should try to get some sleep now," Emmie broke in, glancing back toward the shaded window. It was still dark outside. She looked toward Finn. "We'll all need our strength in the morning to talk with..."

Finn's expression turned somber, and he swallowed. "I'm looking forward to it."

24

Emmie opened the door to the basement. Finn and Sarah came up beside her and they all stared down into the darkness before Emmie switched on the light.

Finn's mother had left for the day to spend time with friends. Perfect. It would give them the privacy they needed to confront Neil's spirit in the basement. Finn's face was full of apprehension, but Sarah would be right there with him.

Emmie glanced back and looked into Finn's eyes. "Are you ready?"

Finn swallowed and took Sarah's hand. "As ready as I'll ever be."

Stepping back, she let Finn go first, with Sarah right behind him. He led them to the back corner where Neil had ended his life two years earlier. There were no physical signs of the tragedy now, although the walls were painted white, just as Finn had mentioned months earlier. His father had painted over everything, seemingly to whitewash the horrible event.

But Neil's spirit was there, just as expected. He sat in the shadow of a chair that had been there at the time of the suicide, and he clutched a shotgun with both hands as he hunched forward, as if deliberating whether or not to use it. But his expression was not as expected. There was none of the inconsolable sadness that Emmie had usually encountered with suicide victims. None of the depression or hopelessness. Instead, his eyes were wide with a stark expectation that something awful was about to happen, and he was mumbling to himself as he looked sharply around the room. So full of fear that it bordered on terror.

Emmie glanced over at Sarah, and judging by the shocked expression on her face, she had come to the same conclusion. Something was... off.

"Do you see him?" Finn asked, watching their faces.

"Yes," Sarah said. "He's here."

Finn stared into the empty space where their gazes had converged, then looked away. "My parents left it pretty much the way it was when it happened, except for it looks like they pushed in more boxes around the area." Finn gestured toward a stack of boxes that had no labels. "This is all his stuff, or at least what's left of it." He opened a flap of one box and glanced inside but closed it again without commenting and turned back to them.

Neil sat in the chair for a long time whispering and seemingly contemplating the fateful decision before finally turning the shotgun back on himself and looking sharply around the room before pulling the trigger. What would have been a deafening shotgun blast was replaced with cold silence. At the instant of his death, the loop started again, with him picking the shotgun up off the floor.

It was all exactly as Finn had said it would be, although Neil's frightened mannerisms held a striking resemblance to his father's spirit in his final moments as the heart attack struck him down.

"I wish I could see him," Finn said. "At least, somehow tell him not to do it."

"I don't think your brother would want you to remember him like this," Emmie said. "It's probably a good thing that the glasses from Whisper House don't work here."

"Maybe." Finn's tense expression showed that he was trying to put on a brave face. "Can you pass along a message for me?"

"Of course," Sarah said. "We can try."

"As you know, they don't often listen," Emmie tried to lower Finn's expectations. "Too absorbed in what happened during their final moments."

"I understand," he said.

Emmie and Sarah both turned to face Neil and called out to him several times, although he made no motion to show that he recognized they were even there. After trying to reach him on a deeper level, Emmie paused to watch Neil's actions, focusing on him a little more in the moments just before his suicide. Neil made repeated cross gestures over his chest, like a Catholic would if trying to protect themselves from an evil spirit.

Emmie turned to Finn. "Was your brother Catholic?"

Finn shook his head. "We're Presbyterians... theoretically. Why?"

"He keeps making the sign of the cross."

Finn had a confused expression. "Neil wasn't religious, I swear."

"Why would he do that?" Sarah asked.

Finn shrugged and glanced down. "Last ditch effort to save himself?"

Emmie tried focusing on Neil more intensely, seeing his spirit in her mind while trying to pull his attention over to her. There were moments when he seemed to sense her presence with a subtle turn, although her intrusion only seemed to annoy him, and he resisted her efforts as if deviating from his plans even for a moment would make things worse.

"Neil," Emmie called to him. "Your brother wants to talk with you."

"Neil," Finn said in a pained voice.

His brother's eyes fluttered for a moment at the sound of Finn's voice before slipping back into the loop once more. Neil's gaze was locked on something just out of sight in his final moments, although the vision only extended as far as Neil's immediate surroundings. Moving in a little closer, Emmie caught sight of something in Neil's hand, even as he lifted the shotgun. It was small and black—made of stone.

"Did Neil own any religious items?" Emmie asked. "Maybe a crucifix?"

"Doubt it," Finn answered.

"Maybe something connected with the occult? A talisman or amulet?"

Finn shook his head. "Do you see something?"

"He's squeezing something in his hand."

Finn stepped over to a pile of boxes and pulled one of them aside while digging through them. "What does it look like?"

Emmie moved in for a better look. "I don't see it very well, but maybe a small statue?"

Finn dug into the box, pulling out most of its contents and laying it across the floor. "I went through some of this earlier. Maybe it's in here?"

Emmie scanned through the eclectic mix of electronics, papers, and other odds and ends, but there was nothing in the pile that matched the object Neil was holding. Instead, a piece of shiny metal clanked against the floor and nearly rolled away from them before hitting another box, coming to a stop a few feet away. The glint was unmistakable, even in that dim light. A gold coin.

Sarah bent down and retrieved it. "What's this?"

Finn seemed as shocked as they were and stared at it as Sarah turned it over in her hand.

But while Finn and Sarah were studying the coin, Emmie couldn't help but notice that Neil seemed to snap out of his suicidal loop for a moment, glancing toward the coin in Sarah's hand with wide eyes at the same moment that she held it up to the light.

"I can feel the suffering in it," Sarah said, rubbing her fingers against its edges.

Neil's expression changed immediately. He seemed to retreat from it. Even in his loop, the coin affected him.

"Guys," Emmie said, "something's happening with Neil. He's looking at the coin."

Sarah studied Neil while lifting the coin. Up, down, left, right. He followed its every movement. "There's something about this. He's afraid of it."

"That doesn't make any sense," Finn said. "He wouldn't be afraid of a gold coin. And it doesn't make sense that he even *had* a gold coin in the first place, since he was broke when he died. I'm sure of it."

Sarah examined the coin a little closer. "It's very old. Maybe it's from the ruins?"

Finn silently stared at it.

Sarah moved around and stood in front of him, looking at him softly with a spark of light in her eyes. "We can try to help him move on now, if you want."

Looking up to meet her gaze, he shook his head. "There's still too many questions. He doesn't communicate with you?"

"He's too absorbed in his trauma. We can try again later."

He nodded, looked at the coin, then at Emmie with tired eyes. "See what your boyfriend can find out about this. My head is spinning."

25

Sarah sat beside Finn on the couch holding his hand while Emmie sat in a chair across from them reading through Jason's text messages out loud as they came in. They had sent him photos of the coin in the hopes that he had time to dig into its background, and he'd responded only thirty minutes later.

Emmie immediately answered each message while Finn and Sarah passed the gold coin between them, examining it, turning it over, and holding it up toward the small chandelier centered over the table above them. Finn took the most time with the coin, inspecting every detail with his usual intense curiosity while scouring through search results on his laptop for clues, not waiting to hear what information Jason had discovered, as if he were an archaeologist after a big find.

Jason's text messages came in sparse, at first, but within minutes he sent a barrage of facts, websites and pictures that detailed some of the 16th-century Aztec artifacts he had found in the underground market. He went into a lot more information than necessary for each object, although Finn seemed to hang on every word, comparing the discoveries to what he had found on his laptop.

Switching over to a call from Jason on speakerphone, Emmie

placed the phone flat on the table between them to allow each of them to ask questions.

"Everything I found was sold by someone matching Liam's description," Jason said, "but not recently. Looks like someone dumped the stuff on the market about two years ago."

"That sounds about right," Finn said. "That fits the timeframe when Liam and Paige disappeared."

"Can you give me any more details about this guy?" Jason asked. "The more info you give me..."

"That's all we have on him."

"I see."

"Didn't you find any names or addresses?" Sarah asked. "You must have some inside information."

"Sorry, it doesn't work that way. This isn't eBay. All the transactions on these sites are anonymous, and there's no definitive way to prove that any of the stuff came from him."

"We were hoping you'd provide us a smoking gun," Emmie said.

"Sorry, Em. I provided the gun, in a sense, but I'm afraid it's cold. If you think you've got the right guy, then I can keep looking, but it's unlikely we'll find anything that connects him directly to this stuff, if he's smart. You're better off looking for signs that this guy suddenly came into a large amount of money and went on a buying spree, stuff like that."

"According to his mother," Emmie said, "he did."

"Okay, so all the circumstantial evidence is there," Jason said.

"We also discovered that his girlfriend, Paige, went missing about the same time, and we know she was murdered."

"How do you know that?"

"We saw her spirit."

The call went quiet for a moment. "I see. Then I definitely wouldn't confront this guy about it if you track him down. Based on everything you told me, you should expect that he'll do anything to keep this quiet."

"Jason, we have to find him," Finn said. "If you run across any more information, please send it right away."

"I'll do that. You might also want to consider getting a private investigator, but that will take time."

"Everyone seems to think they left the country together," Sarah said. "But we saw her, and we don't have the proof to bring it to the police. We're concerned that if we rattle the cage too much..."

"You'll wake the sleeping tiger. Yeah, you should lie low until you know more. I know that complicates things, but he could be anywhere. Unless he comes back to visit his mother or you can track him down through social media, there's no way to pursue this further without arousing suspicion. Maybe you can stealthily get more information from his mother?"

"We tried," Finn said. "She wasn't any help. I'm inclined to break into her apartment..."

"Be careful with that," Jason said. "Using a private investigator might be the best course of action."

"I won't break the law." Finn groaned. "But no time for private investigators. Paige was a close friend, and I'm sure this Liam guy killed her. Maybe he had something to do with my dad and my brother too, I don't know. I think he might have run off with the treasure and stirred up a curse."

"What makes you think that?" Jason asked.

"By the way their spirits appeared to me," Emmie jumped in.

Jason was quiet for a moment. "I wish I could help you more. Sounds like you know what happened then."

"I'll find him," Finn reiterated with an icy stare at the phone.

"I have no doubt you will."

Finn's expression softened after a moment, and he reached toward the phone. "Thanks for your help, Jason."

"Anytime."

They ended the call. The room went silent as they all seemed to contemplate the information Jason had provided.

Finn turned his gaze toward the gold coin in his hand. While turning back to them, the coin slipped out and clanked against the table, jarring him from whatever thoughts had held his focus. It rolled to a stop, and he picked it up again while looking toward Sarah. "What would you do if you were me? Should we go to the police with this, despite having absolutely no evidence?"

"We can't," Emmie said.

Finn scowled. "I'm not going back to Minnesota and leave things like this."

"We won't," Sarah said.

Emmie considered their options. "Would Marc and Amelia help us?"

Finn scoffed. "With what? We have nothing to tell them. And they'd think I was bat shit crazy if I even mentioned our involvement in the psychic world. They're diehard skeptics, like my family. Marc is a doctor. Solidly on the side of science. He used to tell me all the time while growing up to be skeptical about anything to do with ghosts, the supernatural, and all that. He would endlessly mock me just for hanging around with you guys if he knew the truth."

"What if we planted the idea with Amelia that something might be wrong?" Sarah asked. "If we can persuade her to try contacting Liam... You know, plant the seeds of doubt."

Finn shrugged as a wave of sadness swept over his face. "I can't believe this is all happening."

Sarah reacted quickly, taking his hand. "Em and I can bring it up."

"Tactfully," Emmie added.

"I know you will." Finn caressed Sarah's fingers. "Maybe I'm too emotionally invested in all of this to make the right decision, but please be careful. Amelia would never look at me the same if we're wrong." Gripping the gold coin again, he cracked the edge against the table then sat back in his chair.

Sarah gestured to the gold coin. "What if she saw that?"

"There's no absolute proof it came from the ruins," Finn said.

A soft voice caught Sarah's ear. Just an indistinct sound off in the distance that she barely noticed as Emmie and Finn continued the conversation without her. When the voice came back a second time, she turned her head toward it and tried to locate the source. Her friends didn't seem to notice when she glanced around and leaned forward.

"*Help me,*" came the distant voice.

Sarah immediately recognized it as the same shadowy spirit from her dream. But if she was awake, how was that possible? Alex Temper had contacted her in a similar manner months earlier, by communicating telepathically, but he'd been alive. The child in her vision was dead, wasn't he?

When it came a third time, she watched Emmie and Finn for a reaction. Did they hear it too? But their conversation hadn't even paused, and she hesitated to interrupt.

Glancing around, she debated what to do. If the spirit could communicate with her while awake, it would pose a big problem. How could she function? The distraction was unavoidable now.

Oh great, I can't shut it off or turn it down or run away. I'm its captive audience.

A moment later, it repeated, *"Help me, please."*

A sense of urgency swept through her, and she stood up, although her eyelids had become heavy, and she wavered a bit while glancing toward the window.

"Where are you?" Sarah clutched Finn's arm to steady herself. Things in the room started to shift.

Finn and Emmie went silent. They were staring at her.

"What?" Finn asked her.

Emmie stood, knocking her chair backwards. "Sarah? You alright?"

The lights were growing dim as if an eclipse were passing over the room, and her legs weakened within a growing sense that something was wrong. Very, very wrong.

With Emmie and Finn both clutching an arm, Sarah stepped toward the door as if a breath of fresh air was all she needed. Her legs buckled a moment later and she toppled forward, but

Finn slipped his arm around her waist, dropping the gold coin in the process, and caught her moments before hitting the floor. The coin rolled to a stop only inches away, reflecting the overhead light off its metallic surface.

As her friends rushed to move her to the couch, the voice in her head called out again before everything went black.

"Please come, now."

26

Everything stopped. There was a young woman lying on the floor, her hair frazzled and swept over her face, although she looked familiar. Finn and Emmie were also frozen in place, suspended over the woman's body while reaching down as if time itself had stopped. It took Sarah a moment to catch her bearings as she hovered above them, now moving in an ethereal body, but when she finally realized who Finn and Emmie were trying to help, she gasped in that altered reality. That was *her* body on the couch, and as soon as she had that revelation, a darkness swept in from all sides and the smell of toxic fires swept past her in a sickening breeze.

It was just like the vision she had experienced earlier, and the gold coin Finn had dropped was still lying on the floor. Whatever had triggered the vision was taking over as an altered reality surrounded her. Before the scene faded to black, she caught a glimpse of Emmie and Finn, still frozen with expressions of shock.

A shrieking cry for help came out of the darkness. The same spirit she'd encountered in a previous vision, but this time dozens, maybe hundreds, of tormented souls added to the chorus of pain. A field of flames stood between them, as before, but now it grew brighter as she zeroed in on the spirits within the chaos.

She could maneuver within that world, although with great difficulty. A wall of unseen resistance closed in around her as if the darkness intended to extinguish her light at any cost. She was out of her element here—so far from home—but kept trudging ahead toward the singular tormented soul that had connected with her on a deep emotional level. The distant flames grew brighter, hotter, into a sprawling bonfire which lit the surroundings. Fires danced around an expanse of crumbling stone structures with Spanish-style, centuries-old architecture. The tormented voices came from everywhere within the flames. Men, women, old, young, they all contributed to the endless, mournful song. These were some of the same traumatized spirits she had seen at the ruins, caught within the agonizing flames of the curse, and it was clear they had no way out.

But even within the horde of heart-wrenching cries, the single desperate voice from her dreams somehow rose above all the others. The spirit. Its shadowy outline appeared again within the flames, pulling at her heart with such intense emotions as if longing to reunite with an old friend.

She resisted the attraction, but it felt so natural, so logical. Catching a sense of the separation from her friends, a bit of panic swept through her.

Am I dead?

Crying out in a torrent of emotion, she screamed Emmie and Finn's names over and over, focusing with all her strength on her friends.

This can't be hell. Wake up, wake up, wake up.
This is just a dream or a vision or... something worse?

The spirit's magnetism tugged again at her energy. They shared a strange connection on some level, a special bond, like kindred spirits, and it was impossible to ignore.

It hadn't yet joined the others in the flames—not yet—but it hovered just beyond the field of fire as if waiting its turn to pay for its deeds.

There was still time to rescue it, although she had no idea how. The concept seemed so ludicrous in that place. There was no way out, but wave after wave of distress and hope demanded that she save it from the horrible fate.

But...

Who are you?

The spirit's presence seemed to reach across the expanse and nudge her forward. Without invading her space, it led her energy like a gentle hand steering her around the flames, away from danger. Instead of trying to navigate through the fires, like she had in her previous vision, now her connection guided her along its perimeter, hovering at the edge of impenetrable darkness.

A hoard of lost spirits was circling and twisting ahead, although their figures moved in and out of the shifting darkness like drowning victims caught in a deadly ocean current, endlessly cycling to the surface to catch a breath before getting sucked under again. The hopelessness seemed almost tangible in that place. The blackened spirits rose and fell, calling out for someone to save them.

In the grip of the spirit's pull, she traveled beyond the flames, beyond the deafening cries for help, to a darkened terrain that seemed so familiar though surreal. There were hills and barren fields and patches of dead trees along the way until she arrived at the edge of a cemetery lined with rows of small headstones. Passing through without a moment to pause, she arrived at the outskirts of an old Spanish settlement.

A simple stone wall surrounded the small community, which seemed to revolve around a single structure near the middle that rose above all the others. A domed tower crowned with a large white cross. Arched windows on each side revealed a large bell inside. Moving in closer, the main building beneath the tower came into view.

This was the ruins as it had existed long ago, when the Santa Isabella Mission had thrived.

The spirit was nearby.

"Where are you?" Sarah called out.

While waiting for an answer, she tried her best to focus on the connection between them, to draw them out or reveal their identity, but something still stood between them like a fog.

Only a moment later, the spirit appeared just beyond the edge of the mission. The moment of recognition sent a jolt of relief and curiosity through her, but its spirit was nothing like she'd imagined. The thing—and it *was* a thing in this reality—didn't move at all like a human, seemingly twisting and shifting while lifting its borderless frame into view. She tried to make sense of who or what it was. Its contorting appendages lifted and settled in place, as if trying to rise up to greet her on broken legs.

"You're my only hope," the spirit said in a garbled, desperate voice. "Please hurry."

"I don't think I can get to you over there," Sarah said.

"Please," they said between labored gasps of air. "You can't leave me like this."

Sarah struggled to move forward, but found more resistance as she arrived at the wall around the mission. "How do I get over there?"

Their voice faded a bit. "Help me... help me... help me..."

Sarah held the shifting spirit in her mind for a moment, but the mental image of its form took her breath away. This thing looked nothing like a human. If someone could have taken her worst nightmares and manifested them all into one creature, this was it.

Its skin was a web of decaying flesh, with missing chunks and maggots wriggling within barren eye sockets. Worms snaked through its matted, muddy hair while patches of skin hung loose over bone and layers of crumbling tissue. Its jaw dropped open as she stared, and its throat churned out a guttural cry.

How? The word hung in her mind. *How could this be true?*

She couldn't break her focus, either from the terror or its desperate grip on her. Was it the result of some horrible accident or mutation, or a demonic entity from another realm? She had seen so many horrific sights recently, but this entity seemed to encapsulate them all.

She pulled together her thoughts long enough to ask, "Who are you?"

"I lost my way and I need your help. Take me out of here." They extended a twisted limb toward her. A hand at the end of the appendage took shape.

But the more Sarah stretched toward it, the more resistance she encountered. How would she get out of there even if she could pull them toward her? "I can't reach you."

It groaned louder while struggling to meet her halfway. "Please don't give up."

Still, she tried one last time, pushing forward toward it until something forced her backward again. Something behind her also tugged on her spirit, a stronger force. The spirits within the field of flames called out to her, demanding her attention. They had discovered her and would now come to beg for help, just as every spirit did when she drew close to them.

Sarah turned her focus back to the spirit. "What's your name?"

A murky haze swept in around it as if feeding its memory. "I... I can't remember..."

Sarah couldn't help but wonder what the spirit had done to end up damned forever in that place. Such a tragic fate to suffer.

But something was different about this one. They didn't *belong* here. They weren't *of* that place, but it had somehow started to consume its soul anyway, dragging it in slowly... perhaps to prolong the torment?

The other spirits were approaching from all directions. Her light had attracted them in that darkened space, and they would soon circle around like bugs drawn to the flame. And what would happen if they too latched onto her? Would she ever escape that place?

She needed to leave. Immediately.

Sarah focused on the only person who could draw her out. Emmie's light was beyond all the darkness, but her friend's dim light was there, just out of reach.

Pulling her friend's light closer, just a gentle tug to get her attention, Sarah held onto the connection with all her strength. In a moment, a familiar wave of light spread through her heart. Emmie had met her halfway.

As if sensing Sarah's imminent exit, the spirit cried out, "Don't leave me!"

But the hoard of ghastly spirits from the flames had come too close and time had run out. Holding Emmie's light in her mind provided the only escape as she accelerated toward her friend. Glancing back into the darkness before she left, Sarah caught a glimpse of the spirit's face before light and reality filled her vision again.

Sarah gasped at what she saw—its true form.

A young boy with a pale face and wide, bloodshot eyes staring back at her.

27

Sarah awoke in Emmie's arms. They had moved her to the floor with Finn kneeling down beside them, his face full of panic.

"Are you okay?" Emmie's eyes widened as Sarah adjusted her vision and glanced around. "Sarah? Are you okay?"

Sarah nodded but shuddered. "We have to go back to the ruins."

"Nevermind that," Finn said. "We thought you were..." He closed his mouth and pushed his lips together while glancing away.

"Your heart slowed to a crawl," Emmie said. "Finn almost called 911, and I was prepared to do CPR. And I couldn't remember how many compressions to do." She smiled, but the distress on her face was clear. "We thought you were gone."

"I thought I was too." Sarah sat up, although her muscles ached. "Your light guided me back."

Emmie nodded sympathetically. Her expression seemed to waver between relief and curiosity. "I felt you leaving this world."

"I did." Sarah waved away Finn's phone. "No need to call for help."

Finn slipped it into his pocket, but kept his gaze on her. "What happened?"

"You sensed something," Emmie said, "didn't you?"

"More than that," Sarah said. "I saw something, just like in my dreams, except... it was worse."

"Worse in what way?" Finn asked.

Sarah looked toward Emmie. "The spirit I saw in my dreams is desperate for help, and it's definitely a boy, but it kept changing... I can't explain it. It flipped between identities like flipping through TV channels—some of them terrifying. I've never seen anything like it before."

Emmie nodded slowly. "You're okay now. Just stay with us."

Sarah nodded. "I'll try. But whoever it is, they know I'm here, and I know they won't stop contacting me until we act."

Finn looked concerned. "Something doesn't sound right. Why would they single you out to communicate with?"

"I don't know." Sarah rubbed her arm. Her muscles ached, and her vision was still a little blurry.

"Do you think they're somewhere nearby?" Emmie asked.

"I know they are. Somewhere near the ruins."

Finn rubbed his forehead. "Everything seems to revolve around that place."

"We have to go back," Sarah said.

Emmie gently rubbed Sarah's shoulder. "I think you should rest for a minute. You went through a lot just now. We all did. At least get checked out by a doctor."

Sarah smiled, then struggled to stand up. "You always said I'm the best nurse in the world, right? So, who needs a doctor?"

"At least lie down for a bit?"

"No time." Sarah shook her head and trudged toward the door again, then paused and turned back toward the couch. Her strength hadn't yet returned, but the vision had stirred her curiosity and strengthened her resolve. She had to do something, but her head throbbed as if she'd awakened with a hangover and every muscle was screaming for her to slow down. Wavering in place for a moment, she sighed. "Yes, you're right."

Emmie stood attentively beside her. "We'll head over there as soon as you're ready."

Finn joined them as they made their way back over to the couch. Settling into the cushions, she let out a sigh of relief and resignation. The vision had taken a greater toll on her than she'd realized, yet the urgency to act grew stronger like someone had planted a seed of unease at the back of her mind. The child's spirit had affected her deeply—it had gotten to her—but was tracking it down before learning of its identity really the best solution? And how would they deal with all the other tortured spirits connected with the ruins?

A brooding sense swept through her. Were they stepping into something bigger than they could handle? But if they didn't act right away, how long before another vision hit?

Emmie looked into Sarah's eyes. "Are you sure you want to find this spirit? With everything else on our plate?"

"Yes," Sarah said. "Stephen, Neil, this child's spirit. I'm sure there's a connection between all of them and probably plenty of others have suffered the same fate, but I don't have the big picture yet." The coin was still lying on the floor across the room, and she gestured to it. "So, we have Neil's gold coin, but we can't confirm that it came from the ruins. We'll start with that. Who can we talk to with knowledge of the ruins and the curse?"

Emmie and Sarah both looked toward Finn at the same time.

He let out a subtle moan, cringed, and glanced away. "Please don't say her name."

"We have no choice, Finn," Sarah said. "We definitely need to confront Amelia about all of this—Paige, Liam, Neil—but there's something bigger going on. Mrs. Blackstone has more knowledge than anyone about this."

Finn grumbled louder. "You're wasting your time with her."

Emmie looked him straight in the eyes. "Can you think of anyone else?"

He looked down and let out an exasperated sigh. "No."

"Then we'll stop by her house on the way there."

Finn cringed and rolled his eyes. "Listen, she might know about all this stuff, but she is bat shit crazy, I'm telling you. I could find more information on my own."

"We don't have time."

Finn stepped over and picked up the gold coin, then scrutinized it for a moment as if there might be some small details he missed earlier. With a smirk, he glanced over at each of them. "Of course, I won't argue with either of you. I'll support whatever decisions you make and stick with you until the bitter end—"

"Perfect!" Sarah said with a grin. "That's all I ask."

Finn smirked. "But what I was *going* to say is... I'll just keep my mouth shut this time and let you girls do all the talking."

"Again, perfect. Thank you." Sarah looked at Finn warmly. "Should we tell Mrs. Blackstone about my visions?"

Emmie nodded once. "We should tell her everything."

28

Emmie paused before ringing the doorbell and turned to Finn. "Remember, let us do the talking."

Finn scoffed. "You don't give me enough credit. Of course, I can take it down a notch when I need to."

"Two notches."

"Okay, sure. Fine." He looked at Sarah. "I believe everything you told me about what you saw in your visions, but please don't blindly accept that she has all the answers, okay?"

"I learned long ago to never blindly accept anything," Sarah said.

Emmie rang the doorbell and stepped back.

Mrs. Blackstone answered the door a minute later, greeting them with a curious stare, then breaking into a bright smile when her gaze stopped on Finn. "What a surprise! I have to say, I never expected to see you again."

Finn kept his mouth shut, just like he said he would.

"We'd like to ask a few more questions," Emmie said, "if that's okay?"

"Yes, of course, although I'm not sure I have answers. But..." She opened the door wider and gestured for them to come in, while adjusting her yoga pants and loose white shirt as if they might judge her appearance. Her long gray hair hung freely this time, flowing across a white meditation shawl draped over her shoulders. "I'm always willing to listen with an open mind."

Finn pushed his lips together into a forced grin with his gaze down as he skirted past the woman. He seemed determined to push aside his emotions, at least for the duration of the conversation.

After walking through the house toward the same couch where they had gathered the day before, the familiar smell of incense came back to them. Judging by the candle lighter in her hand, she had been lighting some of them just before they arrived. A soft, pleasant scent, but Mrs. Blackstone seemed a little dazed as if they had broken her from a trance.

"What would you like to know?" Mrs. Blackstone looked at each of them curiously and slipped off the shawl, lying it across the arm of her chair.

Finn pulled the coin from his pocket and showed it to her, although he made no motion to hand it over. "We found this. We'd like to know if you recognize it."

The old woman's eyes widened as her gaze fell on the coin. "What's this?"

"Can you tell us if it's a part of the rumored Aztec treasure?" Finn asked in a steady voice.

"Not just a rumor," she said sharply. "A very real tragedy."

Mrs. Blackstone stepped forward to take it from Finn, but he seemed hesitant to hand it over. She paused and watched his face until he finally dropped it into her open palm. Clutching it beneath her frail fingers, she rubbed the surface with a curious grin. "This is real."

Finn scoffed. "We know it's real."

Mrs. Blackstone stared closer at it. "But not just real gold. This is real *Aztec* gold."

Finn opened his mouth again, but Sarah cut him off. "How can you tell?"

"The design, of course, but there is an energy that flows from it." She held it out toward Emmie. "Can you feel its power? Its allure?"

"That's called greed," Finn said.

"Greed, yes," she said and handed it to Emmie. "But the tears of my ancestors went into making this. Do you hear them crying out through the metal?"

Emmie took it and ran her fingers along its surface. There *was* an energy within the gold, on a psychic level, a dark energy. After handing it back, a sense that she'd somehow connected with something contaminated stayed with her. "It feels almost toxic."

"Then you know it's not something to carry around with you. This belongs back with my ancestors."

"You can have it," Finn said, "right after all this is over with."

Mrs. Blackstone seemed pleased, but gave them a curious look. "After *what* is over with?"

Emmie spoke up, "Maybe this sounds weird, but Sarah and I see spirits."

The woman narrowed her eyes and nodded slowly. "I had a hunch about you."

"And we've seen a *lot* of spirits in this area. Sarah keeps having these dreams—visions—about the ruins, about someone, a child, begging her to rescue them."

Mrs. Blackstone looked at Sarah curiously. "Oh?"

Emmie continued, "And when we visited the ruins, I encountered a small crowd of lost souls, although they eluded me. Maybe hiding or too absorbed in their trauma to appear..."

Mrs. Blackstone closed her eyes for a moment as if struck by a jolt of pain. "They are the miners, the missionaries, the local people. Gold is a powerful and sometimes deadly beacon for those seeking a shortcut to happiness. So many souls fell prey to the curse and are trapped within the ruins."

"What traps them there?" Sarah asked.

"Like I said," Finn cut in, "greed."

"You are correct," Mrs. Blackstone affirmed. "Even in

death, they cannot let go of its powerful allure. That is the curse. Like flies stuck in a web of their own making, they cannot escape."

Emmie swallowed. "What can we do to help them?"

Mrs. Blackstone shrugged and handed the coin back to Finn. Picking up her candle lighter, she started lighting a few more candles that sat on a small table against the wall. "What's there to help? They are lost souls, trapped in their desires, forever tormented until they let go."

"With no chance for redemption?"

Mrs. Blackstone tilted her head and furrowed her brow. "Redemption? They are only receiving what they have earned. Maybe if the treasure is returned to my people…"

"The treasure's long gone by now," Sarah said. "Someone has probably sold it or melted it or…"

"Then they are damned forever." Mrs. Blackstone gestured to the coin. "It's best that you return that to the ruins where you found it."

"We didn't find it at the ruins," Finn said. "Neil had it among his possessions when he died."

Mrs. Blackstone stared at him for a moment as her expression wilted. "I'm sorry. Is this visit about what happened to Neil?"

"Did you know he had it?" Finn asked with a strained voice.

"No." She forcefully shook her head, then peered at Emmie and Sarah. "Was he among the lost souls you saw?"

"Yes," Emmie answered. "We saw him, but he died in his house, you know."

Her face saddened. "I know the details."

"What can we do about it?" Sarah asked.

"What is there to do?" Mrs. Blackstone answered. "Return the treasure to where it was found. Dig a hole there as deep as you can and drop it in. Bury it and forget about it."

"But we don't know where the treasure was found."

Mrs. Blackstone tossed her hand as if they'd asked a silly

question. "Then sail out to the middle of the ocean and throw it overboard. Somewhere no one will ever find it again."

"Would that break the curse on Neil?" Sarah asked.

"I doubt it. Only Neil knows what he's done, but you will fall victim to greed if you keep it and suffer the same fate as all the others."

Finn inched forward. "Do you know where the treasure is... or was?"

"I don't." Mrs. Blackstone settled into her seat while staring at Finn. "Many have asked me, but whomever removed this from its resting place has released a great evil into the world." She shook her head. "Is that why you hate me? You think I'm to blame for Neil's death?"

"You facilitated it," Finn snapped back. "Both Neil and my dad got caught up in this curse somehow."

"Stephen?" Mrs. Blackstone asked. "How do you know this?"

Finn held back and looked at Emmie.

"Because I saw his spirit at the house too. He kept saying some Spanish phrases..." Emmie dug in her pocket and pulled out a piece of paper. "I wrote it down. Something like, 'El tesoro robado no puede ocultarse de los dioses.' And Neil's spirit also looked terrified in the basement, as if trying to hide from something awful."

Mrs. Blackstone nodded slowly, as if the revelation hadn't quite processed yet. "I see."

Finn turned to Emmie and Sarah. "I told you this was a waste of time." The frustration in his voice was clear.

"A little patience goes a long way, Finn." Mrs. Blackstone tapped the side of her head. "This old brain takes a little longer to process things after so many years. Your father is saying, 'The stolen treasure cannot hide from the gods.' These are the words of my ancestors, and proof that the curse also touched him. Of course, there's no magic bullet to set them all free. Those cursed will likely remain in that state until they let go of their desire or my ancestors decide to release them, if ever."

Emmie looked into the old woman's eyes. "The child that Sarah mentioned... have you heard of anything like that? Spirits who can change shapes, identities? They keep reaching out to her in the visions."

"That *is* unusual." Mrs. Blackstone looked at Sarah from top to bottom. "I haven't heard of any such thing, but I'd be cautious. Stay far from the ruins. Leave the coin with me, if you'd like, and I'll dispose of it properly."

"What about Neil and Stephen?" Sarah asked. "How can we free them? We won't leave until we do."

"Like I said, I don't see a path to redemption for them. Whatever they did—"

"They didn't *do* anything," Finn jumped in. "They're *victims*, and it's amazing how you've known my family your whole life and you just brush them off like they're nothing. 'Oh well'," he mocked, "'that's the way it goes. Can't do anything about it.' Ridiculous."

The old woman turned her back on them and faced the candles she'd just lit. Taking in a deep breath, she spoke softly, "My ancestors believed in retribution and sacrifice. Those principles belonged to them, and it's something I cannot change. I'll meditate on all that you've said to me, but please temper your expectations."

"My expectations couldn't go any lower," Finn said.

Sarah slipped her arm around his back. "We should head out."

"Agreed." Emmie stepped toward the door with Sarah towing Finn along beside her. "We appreciate your help."

Finn scoffed under his breath. "Help..."

Pausing at the door on the way out, Emmie turned back, even as Finn and Sarah continued. "You mentioned the Aztec believed in sacrifice. What kind of sacrifice?"

Mrs. Blackstone grinned. "I'm sure you've heard the stories, dear. Human, of course."

29

It was just like old times. Finn was sitting in the back of the car clicking away on his laptop as Emmie drove with Sarah in the passenger seat. Every few minutes, Finn glanced up and met Emmie's gaze in the mirror with his expressions shifting somewhere between frustration and bewilderment, although he hadn't said a word in a while, maybe from being asked to take a back seat at Belle's house. Now, he had that same perplexed stare, but seemed to be holding back his opinions with great difficulty.

The poor guy was suffering, and Emmie couldn't take it anymore, so she opened the door for him to vent by speaking up, "So, what did you find?"

"Ah, man, it's unbelievable."

"What's unbelievable?" Sarah glanced back at him.

"I can't find anything on that Liam guy. Usually when someone disappears, they leave a trail with friends and family on social media—*something* that gives away their location. But there's nothing. It's like he truly did disappear with the treasure."

"It's not like the police are hot on his trail or anything like that," Emmie said.

"He could be anywhere—*anywhere*—but I'm sure I could

track down something on him if I just had more time. Maybe he's been lying low this whole time, sipping margaritas on a tropical beach, but after two years of hiding you'd think he'd have left a trail of clues *somewhere* along the way."

"What if he changed his identity?" Emmie asked.

"That's possible."

"The money he made from the treasure would have stood out if he were living it up on a beach. I don't get the impression that he's careless."

"In which case," Sarah said, "we may never find him."

Finn scowled. "Oh, I'll find the bastard."

Turning onto the road leading up to the ruins, a rush of anxiety washed through Emmie's chest. She had encountered so many spirits in her life, but something about the place pulsed through her being in such an uncomfortable way, as if something was nudging her toward the edge of a dark abyss.

Sarah also seemed to pick up on her sudden disturbance. "Want me to drive?"

"You aren't feeling the same?"

Sarah lost her brave face. "I am. Absolutely."

"I got this." Emmie tightened her grip on the steering wheel. "Not looking forward to this place again, but we're almost there."

But braving through the uneasy moment would only get her so far. It was impossible to ignore the growing menace of that place, which seemed to envelop her with icy fingers, digging in and tugging at her soul on a dark, subliminal level. It wasn't just Sarah's experience with the child that stirred her senses. The tragic history of the Santa Isabella Mission still seemed to electrify the air as if it existed in an eternal lightning storm. Definitely not a vacation spot for psychics.

Approaching the ruins, Emmie focused, trying to narrow down the location of the spirits she had sensed there previously, although again it seemed to come from everywhere, eluding her senses like nothing she'd dealt with before. The spirits were there—she could feel the presence of every single one of them—and the impending dread made her skin crawl, but like the previous visit, not a single one was visible. *Were they evading her? Or had some darker energy connected with the curse blocked the doomed spirits from communicating?*

"I don't get it," Emmie said. "I'm sure they're all here, but I don't *see* them."

Finn looked up from the back seat and glanced around as if he might help in the search. "Be careful what you wish for."

"True." Gazing over the ruins, Emmie followed it back until it met with the hills and fields that surrounded them. "How big is this place?"

"The mission is just what you see," Finn said. "A small village developed around it a long time ago, but nothing else survived, as far as I know."

Emmie took the exit up the narrow road and stopped the car in the same area they had the previous day. Staring out the window at the ruins, there was an undeniable sense that a thousand invisible eyes were watching her. A glance at Sarah confirmed her unease. Her friend was clenching her fists as if trying to hold herself together.

"It seems to be a little worse this time," Emmie said.

Sarah smiled nervously. "You're telling me."

"Why is that?" Emmie asked rhetorically.

"Maybe we're tuning into them the longer we stay here?" Sarah said.

As soon as Emmie shut off the engine, Finn threw his door open. "Then let's not stay here longer than we have to, for everyone's sake."

They gathered at the front of the car and Emmie glanced toward Raven House. The vineyards were devoid of workers, which would give them the opportunity to look around without attracting attention.

Finn looked at Sarah and spoke softly. "If you feel sick..."

"I'll let you know." Sarah stepped forward without another

word, heading straight into the heart of the ruins again as if driven by nothing more than her passion to help the spirit in her visions.

Winding through the same structures they had passed the previous day, it seemed they were headed toward the cave opening, but Sarah veered away from it after pausing for a moment to close her eyes.

Emmie and Finn were silent during Sarah's intuitive pursuit, although Finn grabbed Sarah's arm a couple of times to steer her clear of obstacles after she'd closed her eyes without stopping.

"I don't get the sense that the child is in the ruins," Sarah said, "despite what I saw in my vision. But they *are* nearby."

Emmie scanned the area again for any sign of spirits. If they were trying to stay hidden, then they were doing a great job, although she could see them in her mind, hovering at the edge of her awareness. But something was different this time. They were aware of her, fixated on her every move, but even more so, they were focused on Finn.

The realization caught her by surprise. Why Finn? He had no connection to the spirit world, which they had discovered months earlier, but in this place, he had stirred the tormented spirits like a sheep who had wandered into a pack of wolves.

"This is weird," Emmie said as they continued.

"You'll see them eventually," Finn said.

"I don't mean that. I mean, it's weird that they're all focused on you, Finn."

"Me?" He paused and gave a confused look.

Sarah paused too and scrutinized Finn for a moment as if he were hiding something. "Em, are you sure?"

"Positive."

"That *is* weird." Sarah glanced around the area. "I *do* feel that same awful feeling I had in my vision. The dark emotions are getting worse."

"I'm not sure I want to see them anymore," Emmie said.

"They're all around us, but it's like we're walking into an ambush this time."

"Sarah." Finn's voice wavered. "Can you locate that spirit a little faster?"

"I can try." She turned to her left, then back again. "Do you feel that?"

Emmie glanced around. "I feel lots of things right now."

"They're focused on Finn, yes," Sarah said. "I can feel that—which doesn't make any sense at all—but their desires fuel their focus." She closed her eyes, then opened them suddenly and pointed to an area beyond the cave. "Over there."

"That's the cemetery," Finn said. "Nothing over there except a bunch of old headstones and rattlesnakes."

The massive oak in the center of it all stood out, and Emmie glanced at Finn to gauge his reaction. Would he steer them away from the place where he had carved the initials into the base of the tree?

Within the branches of the sprawling tree, a group of ravens jostled about. The breeze rustled the leaves and muted their deep caws, but the sounds grew louder and filled the air as if the birds sensed they were being watched.

"I saw something like that in my vision," Sarah said.

"You think the child is there?" Emmie asked, glancing at Finn again. Still no reaction. Had he forgotten what he'd carved into that tree? Or had Amelia and Paige carved them alone without his knowledge?

Sarah nodded once, then led them straight toward the cemetery. Pushing through clumps of tall grass at the edge of the ruins, they stepped into the midst of headstones, stone crosses, and a few battered monuments that spread out a few hundred feet in every direction.

Each step forward seemed to confirm what Sarah had mentioned, that the energy in that place had a direction, a focus. Emmie could feel it, too. Even if the spirits were hiding themselves from her, they couldn't hide their piercing attention, which all seemed to focus on whatever lay beneath those trees.

The ravens took to flight before they arrived, fluttering away in a storm of deep, croaking calls. Their absence allowed the gang to move beneath the sprawling branches in silence. The carved initials in the base of the tree were hidden on the opposite side from where they stood, sparing Finn the awkward task of explaining their significance.

Sarah stared at the ground—the dark energy in that place had taken its toll on her. She stood tall, but her face told another story. Pale and tense, she was struggling to hold back the pain that permeated that place.

"What are you seeing?" Finn asked.

"Nothing yet—" Sarah's voice cut off.

Emmie gasped at the same time. They must have seen the same thing. There it was. A section of earth that someone had disturbed near the base of the largest tree. Someone had filled it in, and Emmie might not have noticed it at all if it weren't for the glint of metal poking out from the soil, but it was the same glint she had seen on the gold coin in Finn's pocket.

"That's it!" Emmie pointed and jumped toward it until a rush of cold air swept around her chest like an icy hand. An invisible force tried to hold her back.

Before reaching the coin, spirits began appearing to her on all sides. Just a single young Spanish soldier at first, dressed in an officer's uniform reminiscent of the seventeenth century. The man's pale face was twisted into an intense expression of rage. He lunged between Emmie and the coin as if to thrust her away from it. It was *his* icy hands she had felt a moment earlier, tearing at her throat and chest, as he had tried to stop her from reaching the coin before he did. Turning his attention back to the coin in the dirt, he lunged at it as if his life depended on it.

More spirits added to the chaos, charging in from every direction. Some came out of the ruins, and some came from behind the trees and hills. Spanish soldiers, a priest, missionaries dressed in brown robes, and even an elderly woman joined in, hunching forward with her hands stretched toward Emmie like claws. Even more joined them, spirits from every era dating back to the birth of the mission. Young and old, they all held the same insatiable thirst in their eyes, to possess the gold coin and keep Emmie away from it.

While Emmie took in the spectacle around her, Finn plucked the gold coin off the ground. As soon as he picked it up, the spirits turned their attention to him, sweeping through him like a tornado, futilely grasping at the coin in his hand. He shivered, blissfully unaware of all the turmoil surrounding him, then wiped the coin on his pants before examining it.

"That's it," Emmie repeated. "That's why the spirits were focused on you, Finn."

"What's it?" He asked without looking away from the coin.

"The gold coin in your pocket." Emmie stumbled to her feet and took a step away. "It's part of the treasure, and they want it."

"They can have it." Glancing around briefly, he pulled out the other gold coin from his pocket and compared it to the one he had just found. "Right after I'm done with it. They look the same."

"I'm sure they are the same." Sarah looked at Emmie, then back to Finn. "Finn, you're lucky you don't see what we do."

"What do you see?"

"Not good," Sarah said.

"I'll tell you later." Emmie pointed to the section of disturbed earth. "But more importantly, it looks like someone's been digging here."

Finn slipped both coins into his pocket while the spirits continued to work themselves into a frenzy, trying to remove them from Finn in every way imaginable. Following Emmie's gaze to the patch of ground, he crouched down and examined the disturbed soil with wide eyes before scrambling faster to clear it away. It wasn't just a hole in the ground, but instead a natural cavity beneath the roots. "There's something here."

Sarah and Emmie maneuvered around the storm of spirits that still surrounded Finn, but kept their distance.

Without pausing, Finn started pulling stones the size of baseballs from the hole, then larger ones that someone had packed into place with handfuls of gravel. Pushing through the debris until he cleared an opening about two feet wide, a dark hole emerged. He turned back to them with a burning resolve in his eyes. "You're right. This must be it. I know it. The treasure."

"Or what's left of it." Emmie turned to Sarah, who had taken a few steps back. Her friend had turned away and now faced almost directly into the sun. Emmie shielded her eyes to get a better view of her friend. "You okay?"

"No," Sarah said.

Finn stood beside the hole, catching his breath after all the heavy lifting. "This will take all night, anyway. I'll take you home."

"Not home." Sarah didn't turn back to them.

Emmie hurried over to Sarah's side. Her friend's eyes were closed against the beaming sun. "What's wrong?"

"With the spirits focused on Finn, I can see everything clearly now." Sarah lifted her hand and pointed. "We can't leave. Not yet. The child, he's over there."

Emmie followed Sarah's guidance, and she gasped. She was pointing at the far edge of the vineyard toward the flagpole on the Moretti family's property. Raven House.

30

Emmie spotted Amelia standing at the edge of their fire pit across the yard with her arms folded over her chest as soon as she pulled into the driveway at Raven House. A shallow, circular brick wall blocked most of the flames in the pit from view, but the smoke rose high into the air before the gentle breeze swept it away. Amelia broke into a bright smile as soon as they arrived, walking toward them without reservation.

Sarah had gone into a mild trance only a few minutes earlier to confirm they were on the right path, but as soon as the car stopped, Sarah came out of it and put on a brave face for Finn who had expressed his concern that she might lapse back into one of her visions.

Marc's truck was gone. At least they could expect to have a private conversation with Amelia, but if they didn't get the help they needed from her, then at some point they would need to talk with him as well.

Climbing out of the car, they gathered in front of the headlights. Emmie sensed some spirits nearby, although none of them stood out in her mind like the child did with Sarah. Paige's spirit still roamed the area, and it wouldn't take much to track her down again, but everything was pointing back to Raven House and Amelia was their best hope for answers.

Amelia spoke up a few yards before she reached them. "I didn't expect you back so soon."

"Roasting some marshmallows?" Finn called out.

The young woman laughed. "We *should* do that again one of these days, but no. Just cleaning out some trash from the wine cellar."

"Speaking of wine... do you have any more of that Pinot reserve?" Finn gestured to Emmie. "She's thirsty."

Amelia laughed again while removing her garden gloves and looked at Emmie. "You've got good taste."

Emmie opened her mouth to scold Finn for putting her on the spot like that, but Finn spoke first, responding to Amelia. "She knows her wines."

"Well, I'm not surprised." Amelia brushed a bit of soot off her arms and looked at each of them. "Everyone likes our Pinot."

Emmie glanced around. Something about the place was different this time. The fields. A peace had settled across the young vines as if the vineyard had borne a slice of heaven. The tranquil beauty soothed her mind until it struck her what was different. All the workers were gone. Every single one. It wasn't *so* strange, though. No doubt, they didn't work seven days a week, and it *was* Sunday, but the solitude was somehow disconcerting.

Amelia seemed to focus on Sarah. "Are you all right?"

Sarah straightened and smiled. "Just tired."

"Wine won't help that." Amelia turned toward the house and started to say something else, but before she could speak, a group of ravens landed in a tree at the edge of the vineyard. Their harsh cries filled the air as everyone watched them.

"Don't they keep you up at night?" Sarah asked after the noise had died down.

Amelia shrugged. "Not so much at night, but there's no hope of sleeping late in the morning."

Finn glanced back toward the driveway. "I see Marc's gone for the day."

"As usual," Amelia said. "The hospital called him in. No way to know when he'll be home, either. It's always been like that."

Finn nodded. "I remember."

A cool wind swept across their faces and jackets. Amelia glanced back toward the house again, then gestured for them to follow her as she started to lead them around the side to the back porch. "It's a lovely day, for the grapes, anyway. We can sit outside again and share another bottle while we talk. I'll put up a few torches."

Sarah shivered and Finn put his arm around her. "Maybe it's better if we talked inside," he said. "I have a few questions too."

Amelia tilted her head. "Oh?"

The wind picked up and rustled Finn's hair. "I know how you love the outdoors, but we've been outside all morning…"

Amelia nodded with a grin. "You're going soft, Finn. A day like this in Minnesota would have you singing. I thought everyone from up there was immune to the cold."

"We're not in Minnesota."

Amelia laughed, then led them inside. The classical music they had heard on the first visit was conspicuously absent, and the echoes of their footsteps reverberated through the empty house. But even before they moved into the living room, Amelia had stepped over to a digital device against the wall and pressed a few buttons, and the rich, dark melodies of an orchestra filled the air from every direction.

"Robert Schumann?" Finn asked.

"Johannes Brahms. Symphony number four in D minor. Dad's playlist, not mine." Amelia stepped between them to get to the fireplace. "I'll get a fire going. Please, have a seat."

Finn and Sarah dropped into the overstuffed brown leather couch, while Emmie sat on the matching reclining chair and watched Amelia work with the kindle in the fireplace to get the logs burning. The young woman glanced back at them every few seconds with an apologetic smile as if it were her job to keep them entertained while she worked. Emmie felt the urge to help, but knew nothing of how to get a fire started properly, and Finn didn't appear to be concerned.

"Don't you love the music?" Amelia asked while still facing away from them. "Dad says music heals all things."

"It's beautiful," Sarah said.

"I thought Marc had a smaller stereo system?" Finn asked.

Amelia nodded. "He upgraded since you left."

"It's a huge improvement."

The fire started a moment later and Amelia closed the glass doors to the fireplace while turning back to them with clasped hands. "Now, let me get you some wine." Before anyone could object, Amelia hurried away.

Emmie spotted the same stuffed raven from their previous visit, still staring back at her from across the room, its dead eyes daring her to look away. She gestured to it. "I never liked ravens... crows... blackbirds... any of them."

Sarah and Finn followed her gaze.

"Then you wouldn't have liked it much out here when I grew up," Finn said. "Lots more back then. I suppose all the development has driven most of them away. They can be scary, but they're highly intelligent too."

"I don't care how intelligent—don't like them." Emmie frowned.

Sarah leaned into Finn, and he reciprocated while looking into her eyes. "How are you doing?" he asked.

Sarah spoke softly. "We're in the right spot."

Finn glanced around. "The house is old. I'm sure Amelia would know its history. I don't think it was part of the mission, but... do you want me to ask?"

"Yes, but wait until I get back." Sarah stood and glanced around.

Finn seemed to pick up on her needs and stood up while

gesturing down a long hallway on the opposite side of the living room. "It's down there. Do you need help?"

She smirked. "I'm a big girl."

"Sorry." Finn sat again as Sarah hurried away.

Only a moment later, Amelia shuffled out from the kitchen holding a tray with four glasses and a half-empty bottle of red wine. "I poured our finest Pinot reserve. Dad was saving it for a special occasion, but what's the use of having it if you can't share it with friends?"

"Exactly," Finn said.

Amelia glanced around the room. "We've lost one."

"She'll be back in a minute," Emmie apologized.

"I see." Amelia looked toward the hallway, then back to them while distributing the drinks. Sitting on the couch beside Finn, she sipped the wine and leaned back. "So, Finn, what's on your mind? You said you had some questions?"

"I do." Finn held his glass with both hands. "I'm just a little concerned about Paige. Do you have her phone number? I know you said she was off the grid for a while, but I would love to give her a call sometime, just to keep in touch. Or maybe you know when she'll be back?

Amelia looked down. "It's hard to say."

Finn inched forward in his seat and leaned toward her as if to share a secret. "Listen, don't you think it's a little strange that Paige has been gone this long without letting you know exactly where she's at? It's not like her. She was meticulous about that stuff, and I remember Marc even forcing her to carry a cell phone to school just so he could make sure he knew where she was at all times. And I have a few questions about this Liam guy..."

Amelia's pleasant expression faded as the muscles in her face tightened. Pushing her mouth shut, she opened it only a little to speak. "He is quite a character."

"Do you trust him?" Finn asked. "With Paige, I mean."

Amelia paused, then shrugged before looking into Finn's

eyes. "I can't be there to protect my sister all the time. She's got her own life."

Finn swallowed. "That's what I wanted to ask you about. Please tell me the truth. When was the last time you spoke with Paige or had *any* communication with her at all? Text, email..."

Amelia spoke softer and looked down. "It's been a while. But I don't think it's anything you need to worry about."

Finn let out a quick sigh as if holding back his frustration. "I *am* a little worried, actually. How long has it been? A week? A month? Two years?"

Amelia looked up sharply. "What are you trying to say? She calls Dad all the time. I don't know. Maybe you should talk to him."

"This is important, Amelia. When was the last time he talked to her?"

She raised her voice. "I'm not sure. You'll have to ask him."

Finn nodded. "I'd rather hear it from you."

"Why?" Amelia yelled.

A silence fell between them, and the raven across the room caught Emmie's gaze again. The thing stared at her as if trying to peer into the darkest parts of her soul. The words of Edgar Allan Poe came back to her, "Quoth the Raven, nevermore," which Marc had quoted during their previous visit. But now Marc's fascination with Poe's words reverberated through her mind, and something didn't feel right.

Quoth the Raven, nevermore.

Nevermore...

A chill swept through Emmie, and she couldn't hold back, staring into Amelia's weakening eyes. "You know where she's at, don't you?"

Amelia recoiled and scowled. "Don't talk to me like that."

"But you know where she's gone."

"We know something happened to Paige," Finn added. "We have to know the truth. You must know how much I care about you both."

"Everything's all right," Amelia growled. "Just leave it alone."

"Leave what alone?" Finn asked. "Why won't you talk about your sister?"

"It's too painful."

"What's too painful?"

Amelia clenched her fists as if to strike out at Finn. "That she *is* gone."

"Gone where?"

Amelia's eyes watered. "Gone. I don't know where. That's the truth. We haven't seen her in a long time."

Emmie spoke softly. "She's dead, isn't she?"

Amelia stared back, her eyes sharpening one last time at Emmie before they softened. Standing suddenly, Amelia turned her face away, and her body shook as she wiped her eyes and covered her face. "Of course she is. Why doesn't anyone know it?"

Finn stood a moment later but kept his distance. "Whatever happened... we'll get through it. It's going to be okay."

Amelia shook her head. "No, it's not."

Marc's voice erupted from the doorway. "What did you tell them?"

31

Sarah exited the bathroom a little dazed and paused for a moment. Finn's voice came from the living room, a little harsh in tone, which drew a sharp response from Amelia, although none of that seemed to matter right now. The cry for help that she had heard earlier now came from somewhere deep inside the house. But this time it hadn't come as a vision or a dream, but something even more disturbing. The cries of a tormented spirit never sounded like this, and the realization caught her off guard.

She wasn't pursuing a spirit at all, but a living being.

Instead of returning to her friends, she followed the faint cries toward the back of the house as the classical music faded into the background. The voice seemed to echo up through the walls, and it was getting louder as she moved ahead.

Turning left and right, she adjusted her path.

Hang on. I'll be there soon.

So much desperation and longing in that muffled cry. But it *was* the child, no doubt about that. The energy and tone were the same, and the connection between them was as clear as if they were whispering in her ear on some private frequency.

Turning a corner toward the back porch, the emotional

agony coming from the source threatened to drain her energy, although she had learned from previous encounters how to manage it. Judging from the tone of the cries since the last vision, the entity's physical and emotional pain had snowballed into a crisis. They were dying.

But was this the pleading cries of an innocent child as she had seen in her vision? It was impossible to tell, even now, but did it make any sense that a child had gotten trapped somewhere in the house without anyone knowing about it? Nobody had mentioned anything about children in the Moretti family, but the energy that surged through her now had that same sense of innocence—a sweet child in danger—and it was impossible to ignore. She couldn't go back into the living room now to get help from her friends, even if she wanted to. She was on her own.

Shuffling past a door near the end of the hallway, with framed family portraits and flowery painted artwork on all sides, she paused and turned back. She had gone too far. Her internal compass guided her back to the door she'd passed and the urge to open it grew like a compulsion.

Still, she hesitated. Whoever had brought her to that moment had not only picked up on her psychical frequency but had also drawn her into the same house connected with the unsolved murder of a young woman.

Was this another victim of the same killer?

And was that killer sitting now in the living room chatting casually with her friends, who were oblivious of the dangers literally staring them in the face?

Sarah's heart beat faster as she considered the implications. If she found the victim alive, how would she rescue them without drawing the attention of the Moretti family? She had no plan to get them out.

You can't stop now.

The heart wrenching energy coming from behind the door ahead pulled at her as if drawn by a powerful magnet. Regardless of the logistics of the rescue, she had to do something.

Grabbing the door handle with great care, she turned it and pulled.

Locked.

There was a deadbolt on the door, but it was... backwards. The mechanism to unlock the door was facing her as if to prevent someone on the other side from opening it.

Turning the latch, the door swung open with a creak that she minimized by holding her hand against it. The light spilling in from the hallway illuminated the darkened area inside enough to see a staircase leading down into the basement. A cool air drifted around her. But California houses rarely had basements. No, not a basement. A cellar, of course. A wine cellar. The faint fruity smell filled the air, along with the rising moans of someone trapped in that place.

After switching on the light, Sarah descended the staircase with great care, her footsteps rustling noise from every wooden step, although she shifted her weight slowly and held both handrails to steady herself. The musty smell grew stronger as she descended, and as she reached the bottom of the stairs, the noises stopped.

They know I'm coming.

She didn't dare call out to them. The ceiling at the bottom of the stairs was heavily insulated, judging by a section of padding that had broken loose along one seam, but her voice would carry upstairs to some degree. The rest of the wine cellar had walls and an arched ceiling built with laid stones by hand. Rich mahogany wine cabinets full of bottles stacked to the ceiling and several wooden barrels lined both sides of the room, but a longer corridor lay ahead that must have stretched out beyond the edge of the house.

It was at the end of that passageway that she spotted a single door, and she knew on a deep level that the person who had called to her was just behind it. Sarah's breath became the only sound as she stealthily moved forward.

The racks of wine bottles were well organized, labeled by

year and type, with several of the slots empty. There must have been hundreds, maybe thousands, of bottles down there.

This is where Amelia went to retrieve the wine during their previous visit, only a few steps from the person behind the door. Certainly, she must have known.

Arriving at the thick wooden door, she unlatched the two deadbolts and looked over at a small table beside the door. A military-grade knife sat ready—for trouble?—along with several sets of earplugs, some of them still in the package, and a couple of flashlights.

A knife and earplugs. The unsettling mental image made her shudder.

Listening for any signs that someone had followed her, she opened the door and switched on the single, unshielded overhead light.

The room had the setup of a hospital room, with a single hospital-grade bed occupying most of the dark space in the middle, an IV station beside it, and a pile of soiled white sheets in the corner. A table beside the bed held an open box of latex gloves, antiseptic pads, and syringes.

Someone lay in the bed, although a white sheet covered them. It shifted and rose as Sarah approached until a disheveled and gaunt face poked out from under the sheets.

It was the same boy she had seen in her vision, struggling to get free, held captive by several restraints. Wavering as he lifted a hand toward her, the restraint around his wrist tightened. Bloody bandages covered the side of his head above his ear and medical tape held it all in place.

Is this how they had used the knife? Sarah's stomach churned.

He spoke in a weak voice, "Hurry."

32

"I didn't tell them anything." Amelia wiped her eyes and stepped toward him.

"Liar." Marc glared at each of them. Still dressed in his surgical scrubs from the hospital, he removed his keys from his pocket and tossed them onto a nearby table. "After all we've been through."

"What are you hiding?" Finn asked.

"What am *I* hiding?" Marc shot back. "You have no idea what you're asking me. Now go home."

Marc's pitbull, Lenore, barked from the next room, then tried to squeeze its nose through the narrow crack in the door.

"What happened to Paige?" Emmie asked. "We know she's dead."

Marc looked sharply at Amelia.

"I didn't tell them anything," Amelia repeated, shaking her head. "I swear."

"We'll see about that." Marc turned his attention back to Finn and Emmie. "I need you to leave right now, or I can't guarantee your safety."

"Whoa." Finn held up his hands. "Are you threatening me?

Now I definitely know you're hiding something. Did Liam find the treasure?"

"Go home," Marc repeated, a little louder.

"And he killed Paige, right? Or did you find the treasure and then kill Liam to keep him quiet? Which is it?"

Marc stepped toward Amelia but glared at Finn. "You're pushing my patience."

"Or worse," Finn continued, "did *you* kill Paige?"

Marc forced a smile and narrowed his eyes while his face turned red. Pressing his mouth shut until he reached Amelia's side, he latched onto her arm and spoke in a calm voice as if he hadn't heard what Finn had asked him. "Get my bag."

"No, Dad, please," Amelia pleaded.

He yanked her sideways toward the door. "Hurry up."

Nursing her injured arm, she covered her chest and stood in place with her head down. "I can't."

Emmie spoke up. "We found all the documents in Stephen's office, everything related to the ruins. He was onto something here, we know that."

"Stephen should've left it alone."

"You had something to do with my dad's death too?" Finn asked Marc accusingly. "What did you do?" Even before Marc had a chance to answer, Finn nodded and continued, "You did, didn't you, you son-of-a-bitch? He had a heart attack, but you're his cardiologist. You're his *friend*. He trusted you with his *life*. Did you mess with his prescription? Slip him a fatal drug? Is that what—"

"He wouldn't leave it alone," Marc yelled. "I warned him, but he wouldn't mind his own business."

"So you killed him?"

Marc spoke in a matter-of-fact tone. "I couldn't let him interfere."

"Interfere in what? Did you threaten him just like you're threatening us now? Why? Because he figured out you killed Liam? Or Paige? Or maybe you killed all three of them?" He turned to Amelia. "How can you just stand there and stay silent through all of this? Tell me what happened to them."

Amelia wiped her eyes again and shook her head.

Marc grumbled and glanced down as if he were about to confess, then lunged at Finn's throat, catching him off guard. They collided a moment later, knocking Finn back and then sideways to the floor, even as Finn struck his fists into Marc's chest. Lenore erupted on the other side of the door at the same time, growling and barking, drowning out the grunts and gasps of the two men fighting for control of the situation.

Amelia seemed to recoil from the scene, so Emmie slipped out her phone to call 911. But before she could even dial the first number, Amelia had reached into a nearby drawer and pulled out a pistol, aiming it at Emmie's chest with trembling hands. Emmie froze. Amelia's expression wavered between cold detachment and panic, but Emmie wasn't about to doubt the young woman's resolve to help her father.

Finn knocked Marc backwards after a violent struggle until they stood across from each other while trying to catch their breath. Marc's scrubs had torn down the front, with a section of fabric dangling over his chest, revealing a patch of blood that had pooled from a gash on his neck. Finn took the moment to beg Emmie to call the police, but she didn't dare move. Amelia still had the pistol pointed toward her.

But would she really shoot Finn if it came to that? Her lifelong friend? Maybe out of desperation, to cover for her dad, as she must have been involved with what had happened to Paige and Liam to come to his rescue like this.

Finn jumped forward again in a fit of rage, but Marc's fists cracked across Finn's face, knocking him to the ground as blood trickled from his nose. But it continued, and Marc kicked at Finn's chest, again and again as he dragged himself along the edge of the wall toward the couch while gasping for breath. The blows seemed to have knocked the wind out of Finn's struggle.

"Amelia," Finn said weakly, "how can you let this happen?"

Blood ran down Finn's forearm, coming from a source hidden somewhere beneath his shirt. Marc was hunched forward while standing over Finn, but from the look in his eyes, he still had enough rage in him to do it all again if he had to.

"Dad, please don't," Amelia screamed. "Please stop."

"Give me the gun," Marc demanded. "I'm going to finish this."

Amelia shook her head. "Dad, no, I can't."

"Lenore! Where are you?" He glanced back at the door where the dog had worked itself into a frenzy, growling and scratching and tearing at the door's edge with its teeth. The wood visibly strained under the weight of its body, and it had already torn a small hole large enough to push its nose through. It wouldn't take much longer before its head came through, then its body, then...

"Give me the gun!" Marc shouted at her, his face reddened.

"No!" Amelia screamed and turned the gun on Marc now. Her hands trembled as she stepped toward Emmie, never veering her aim from his chest. "Stay away from him."

"You've got to be kidding me," Marc said. "After all we've been through with this. He's just a punk."

"It's over, Dad." Amelia's eyes watered.

"Sure." Marc inched toward her. "I won't kill him, if that's what you want. But nobody leaves. Now give me the gun." He extended a palm.

Amelia moved in beside Emmie. The pistol was within reach, but Emmie could only assume that Amelia would defend her father with more violence if she tried to grab it. Still, there wasn't much time to act.

Emmie's heart pounded as she calculated how she would rush Amelia and grab the gun. Just a quick thrust to the side and rip it from Amelia's grip. It couldn't be too difficult—the young woman wasn't as fit as her father. Emmie tensed while focusing on the pistol's barrel.

"Here." Amelia thrust the pistol into Emmie's hands and backed away. "I can't do it."

With a shudder, Emmie took it and aimed at Marc's chest, while watching Amelia from the corner of her eye.

The man stopped. The rage swelled on his face, baring his teeth at Amelia. "What have you done?"

"It's over, Dad." Amelia wilted and took another step back.

Finn used the back of his hand to wipe a streak of blood from his face, then crawled to a standing position beside the couch. "You must have killed my brother too."

"No." Marc clenched his teeth and met Finn's gaze.

"Don't lie. We found the gold coin, so we know he was involved. Did you threaten him or blackmail him into keeping silent? I'm sure you knew of his drug use. He trusted you. Or maybe you were there in the basement to help him pull the trigger after giving him a little *medicine*?"

"That's bullshit and you know it."

"What happened to Paige?" Finn stepped over beside Emmie.

"I don't know," Marc finally seemed to calm a bit. "Don't you think I'm doing everything I can to find her? She can't rest until I do."

"So, you *do* know she's dead. Who killed her? Did Liam do it?"

"Of course he did. I could never kill my little girl. Are you serious?" Marc looked at Amelia with pained eyes. "Nothing is more important than finding her. That punk tricked her into following him somewhere at the ruins to find that treasure. I think the bastard found it, although I don't have any proof." Marc turned his attention back to Finn. "He killed my Paige, and I don't know where she is."

"Why didn't you go to the police?" Emmie asked.

He scoffed. "The police? You don't understand. This guy..." Marc pressed his mouth closed.

"What about him?" Finn asked.

"Amelia and I looked everywhere for her," Marc said. "*He* knows where she is—the only one who does. I can't let the police have him. He'll be out on the streets the next day."

"That's not how it works," Finn said.

"That's how it works with this guy."

Finn glared at Marc. "So, you know where he is, right? Tell us."

Amelia was silent and still.

Finn moved toward Marc with his fists clenched as if he might take a swing at him. "Did you kill Liam?"

Marc laughed. "Not yet."

"So, you know where to find him."

"What do you care? He deserves everything he got."

"Where is he?"

Marc's gaze dropped to the floor.

Emmie also glanced down and the answer flashed through her mind. "The wine cellar."

"Leave it alone," Marc spoke low and clear.

Finn's expression brightened while staring at Marc. "He's down there, isn't he?"

Lenore had nearly torn a hole through the door. Only a few more minutes and he would be free. As if sensing Emmie's fear, Amelia stepped over to the door and kneeled in front of the hole. In a calm voice, she repeated, "It's over, Lenore. Now we'll never find Paige."

Finn stepped back. "We'll find her, but not *your* way."

"You're an idiot," Marc said with a sneer. "Just like your father."

Finn's face reddened again as he turned back toward Marc, but someone's voice came from below the floorboards. He looked down then around the room. "Where's Sarah?"

33

Sarah hurried to the boy as the putrid smell of filth hung in the air. On a shelf in the corner sat a pile of men's clothes, judging by the size—nothing a young boy would wear—a pair of jeans, gray socks stuffed into a pair of running shoes, and a green flannel shirt.

A single red wastebasket sat beside the hospital bed, stamped biohazard, with an orange liner. Glancing inside, there was a handful of needles and used syringes, along with a few tiny glass bottles that she instantly recognized as the same type she routinely administered to her own patients in the hospital. Reading one of the bottle labels, she recognized the medication.

Morphine.

Something only an addict or a medical professional would have access to. Someone like Dr. Marc Moretti.

Staring back at the boy's gaunt face, her heart sank. How long had they kept him down in that dank cellar? And why? A torrent of emotions swept through her like a tornado as she contemplated what to do. Of course, she had to get him out of there, but she couldn't allow her heart to blind her.

Squinting and maneuvering himself toward her, the black straps attached to his wrists and ankles rustling with every movement, the boy's face filled with hope. He spoke with a dry, raspy voice, "I knew you'd find me."

"What happened here?"

He shifted to the left and right, then shuddered as he slipped his foot out from under the sheet as far as the restraint around would allow. The dry, cracking skin around his toes was soiled, as if he hadn't bathed in weeks. "No time," he pleaded in a drowsy voice. "Please, get me out of here."

"Yes," Sarah answered. "Of course. But what's your name?"

He turned his eyes up and furrowed his brow while straining. "I... I don't remember. They kidnapped me."

Sarah's aching heart pounded as she reached toward the phone in her pocket. "I'll get the police."

The boy held out a hand and looked toward the ceiling. "No. They'll kill us all. We have to leave."

Sarah had a million questions, but he was right. A call to the police might escalate the situation and put Em and Finn in danger upstairs. They all had to get out of there, as far away as possible, before notifying the authorities. Whatever the Moretti family had done to the boy down there wouldn't get settled with a simple 'Knock at the door. You're under arrest.' They obviously had gone to great lengths to keep this boy imprisoned and they would no doubt defend their secrets with more violence. Run first, get help later.

But she would need to get him out of the restraints first. The straps were hospital-grade—no doubt Dr. Moretti had acquired them for just this purpose—and she unbuckled all four of them in seconds, exposing the boy's inflamed, raw wrists and ankles. With his hands and feet free, he touched the sores briefly, then struggled to crawl off the bed.

He wore a hospital gown with blood stains down the front. The back of the gown was open, revealing an emaciated frame with signs of malnutrition and neglect on a scale she had never seen before. This was not only criminal, this was inhumane. They had treated this boy like an abused animal.

Sarah instinctively reached out to help him stand, but he waved her away and recoiled. "Don't touch me."

"Sorry, but I am a nurse."

He shook his head and pulled away further. "I don't like when people touch me. Especially nurses."

Sarah remembered Amelia was studying to be a nurse. Marc's daughter must have actively participated in the abuse, using her training to aid her father. "I don't blame you."

His bare feet slapped against the cold cement floors as his drowsy eyes peered at the open door. "Are you all alone?"

"My friends are upstairs with... them."

He glanced at her curiously on the way to the door as if doubting the trust he had put in her. She smiled warmly in return, but avoided touching him as he'd requested. Those were the same desperate eyes she had seen in her vision, and the way his vulnerability seemed to penetrate her heart gave her the strength to do anything to get him out of there alive.

How was she going to get him upstairs and out the back door without attracting attention? Maybe he already knew the way out and had been preparing for such a moment as this. Maybe he'd been planning his escape for months, even years? By the way he struggled forward with a stoic determination, she trusted his judgment better than her own. But he was wobbling, grasping at the wall for balance as they trudged across the room toward the door, and getting up the stairs seemed a daunting task.

Stepping out into the hallway, they paused at the small table just beyond the door. The boy observed the items on it for a long moment, then finally picked up one of the flashlights and knocked the earplugs off the table with the back of his hand while rolling his eyes in silence. What were the earplugs for? To drown out his screaming? Another thing she would ask him later.

He also picked up the knife. Holding it in his shaky hand, he stared at the blade. His emotions flared a bright red. Revenge?

Sarah reached toward the knife. "I better take that."

Reluctantly, the boy relinquished it. "Sure."

The blade glimmered in the cellar's light, but instead of placing it back on the table, she held it down at her side. It offered a little security, but would she actually use it against Marc or Amelia? She squeezed the handle and thought of what she had just witnessed in that room.

Yes, if I have to.

The boy picked up his pace, even as he winced and gasped with each step, but instead of heading back down the hallway toward the stairs, he made a sharp turn toward a door nestled between two tall wine racks. Opening it with ease and flipping a light switch, he glanced back and gestured for her to follow him into the dimly lit stairway. "We'll go out the back."

She studied his small, crooked frame for a moment. Could he manage the stairs by himself? She could carry him—he couldn't have weighed more than eighty pounds—but the narrow passageway would make it difficult. And how old was he? Twelve? Thirteen? Such horrible things to endure for someone so young. She couldn't, or wouldn't, imagine any of it.

Why?

It was heartbreaking. In any case, how could the Moretti family have continued on, knowing the boy was down in their wine cellar suffering every day—the emotional, physical, mental pain he must have gone through? Such horrors.

Seeing the boy recover so quickly brightened her heart, but after he rushed to the bottom of the stairs, he stumbled for a moment, and she instinctively reached out toward him while holding the knife off to the side.

He seemed to sense her hand and pulled away at the last second, looking at her again with wide eyes.

"I'm sorry," she whispered.

Without saying another word, she followed him up the stairs into what looked like a small storage shed, although it was dark and empty, except for a broken wine barrel, some discarded tools, and a pile of rags. A stench hung in the air. Dried blood? She hurried ahead to work the latches on the door, hoping someone hadn't locked it from the other side, but when the door finally clicked open, she let out her breath and escorted the boy outside.

As the sunshine touched the boy's face, he looked toward the bright sky and closed his eyes for a moment. "I never thought I'd see the day."

They stood at the edge of the vineyard, but not too far from the house. Sarah glanced back, although there was no sign that anyone inside the house had noticed their escape. Gesturing forward, she gazed down again at his thin frame. The full extent of his injuries became clear in the crisp, bright air. So many cuts and bruises, and it was a miracle that he could stand at all with his arms and legs so weakened by neglect. "We should keep moving. I'll call the police once we're safe."

The boy nodded and hurried forward while hunkering down as if it might help, but there were plenty of windows facing them on Raven House, with no trees to shield them from view. She could only hope that Marc and Amelia didn't glance outside and see them escaping.

Rushing along the edge of the vineyard, the ravens cawed in the trees nearby, probably watching them with interest as they crouched and scurried like animals between the rows.

The boy seemed to know the terrain better than she did. He moved through the maze of trees and vines with ease until they came out on the other side near the ruins ten minutes later.

A sickening wave of suffering swept through her. They had barely paused to catch their breath, but the tormented spirits caught in that place threatened to end their escape sooner than she had hoped. She kept going, despite the growing pain, but stopped when they passed behind a narrow stone wall. They were far out of sight from Raven House, but it wouldn't take Marc and Amelia long to find them such a short distance away.

"Maybe now is a good time to call the police." Sarah dug into her pocket and started to pull out her phone.

The boy reached out and grabbed her arm. "No."

When his icy hands touched hers, something flashed through her mind. A brief glimpse of the boy's true identity as some sort of veil seemed to melt away. She had seen that face somewhere before. Not just in the visions.

His mouth gaped, and a bit of panic flared across his face until he grabbed the knife from her hand and knocked her phone away. Squeezing her arm tighter, he pressed the knife's blade against her chest. "Don't scream."

34

Finn didn't waste any time in rushing through the house, searching every room for Sarah while Emmie held Marc and Amelia at gunpoint in the living room. He steered clear of Marc's office, where Lenore had nearly ripped a hole through the door, but Sarah wouldn't have gone anywhere near there anyway. She had stepped away from them to use the bathroom, hadn't she? But even after calling her name several times, there was no sign of her. During Finn's mad dash through the hallways, Lenore's barking and growling echoed throughout the house.

Returning to the living room, he called out her name again without a response, then turned to Emmie in exasperation. "Where is she?"

"She couldn't have gone far," Emmie said.

"But I looked—" There was only one place he hadn't searched. The wine cellar. But Sarah wouldn't have gone down there on her own unless...

...something powerful had drawn her there. Something or someone.

And the wine cellar door was near the back of the house, next to the bathroom. Hurrying down the hallway again, he wondered how he could have overlooked it before. But throwing the door open, he stomped down the old wooden stairs while calling Sarah's name.

Bracing himself for the worst, he spotted a door at the end of the cellar that had once housed stacks of wine barrels, but now it was wide open. The edge of a hospital bed caught his attention and a chill passed through him. If Marc had held Liam in that place and Sarah had somehow wandered down there, she might have gotten...

In his panic, all sorts of images flashed through his mind, even as his heart pounded faster, and ran toward the open door. The hallway was so dark, as everything seemed to close in around him, until he ran into the dimly lit room and called out Sarah's name once again.

An empty hospital bed sat on one side of the room, with soiled linen on the floor, and no sign of Sarah.

As the full nature of the makeshift hospital room surrounding him started to sink in, the stench of what must have happened there made him gag. Liam had been there... and for a long time. Marc and Amelia had held him captive in that dank room, just as they'd said.

But Liam was gone, and Sarah too. Finn had found the doors open, he reasoned, so Sarah must have either taken pity on Liam and brought him outside, or the scumbag had kidnapped her. Sarah was the epitome of compassion as a nurse, but she never would have gone with Liam voluntarily. Not after everything that had happened.

Without wasting another moment, Finn ran upstairs and met Marc's stern glare from his spot on the floor where Emmie still hovered over him. Marc's face was full of apprehension and anger, as if anticipating the dreaded news. "What did you do?"

"He's gone," Finn said. "Sarah too."

"You son-of-a-bitch!" Marc tried to stand while slamming his fist into the wall, but Emmie pushed him down again. His fist left a deep impression in the sheet rock. "You let him go? You've got to be kidding me. He's the only one who knows where she is."

"I didn't let him go. Sarah—"

"That bitch!" Marc yelled.

Finn's face warmed and he clenched his fists. "Say that again and you'll regret it. She must have gone downstairs to explore. Maybe she heard him screaming. You had him locked in the wine cellar like a rat in a cage. You should have called the police after Paige disappeared."

"I don't think you understand the situation," Marc said condescendingly. "You think the police can handle a guy like that?"

"Why couldn't they?" Emmie asked.

"He's got a *way with words*," Marc said mockingly. "And I don't mean he just puts on a little charm to get what he wants. This guy has one of those reality distortion fields around him, like a cult leader. Anything he says... you believe him. It messes with you."

Emmie glanced at Finn. "The child?"

"What child?" Marc asked.

Finn nodded. "Liam must have appeared as the child in Sarah's visions. He's from a psychic family. Remember what his mom said about his abilities, that 'he could charm anyone into seeing things his way.' Maybe that wasn't just a figure of speech, but that he can do exactly that, make others *see* things. An empath like Sarah would pick up on that sort of emotional persuasion right away. Visions of a helpless child would pull her right in."

Marc laughed. "For two years we had things under control, and we almost broke the bastard. We almost had it, but you messed it all up. Maybe he doesn't have a lot of strength left after being down there, but all he needs is to get to someone, say a few words."

Finn turned to Emmie. "Can you see Sarah in your mind? Or try to sense Liam? Get his location?"

"I'll try." Emmie pushed her eyelids together for a moment then opened them again and shook her head. "Finding a spirit is one thing, but a human? I don't see either of them."

Finn turned to Marc and Amelia. "I'll never forgive you if something happens to Sarah."

"What about my Paige?" Marc pleaded.

"We won't let Liam get away—I'm sure Sarah's with him—but you're not going anywhere either. You're done."

Marc and Amelia looked at each other as if reading each other's thought until Marc spoke up, "Listen, he's probably on his way to the airport by now to book the first plane out of the country. He had plenty of money stashed away."

"From selling off the gold treasure he found," Emmie said. "We heard."

Marc seemed to study her for a long second. "So, he's probably running back to get the rest of it."

"Where is that?" Finn asked.

"Do you think he told *me?*" Marc grumbled. "Only Liam and Paige knew where it came from, and Neil, but he isn't talking." He glanced down for a moment as if he regretted his choice of words, then continued, "But I don't care about the treasure. All I care about is my Paige, and now you've messed up everything, and we'll never find her body."

Amelia inched toward her dad. "It took us a while to realize that Paige was gone—too long. Like Dad said, Liam has a way with words. We believed she was in good hands when he disappeared with her for the longest time. But then when he showed up without her and started avoiding us, that's when Neil went looking for her too. He wasn't as taken in by the lies as we were, not at first. I think Liam tried to pay him off to stay away because of Neil's financial situation, but then things escalated. Neil got in a fight with Liam at his mother's psychic shop, and the next day, Neil died."

Finn looked into Amelia's eyes. "Tell me the truth. Was Neil on drugs before he died?"

Amelia shook her head. "I don't think so. Like I said, he was desperate for money, but not from that. You know he wasn't good with finances. But when he died, that's when we realized something was seriously messed up. We snapped out of it, and tricked Liam into going downstairs. We had to wear earplugs to keep him from getting in our heads again. I know Liam had something to do with Paige's disappearance, although we never got any answers. He never talked." Her eyes watered. "We just wanted to find her body."

"We kept him sedated most of the time," Marc said, "to one degree or another. Can't take any chances with all the workers nearby."

"But when his mind cleared," Emmie added, "He found Sarah and tricked her into coming here."

"That's right," Marc said, jabbing his finger into the air toward Finn. "That's what he does. Somehow, he messes with your mind in a way that you believe everything he says. We started using the earplugs after Amelia—" He winced and clamped his mouth shut.

Amelia finished his sentence, "After I almost killed myself in front of him with that same gun." She pointed to the pistol in Emmie's hand. "He somehow got me to turn it on myself and I almost pulled the trigger."

An image of Neil's suicide passed through Finn's mind. Liam and Neil had spent time together before his death. "If Liam had anything to do with Neil..."

"I bet he did," Marc said. "Take us with you and we'll find him faster."

"You're not calling the shots anymore," Finn interrupted. "You murdered my dad, remember?"

"I only did what I had to do. For Paige." Marc softened his voice. "Stephen's days were numbered anyway because of his heart condition. I just wanted him to give me some time to find my little girl. But for God's sake, don't kill Liam, at least not until we find her. Or just bring him back here and let me deal with him."

"You had your chance." Finn turned away.

"I'm sorry," Amelia said, wilting a little further toward her dad with deep remorse in her eyes. "We followed the wrong path."

"We *will* find Sarah and Liam... and Paige," Finn said.

Marc settled back against the wall and scoffed, "Good luck, Finn. But don't let him say a word to you if you do find him. Wear the earplugs. He'll get to you too."

"And then what?" Finn asked. "You slip us the same drug you used to give my dad a heart attack?"

Marc stayed silent and looked away.

Emmie waved the pistol toward Marc and Amelia. "What should we do with them?"

Her question hung in the air, along with a sense of urgency to run outside and chase after Liam, although they couldn't just leave Marc and Amelia in the house unguarded.

Finn glanced down and tapped his shoe on the floor. "There's a nice clean room for them in the cellar."

"Perfect."

Emmie led Marc and Amelia down the stairs at gunpoint to the back of the cellar and locked them in the room that Liam had escaped from only an hour earlier. Finn watched from the doorway as Marc seemed resigned to his fate, although he stood battered and bruised next to the same bed where he must have tormented Liam over the past two years.

Amelia gave a final plea before they shut the door. "Please don't give Liam over to the police until he tells you where Paige is at. Force him to lead you to her body. That's the only way, but keep your ears closed and your eyes open."

Marc grumbled, "He's a slimy son-of-a-bitch."

"Too bad you sunk to his level," Finn said and pushed the door closed.

With the room secured, they made their way back upstairs

and Emmie handed Finn the pistol, suggesting that if Liam was as strong psychically as it seemed, then less was more in that case. Finn accepted it with an unsettling confidence.

Hurrying through the house toward the front door, Lenore pushed his snout through the opening in the door he had carved out, baring his teeth and sniffing at the air as they passed by. His growls filled the air behind them as they stepped outside and paused for a moment on the porch, scanning the fields for any signs of Liam. The fugitive was nowhere in sight.

At that moment, a group of ravens let out a series of menacing cries as they gathered in a tree at the edge of the vineyard.

Emmie looked toward the skies. "He can't hide anywhere without disturbing them." Her gaze stopped on a swirl of black dots scattering from a tree at the opposite end of the vineyard in the direction of the ruins.

Two figures walked below the circling birds: Sarah and a man in a hospital gown.

Liam.

35

Emmie glanced at the pistol in Finn's hand as she climbed into the car's driver's seat. "Maybe we *should* let the police handle this." The safety was on, but would any of them *actually* shoot someone?

"We need to listen to what Marc said." Finn inched the pistol down as if to ease her fears. "He's dangerous, and we're the right people to tackle this. We know how to deal with this stuff."

"He's probably unarmed." Emmie started the car and headed out toward the ruins.

"He's got *Sarah*. And without Paige's body," Finn said, "the police would probably let him go like Marc said. If Liam hasn't caved in all the time he's been locked up down in that wine cellar, what makes you think he would give up her location for the police? Not going to happen. If we don't get it out of him, then nobody will. He kidnapped Sarah, and we need to find Paige, not just for Marc and Amelia, but for me."

Emmie gestured at the pistol. "Just be careful."

Finn scoffed. "I've owned weapons before. I promise I won't shoot him... Not unless he *really* pisses me off."

"That's what I'm afraid of."

Turning onto the road that led to the ruins, Emmie tightened her grip on the steering wheel. A dark energy hung in the air. Something had stirred up the hostile spirits and the unnerving sense of dread seemed to grow as they got closer.

Parking the car while keeping her eye out for any signs of Liam or Sarah, they rushed across the ruins toward the flock of ravens still circling overhead. Navigating the crumbled structures, a flurry of tortured spirits appeared ahead, wavering at the edge of transparency like a mirage as if daring them to continue. She caught a glimpse of their madness at times, faces full of defiance, and they echoed the violence they had committed, although it failed to slow them.

Rushing back to the large oak tree beyond the ruins, they found the same opening they had discovered during their previous visit, but now the signs were everywhere: they had missed Liam by mere minutes. The stones blocking the hole were now lying beside it, and someone had ripped away at the soil and stretched the tree roots aside, creating an opening between them large enough for a man to crawl through.

"I knew it," Finn said. "I knew that's how he got into the cave, and I know the treasure is also down there. Why else would he come back here first?"

"He won't get away," Emmie said.

Finn seemed not to hear her. He dropped to his knees and carefully set the pistol aside before ripping away at the tree roots, dirt and stones along the edge of the hole. "The bastard is down there with Sarah."

The darkness was thick in the hole. "How can he see anything?" Emmie asked.

Finn gave a wry grin. "Maybe he's gained an ability to see in the dark after living in the cellar for so long?"

She played along, then took out her phone and switched it into flashlight mode. "I don't think that's how human eyesight works."

Finn used her phone to light the hole. "At least we've got the rat cornered."

Digging out the earplugs from her pocket, she offered Finn a pair. "Just in case..."

Finn waved them away, then handed the phone back to Emmie. "Not sure if we can use the earplugs down there. We'll need all of our senses just to get around."

The darkness was daunting, but before Finn could object, Emmie pushed in front of him. "I'll go first."

He moved back to give her room.

Sliding into the hole feet-first, the cold dirt chilled her body as she snaked along the ground for only a few feet into the darkness until the ground sloped sharply downward. "There's a drop."

"Go slow."

She tapped her foot into the empty space. "How did he get down there?"

"Does it go *straight* down?"

"I think so." Dropping a little further, her shoe touched something like a soft tree root. Tapping and pushing against it, she went a little further and aimed the light in far enough to see that it was some sort of rope ladder. "Well, that answers my question."

Catching her foot onto one of the rungs, she descended the ladder with great care to keep the surrounding debris from crashing below. Even in that small space, there were spirits frantically crowding in front of her as if trying to prevent her from continuing. Their futile efforts made no difference, although their rage sent a chill down her spine. The greed still burned in their souls, and they would no doubt kill her if given the opportunity.

Finn came in right behind her, and she directed his every step until they both stood together on a solid floor caked with dirt. Stepping over a mound of stones and debris, they came into a larger cave the size of a small bedroom. The space was filled to the ceiling with all sorts of wooden and stone relics, from Spanish swords, spears, and shields to stacks of chairs and a table. Pottery and carvings sat covered in dust beside a thick leather-bound book surrounded by stacks of rosary beads and ornate crosses the size of a small child. These were all the things the mission had either discarded or hid at some point in its past, but there was still no sign of the treasure, or Liam and Sarah.

Finn scanned the items and seemed to confirm this with a brief unimpressed glance, then focused his light on a smaller wooden chest that someone had broken open. It was empty. "He must have grabbed as much gold as he could handle with Paige's help and then planned to come back for the rest before Marc and Amelia got to him."

Shining their lights in every direction, there was no sign of Liam, although two passageways branched off from the room in opposite directions. The light didn't reach far enough down the passages to see if anyone was there, either waiting for them to leave or preparing to pounce.

But something was very wrong. The putrid smell of death hung in the air. And how far had Liam and Sarah gone into the cave? Emmie swallowed her panic.

Only a moment later, Finn gasped. Emmie followed his gaze to a partially obscured young woman's decomposing body lying within the shadows not far from the passageway ahead.

Paige.

Finn charged forward and dropped to his knees beside his childhood friend, although he didn't touch her. "Paige," Finn said with a moan. "Oh God, we found you."

Paige's hair was matted with blood and the stains covered her shirt, just as Emmie had seen on the young woman's spirit in the vineyard. The decay had slowed from the cool air inside the cave, but the injuries were clear, and everything was the same down to the bare foot and missing sneaker, which sat on its side beside the body.

Shining her phone's light into the opening, Emmie caught a whiff of something burning and the faint sound of a young man chanting. "Finn," she whispered.

He gazed up at her mournfully, his eyes watering.

"Do you hear that?" she asked.

They stood motionless as the chanting continued until Finn nodded and stood again. Wiping away the tears, he straightened and gestured toward the source. "Let's go."

Slipping through the opening first, Emmie dimmed her phone to hide their presence. The narrow passageway extended another twenty feet to a larger room ahead that was lit by flickering flames, the dancing lights reflecting off the damp walls.

They crept carefully over the dirt and stones. Finn moved beside her, pistol raised. The chanting helped to drown out their stealthy but flawed approach, but it stopped suddenly moments before they turned the corner and peeked inside.

The stunning, torch-lit sight took their breath away. Gold objects filled every space. Piles of bead necklaces and stone tablets sat among a massive hoard of priceless gold treasures that would have sent any treasure hunter into ecstasy.

But all that wealth faded into the background when she spotted Liam holding a black dagger over Sarah's bare chest as she lay motionless on a massive, intricately carved stone disc.

An Aztec human sacrifice altar.

36

A wave of panic swept through Emmie as she lurched forward. "No!"

Finn did the same while raising the pistol toward Liam.

But both of them stopped suddenly when Liam raised the dagger over Sarah's chest, squeezing the handle threateningly as if he might plunge it into her flesh at the slightest provocation. "Stay away or..."

Sarah's limp body was draped over the top of the stone altar facing up, with her head and arms held in place by ropes tied around stones near the ground, while her bare chest arched toward the ceiling over the center. Despite their presence, she wasn't struggling. The cryptic figures and symbols carved into the sides of the altar mirrored the ghastly designs of other objects in the room. Dark streaks ran through a carved channel across the top of the altar to the side of the stone.

Dried blood?

A legion of spirits had gathered, crowding in with burning eyes, ripping and clawing at each other with unbridled greed. Each of them desperately strained toward the treasure as if it held the key to eternal bliss, but something, some unseen barrier, was keeping them from reaching their prize.

Finn inched forward and cried out, "Sarah!"

"Don't bother," Liam said. "She can't hear you. Take another step, see what happens."

"Let her go," Finn demanded.

"Not after all that work." Liam looked at Emmie and laughed. "Would you like to take her place? It's the only way to satisfy them, you know."

"What did you do to her?" Emmie asked, looking to her friend for a reaction. *Any* reaction.

Liam brushed Sarah's hair with the back of his hand, glancing down at her for only a moment before locking his gaze on Finn again. "Hush. You'll wake her up."

"Sarah!" Finn yelled louder.

"That won't work," Liam said. "She's gone far away from here. And she won't wake up—ever—if you pull that trigger."

"You're psychic," Emmie said. "So, you're controlling her mind or hypnotizing her…"

Liam looked back curiously. "Hypnosis is for hacks."

Emmie could only think of Sarah and how to stall for time. "How are you doing it?"

"What you *really* mean is, what can you do to stop me? Well, it's quite easy, actually, at least for me. It's all about believing in yourself. I *believe* I will soon possess all the treasure in this room, and so… it will happen. It's my gift. I create my reality, and I sometimes share that gift with others, like your friend here, creating a reality for them too."

"I *believe* you're a piece of shit," Finn said.

Liam laughed. "But none of you will survive much longer."

A wave of dread swept through Emmie's mind. A feeling of disconnect from reality. Staring at Liam, she refocused her thoughts. Sarah stirred briefly within the constraints, then settled again.

"You see?" Liam said. "You believed me for a moment. And as soon as—"

"You can't control all of us at once," Emmie said. "Sarah's still alive, so you can't risk letting go of her mind to get at us."

Liam grumbled. "The drugs have taken their toll, but the serenity of the cellar also clarified what I need to do. Don't tempt fate."

Emmie watched Sarah's chest rise and fall beneath the dagger's blade. "Why her?"

"It's the only way to satisfy them."

"Satisfy who?" Emmie asked.

"The Aztec gods, of course." Liam gestured toward a gold idol with jeweled eyes sitting on a wooden chest above them, staring down at them like a gargoyle. "That one piece is worth more than a mansion, and it's not so difficult to sell. There's more than plenty for everyone here, if you think you can play nice. We can share everything in this room."

"I don't want any of it," Finn said.

"I don't believe you," Liam mocked and glanced around. "But I must admit, I wasn't expecting guests at the ceremony. Did you follow me? Where are the others? Is the Moretti family waiting for me outside?" He stared intently at Finn's pistol.

"No, they're not, are they? They don't know you're here… or perhaps you killed them?" He laughed. "Now we can be partners."

"Wasn't Paige enough?" Emmie pleaded, if only to distract him for a little longer. "She suffered so much because she loved you."

A flash of pain seemed to sweep over his face. "I made a mistake with Paige. Killed her in the wrong way. I needed to remove the heart to satisfy the gods. You know, it's all about the heart with the Aztecs. And the blood."

"It won't work," Emmie said. "Just let her go."

"Or I'll shoot," Finn added.

"You might," Liam said. "But it wouldn't take much for me to slice her open before I die. The obsidian stone used in this dagger is still razor sharp after so many years. Can you believe that? Such an advanced culture, the Aztecs. It cuts flesh apart like a scalpel. Is that what you want?"

Finn didn't answer.

"You won't get out of here alive if you hurt her," Emmie said. "It's over."

"The gods might disagree. Don't you think they'll protect me? They want her blood more than I do. Funny, I might not have risked coming back here at all—better to get as far away from Raven House as possible after all I've been through with those psychopaths—but she..." Liam touched the skin between Sarah's breasts. "The opportunity to perform the sacrifice correctly this time was just too much to resist when she answered my call for help."

"Don't touch her," Finn yelled.

"I'll do more than that."

Emmie spoke up, attempting to diffuse the situation by aiming at his ego. "So, you *did* manipulate Sarah through the visions."

"Impressed?" He made a little grin.

"Hardly," she said. "You've got a psychic gift, I know that, but you're also a coward and you failed. She didn't see a child at first. She saw a monster."

Liam scowled. "The drugs interfered. After I sensed a receptive psychic nearby, I couldn't focus well enough to send a clear signal from the cellar, but I knew it would work. A child in danger, an Aztec god, a monster. Whatever it takes to stir their emotions. Do you think she would have run to my aid if she knew the truth?"

"So, you did the same to Neil when he started looking for Paige after you killed her?"

Liam's eyes widened. "You're good."

Finn's voice cracked. "You killed Neil."

"It didn't take much," Liam admitted. "He was already so destitute and depressed, and he had access to plenty of weapons in the house. I just had to set the stage in his mind, plant some terrifying visions about Aztec gods coming to drag him to hell for receiving some of the gold. I gave him some, to keep him quiet, although he didn't stop, so I had to take drastic measures. The stories of the curse helped to set the stage. He did all the rest."

Finn was visibly shaking. His finger hovered over the trigger. "I *will* kill you."

Liam lowered the dagger and touched the tip against Sarah's chest. "Then we'll both go together."

He stared at Finn for a long moment, as if contemplating his next move, when the earth rumbled, kicking up a cloud of dust as the ground swayed for a few seconds.

"Now look what you've done," Liam said with a grin. "You've angered the gods. They want their sacrifice."

Emmie held out her arms to steady herself as the ground swayed and cried out, "Let her go. We don't care about the treasure. You can have it."

"Of course I can. Right after the gods release it to me." Liam tensed above the dagger, then thrust it down.

37

At the same time Liam plunged the dagger, Finn squeezed the trigger. The round caught Liam in the shoulder, spinning him around as the dagger went flying, landing several feet away.

A trickle of blood erupted from the point where the dagger had made contact against Sarah's chest, and she squirmed in place, with muffled moans escaping through the gag's edges as the tremors continued.

Emmie rushed to Sarah's side. "Sarah, I've got you."

Finn lunged at the dagger, retrieving it a moment later, while firing off two more deafening rounds at Liam, both of which exploded against the wall of treasure behind him and ricocheted back across the room.

The rumbling noise and volley of curses between Liam and Finn continued as Emmie struggled to remove the ropes from Sarah's wrists and ankles. Her friend gagged and coughed beneath the rag in her mouth until Finn rushed over with the dagger and used it to cut through the ropes.

Liam had fallen on his side with blood soaking through his hospital gown, but now attempted to stand up as they scrambled to get Sarah out of there.

Within the sound of cracking earth and rattling treasure, several small chunks of stone rained down on them from the ceiling, although Emmie feared the greater danger was that the entire cave might collapse before they got to safety. No doubt the cave had survived numerous earthquakes over the years, but the magnitude of that moment was stronger than anything she'd ever gone through.

In the frenzy of getting Sarah out of the room, Finn stumbled and dropped the dagger. Liam's gaze fell on it, and he seemed to recover with renewed strength, scrambling toward it while hunched forward and nursing his injured shoulder. Finn maneuvered toward it at the same time while embracing Sarah and kicked it into the corner moments before Liam reached it.

Liam cursed, his voice drowned out by the growing chaos, but instead of following his charge toward Finn, he veered back toward the dagger as if retrieving it held his last chance for salvation.

Emmie took in a deep breath and let out a series of deep coughs. Sarah did the same, and seconds later as she seemed to come out of her trance as they closed in on the exit. The dust obscured most of their view, made worse by the light from their phones, which reflected off the particles to produce a thick, glowing fog, but it was their only source of light in that space.

The opening was straight ahead, but before leaving the room, Emmie glanced back and spotted the dagger in Liam's grasp as he struggled toward them. He stared with a burning hatred in his eyes, but slowed instead of making a final charge to try to stop them. Instead, he veered toward the gold idol he'd pointed out earlier, wrapping his good arm around it along with the dagger. Weighed down by the priceless object, he moved toward them in bursts, cradling the object against his chest like a cherished prize.

After Liam boldly swept away the gold object, the spirits crowding into the space worked themselves into a frenzy to stop him from stealing what they believed to be theirs. Each one clawed at a different part of Liam's gaunt frame as if trying to pluck the idol out of his hands before he made off with it. The rage on the faces of those who had tried to plunder the treasure for themselves was clear and terrifying. Was this fury the result of the curse or the source of it?

Crawling through the narrow opening separating the two rooms, the ground continued to sway, threatening to topple them over with each advance, but they worked as a team, silently synchronizing each step to move forward until they passed through the room full of Spanish relics without pausing.

The rope ladder creaked and swayed as Finn helped Sarah up each step, although she moved without any signs of Liam's influence now. Emmie went next.

Meeting outside in a patch of brown grass within the shade of the tree, Emmie removed her jacket and slipped it over Sarah's bare shoulders while checking her friend's wound. The dagger had cut through her skin, but at least the bleeding had stopped. Still, she needed to get her friend to the hospital as soon as possible.

Finn came up the ladder only a moment later, straining and gasping for air as he crawled out of the hole while Liam's hoarse voice called out from somewhere in the darkness below. Instead of joining Sarah and Emmie, Finn swung around and dropped onto his chest beside the opening while reaching down and struggling with the top edge of the rope as if to release it. Thrusting it sideways, the ladder wavered, but Liam steadied it while rising toward them.

"You won't escape." Liam coughed, still grasping the dagger and gold idol as his head and chest rose from the hole. The blood had soaked the area below his wound. "I can get to anyone, anywhere. I wasn't even in the room with Neil when he pulled the trigger, and I can do the same to you."

"Rot in hell." Finn twisted around and smashed his foot down against the ladder's top rung while still gripping the pistol. The old rope strained, but it held together. Climbing to his feet,

Finn raised the pistol and aimed it toward the hole. "I know how to solve this."

"No, Finn," Sarah pleaded. "Let the police handle it. Don't become part of the bad energy here."

His hands trembled as an internal war waged inside him.

A breeze swept over them, and the leaves stirred through the branches above. The cries of ravens filled the air as the ground rumbled to life again.

Finn glanced back at Sarah, then down to the wound on her chest and squeezed the pistol in his hand a little tighter before nodding slowly. "Em, you better call them. Call them now, before I lose my patience. I'm not letting this bastard out of my sight."

Before Emmie could bring out her phone, the ground rumbled and swayed. Finn fell sideways and Liam's voice filled the air.

"Call the police," he said. "It won't matter. You see—"

The ground shook violently, and Liam dropped back into the hole followed by a rising cloud of dust and the sickening thud of a body hitting a solid surface. Tree branches swayed. Ravens scattered in a chorus of panicked cries. All around them the earth had liquified and the rolling ground tossed them from side to side helplessly. The opening to the cave collapsed as wave after wave of rocks and dirt filled it in.

When the tremors finally stopped a few minutes later, leaves and small branches littered the earth, and the air fell silent, except for the pounding of Emmie's heart. Liam's voice had stopped, and the ravens were gone.

Emmie was the first to stand again as Finn crawled to Sarah's side. The tree they'd sheltered under had sunk several feet in the upheaval, leaning heavily to one side now, as if it might topple over with the slightest breeze. The tree's roots were exposed on one side, jutting out like boney fingers grasping at the earth for balance, while the roots on the other side had seemingly drawn in the soil and stones to heal the gaping wound before others fell prey to the evil beneath it.

38

The silence continued as Emmie dug out her cell phone and called for an ambulance. They couldn't simply walk away from everything that had happened or leave Marc and Amelia trapped in the basement of their home despite what they'd done to Liam and Stephen. If there was a curse on Raven House and the mission, then it seemed alive and well. Although, if Liam had survived the collapse, then the police would interrogate him and he would no doubt use whatever psychic skills he had developed, the same ones he had used on Neil and Sarah, but it seemed impossible that he could have survived a gunshot wound and being buried alive.

Sarah seemed to have the same idea, staring down at the rubble while clasping shut her torn shirt. "Did he survive?"

Emmie closed her eyes for a moment to focus on Liam. She pictured him in her mind clearly. He was there beneath them and sensed his spirit trapped among all the others in that place, so full of dark energy. It would take a long time for him to work through all that he had done. "No. He's gone. The curse claimed another soul."

The ravens slowly returned to perch in the tree above them as they started walking toward the ruins. All the chilly air—the cellar, the underground passageways, the breeze sweeping in off the ocean—had taken its toll, and the afternoon sun did little to warm them up. At least they could sit in the car and rest until help arrived.

Sarah and Finn walked arm in arm, and he seemed to support her as they trudged ahead, although the day's trauma showed on his face. So much pain behind those eyes. He had almost lost another loved one in that place.

Passing through the ruins, Sarah paused and gestured toward the vineyard. "She's there."

Emmie turned and spotted Paige standing at the edge of the vineyard, watching them with a warm smile. The young woman's aimless flight to find her lost love had ended. Had she seen Liam die from that distance? By the look on her face, at least she knew the truth.

"We should help her." Sarah headed toward Paige without waiting for a reply.

Finn and Emmie followed, and within a few minutes they stood in front of her. Now the brutality of Paige's death became clear. Liam had tried to sacrifice her to the Aztec gods without using the dagger, judging by the wounds across her head. The senseless death had led to more bloodshed, following the same pattern of greed and vengeance that had no doubt occurred there countless times before.

"Is she here?" Finn asked.

"She's here." Emmie looked at him. "Would you like to say something to her?"

Finn swallowed and his eyes watered. "I would. Tell her I'm sorry I wasn't there to protect her."

Emmie relayed the message and gave Paige's response. "She says she doesn't blame you."

"Neil tried to help," Finn added. "He came to your rescue... a little too late, but still..."

"She says, I know," Emmie relayed. "And she says she hopes to see Neil again soon."

A tear streamed down Finn's cheek, and he wiped it away before it reached his chin. "Me too."

Paige's spirit brightened as she spoke again, and Emmie relayed the message. "She wants to go now."

Finn nodded and stepped back. "Let her go, then. Do your thing."

Sarah reached toward Paige, just as she had for so many spirits before, but this time Sarah's light wasn't necessary. Paige looked to the sky then burst into a glowing ball of energy that flared upward and then disappeared.

"She moved on without our help." Sarah glanced at Finn then Emmie.

Finn looked away as if ashamed for crying in front of them. "She's at peace."

The sound of sirens came from off in the distance as they continued toward their car. Maybe the damage from the earthquake extended further than they knew, and the emergency vehicles were coming for someone else in need, but they grew louder until the flashing lights appeared down the road. Two police cars, a fire rescue, and an ambulance.

Finn seemed to swallow his emotions as his stoic stare returned, no doubt preparing for a flurry of questions from law enforcement. "I hate this part."

Emmie gave him a warm smile. "If only we could tell them the *truth*."

39

The police had subjected them all to an exhausting barrage of questioning at Raven House. Still, Marc and Amelia had remained silent throughout the process, even after the police discovered the makeshift hospital room in the wine cellar where Liam had suffered for years. It wasn't until Finn led them out to the location of the treasure and revealed the spot where they would find the bodies of Paige Moretti and Liam Carver in a collapsed tunnel beneath the large tree that Marc finally broke down and confessed to everything, including Stephen's murder.

When they arrived back at the Adams' home late that evening, Tiffany was still immersed in sorting through a pile of papers in the living room, although she broke away from it when they arrived and gave Finn a firm hug. Pulling back, she eyed their faces and the dirt smeared across their clothes. "What happened to you?"

"We found the treasure," Finn said with tired eyes.

She smirked. "No, seriously."

"Seriously, we did. But it doesn't matter right now." He looked at the ceiling. "We need to take care of something."

The confusion spread across Tiffany's face as she eyed each of them one more time. "I'm afraid to ask."

"We'll explain everything tomorrow." Finn led them upstairs to Stephen's office. Opening the door, Stephen stood in the same place he had during their last visit, although the man's panic seemed to have faded a bit. He looked more dazed now than anything, and Emmie smiled at him when he glanced toward her. "He sees me."

"He's not at peace yet," Sarah said.

Emmie stepped over beside him and caught Stephen's attention. "Do you know where you are?"

He looked around, then toward the open safe on his desk and his face showed an escalating panic. "In my office. Neil was on to something before he died. Liam and Paige went to the ruins, and I think they found the treasure. Dr. Moretti—"

Emmie spoke in a soothing voice. "The police caught him. It's over now."

Stephen stared at the ground. "They fell victim to the curse. I thought Marc would help me."

"He chose the wrong path," Sarah said.

He looked toward his office chair. "I don't know what happened after I sat down."

"You had a heart attack."

"Yes." He pressed his hands to his chest. "I did. But if that's true..."

"You died."

His expression shifted a moment later as if the reality had finally set in. He seemed to take notice of Finn now, staring at him with a growing smile. "You came to visit me."

"Finn was at your funeral," Emmie said. "We were all there."

"How strange." He moved toward the piles of papers on his desk and reached his hand through them with no effect. "I suppose I am dead."

"It's okay," Sarah said. "We're here to help you move on."

Stephen nodded and gestured to an empty pill bottle. "I remember now. Marc urged me to take those pills... to relax and get some rest as soon as I got home. Do you know he threatened me when I asked him about what I'd found in Neil's safe? Why would he threaten me? He was one of my closest friends. The Godfather to my son."

"He confessed at Raven House," Emmie said. "Told the police he knew the pills would induce your heart attack."

"He murdered me..." Stephen showed acceptance on his face now.

Sarah gestured to Finn. "Finn solved your murder."

Stephen smiled at him and turned to face him directly. "You always were good at that sort of thing."

Emmie repeated the words to Finn.

Finn swallowed, then stared into the space that his dad occupied. "I'm sorry I wasn't here to stop all of this from happening."

"Don't blame yourself," Stephen answered, and Emmie repeated everything for Finn's benefit. "I'm so proud of you and your brother. I know I wasn't the perfect father..."

"You did your best," Finn answered as his eyes teared up.

"I suppose I did," Stephen said.

Finn nodded and spoke softly, "Love you, Dad. See you on the other side."

"Love you too, Son."

A moment of silence passed between them before Sarah reached out and swept her hand over Stephen's spirit to help him move on. Finn watched the process with interest, although he couldn't see the brilliant light that his father had become, rising through the ceiling in a flash before he was gone.

∽

ONLY A SHORT TIME LATER, THEY STOOD AT THE TOP OF THE stairs, ready to once again help Finn face the spirit of his brother in the basement. Despite everything that had happened, he still showed signs of anxiety, rubbing his hands together and clenching his jaw with the same stoic stare he always made before facing emotional headwinds. Sarah grasped one of his hands with both of hers as he took a deep breath.

"All right," he said, "it's time."

They stepped down the creaking stairs and across the room to the corner where Neil had died. His spirit stood in the same place, although he was transformed. His light shined much brighter now and he seemed to welcome their arrival as if he'd been expecting them.

"What took you so long?" Neil said to Finn as if continuing a conversation they had started earlier that day.

Emmie relayed to Finn what Neil had said.

Finn stared forward longingly, then cracked a slight grin. "Still the smart ass. I only wish I could see him say that."

Sarah looked toward Emmie. "Maybe. Let me try something."

"Try what?" Finn asked.

"Like what I've done with other spirits, I can merge with Neil so he can talk through me, and you should be able to see him that way. It wasn't possible before when he was so fixated on his trauma, but now..."

Finn's face brightened and he nodded. "Yes, please, try that."

Sarah stepped in front of Neil and gained his full attention before speaking. "Neil, I want you to put your hands on mine."

Neil did and erupted in a delightful laugh when his spirit passed through her. "That's weird."

"Hold it there," Sarah commanded.

Neil refocused on her, matching the position of her hand to his as closely as possible. "I think I got it."

"Good." Sarah removed her hand, then turned around and faced Finn so her back faced Neil. Speaking a little louder, she said, "Now, I want you to take a step forward and walk into me. Position your whole body in mine."

Neil glanced toward Finn and then Emmie before focusing

again on Sarah as he moved into her just as she'd asked. "Oh, this is even more weird. I can almost see—"

Sarah's mouth moved and the rest of his sentence came out through her loud and clear, except the voice didn't belong to her. It was Neil. "—like I did before."

A wide grin spread across Sarah's face before Neil's appearance took over. The glowing energy shifted around her like a silk veil until his form came into view and she became him. A moment later, Sarah was gone, replaced by a handsome young man in physical form with none of the violent trauma.

Neil looked at Finn with wide eyes. "Can you believe this?"

"I can." Finn mirrored his brother's shock.

"Is that all you got to say?" Neil said sarcastically.

Finn jumped forward and hugged his brother for several seconds before backing away. "I never thought I would see you again."

Neil glanced at Emmie. "I never thought I would see you hanging out with two girls?"

Finn's eyes watered. "You haven't changed a bit, asshole."

Sarah's voice broke through the veneer. "Finn, I'm sorry, but I can't do this much longer."

"Whoa," Neil's voice returned. "It feels like I'm talking through a puppet."

"That puppet just saved your life," Finn said. "That's Sarah, my girlfriend."

"She's a keeper," Neil said. "*Thank you*, Sarah."

"You're welcome," came Sarah's voice.

Finn looked into his brother's eyes. "We might not have found Paige's body if it hadn't been for you. The gold coin we found..."

Neil nodded and frowned. "I never should have accepted it, but... gold. They found the treasure, Finn, and Liam gave me the coin to keep me quiet. He knew I was broke, so he bought my silence. But after Paige disappeared, I knew something was wrong. I figured out where he buried her—under the oak tree in the cemetery, along with the treasure—and I even bought a shovel to go dig her up, but he did something to me before I could get to her. He told me I was cursed for taking the gold, and I don't know how, but I started having bad dreams—nightmares, really—about all the stories we heard as kids. The sacrifices, the creatures, the blood and screaming... and Liam was right there in my nightmare with them, although it wasn't *him*. He was some sort of shadow figure off in the distance, as if orchestrating the whole thing with his mind. He got into my dreams, Finn. But then I started seeing shadow figures in the basement, right there in front of me, like the most god-awful ghosts you could ever imagine coming to drag me away. They convinced me to do it, Finn, to pull the trigger. That it was the only way out."

"I believe you," Finn said softly. "It's okay. It's over now."

"Thank God," Neil said. "I think Sarah's getting tired. And I hear someone calling me. I think it's Dad's voice."

Finn was silent for a moment, as if trying to delay the inevitable, then nodded. "You better go."

Footsteps came up behind Finn. "Please, wait." Tiffany appeared behind him with tears running down her cheeks as she stared at her son in disbelief. "It's you, Neil. You're really here?"

Neil turned to face her. "I'm here, Mom. But someone is calling for me to go with them. Not the bad people. I never gave up."

Tiffany laughed with tears in her eyes. "I knew it couldn't be true."

"Dad is there too. He wants me to tell you I love you. Well, *he* loves you. And I do too."

"I love you too." She swept her arm around Finn. "All of you."

Sarah's voice cut in again. "I have to step out now."

"Love you, Brother," Finn said.

"Right back at you," Neil said as his appearance faded. The light from Neil's spirit grew brighter as Sarah repeated the same process that she'd done to Stephen. Her hands swept through his spirit in a soft, gentle motion, and his light flowed up through the ceiling in a burst before he was gone.

Finn turned to his mother and opened his mouth as if to say something.

She spoke first. "I never would have believed it if I hadn't seen it with my own eyes. There's so much I don't know."

Finn embraced his mother. "It's probably better that way."

40

Emmie parked the rental car beside the cemetery's narrow path, beneath the canopy of a live oak tree. There were no signs of the funeral that had taken place a few days earlier at that spot except for a fresh layer of sod blanketing Stephen's grave. They were alone in that section of the cemetery, although a group of workers labored in the distance beside a mound of dirt, maneuvering a backhoe back and forth to carve out another grave.

The mid-morning sunlight peeked through the leaves and brightened the car's interior as the branches waved in the light breeze. The aroma of freshly cut flowers filled the air. Finn had picked them out himself from his mother's flower garden in the backyard. Two bouquets of white roses, and a single red one.

He cradled the two bouquets in the backseat, where he sat with Sarah, but had handed the single red rose to her before getting in the car with an elegance they'd rarely seen. Sarah had accepted it with a gracious smile and kissed him.

She still held the rose close to her chest when Emmie switched off the engine and waited patiently for instructions. It didn't matter that she was playing the chauffeur again. Finn had gone through so much, and she wasn't going to rush it.

Finn glanced at each of them before speaking. "I've decided to stay for a few more days and help Mom go through her stuff."

"I thought you might." Sarah smelled the rose and smiled. "She needs you too. Come home when you're ready."

After Finn opened the door, they stepped out into the crisp air and walked beside him to the graves of Stephen and Neil a few yards away. A temporary grave marker, a simple black sign stuck into the ground near the head of the grave, displayed Stephen Adams's name and date of birth and death. Finn walked to it reverently, holding the two bouquets against his chest.

Emmie stayed back beside Sarah to give him privacy while he stepped forward and placed the first bouquet over his father's grave. He bowed his head and whispered to himself for a few seconds, then turned back with watery eyes toward Neil's grave.

Neil's headstone lay flat against the ground, his name obscured by dirt and grass clippings. Only the edges of the stone protruded through the soil, and she might have missed it if Finn hadn't squatted down in front of it and brushed away the debris. He placed the second bouquet of roses beside the stone, then spent a few moments clearing away some of the grass that had sprouted along the edges.

"Rest in peace, Brother." Finn ran his fingers over Neil's name etched in stone, then stood up and stared down at it reverently.

While Finn stood silent, Emmie glanced back at the men who were digging the grave in the distance. The face of the man driving the backhoe looked oddly familiar, and it took her a moment to remember that he was the man she'd mistaken for Stephen during the burial ceremony. But the man's clothes and his stance and appearance looked nothing like Stephen. Had the light and shadows played tricks on her eyes during the gloomy burial?

Glancing back toward Finn, he scratched at the bruises and cuts on the back of his arms where he'd injured himself while scrambling to get out of the tunnel before it collapsed. A small price to pay. Things could have been so much worse.

A raven cawed in a tree overhead, and she couldn't help but hear the famous word from the Edgar Allan Poe poem in her mind.

Nevermore.

Finn must have been thinking the same thing because his gaze followed the sound up into the tree before he turned back toward the girls. "I'll never look at a raven the same after today. I used to think they were kind of cool... but now I never want to see another one again."

"It's not their fault," Emmie mused. "They're just like all the other birds."

"Not the same," Finn added. "Other birds aren't plotting to eat your soul."

Emmie searched the branches and spotted the raven's blackened eyes peering down at them. "You've got a point."

Finn took a mournful glance back at the graves, then started walking back toward the car. "We can go. I've already made my peace with them back at the house. Not many people get that opportunity."

Emmie lingered behind and scanned the cemetery while taking in a deep breath. "So peaceful."

"Let's keep it that way." Finn opened the door for Sarah. "After you, my sweet living angel."

Sarah let out a little laugh while climbing into the backseat with Finn. "Should I get into a car with a man wearing a devil's grin?"

"I always look that way." He climbed into the backseat next to her but took one last look toward the sky before closing the door. A flock of ravens had scattered into the air, and his gaze followed them for a few seconds. "Perfect day to fly."

Get Book 7 in the Emmie Rose Haunted Mystery series and a free short story on the next page!

Get the next book in the Emmie Rose series!
Amber House: An Emmie Rose Haunted Mystery Book 7

∽

AND get a **FREE** short story here or at my website!

www.deanrasmussen.com

★★★★★
Please review my book!

If you liked this book and have a moment to spare, I would greatly appreciate a short review on the page where you bought it. Your help in spreading the word is *immensely* appreciated and reviews make a huge difference in helping new readers find my novels.

Shine House: An Emmie Rose Haunted Mystery Book 0
Hanging House: An Emmie Rose Haunted Mystery Book 1
Caine House: An Emmie Rose Haunted Mystery Book 2
Hyde House: An Emmie Rose Haunted Mystery Book 3
Whisper House: An Emmie Rose Haunted Mystery Book 4
Temper House: An Emmie Rose Haunted Mystery Book 5
Raven House: An Emmie Rose Haunted Mystery Book 6

Dreadful Dark Tales of Horror Book 1
Dreadful Dark Tales of Horror Book 2
Dreadful Dark Tales of Horror Book 3
Dreadful Dark Tales of Horror Book 4
Dreadful Dark Tales of Horror Book 5
Dreadful Dark Tales of Horror Book 6
Dreadful Dark Tales of Horror Complete Series

Stone Hill: Shadows Rising (Book 1)
Stone Hill: Phantoms Reborn (Book 2)
Stone Hill: Leviathan Wakes (Book 3)

ABOUT THE AUTHOR

Dean Rasmussen grew up in a small Minnesota town and began writing stories at the age of ten, driven by his fascination with the Star Wars hero's journey. He continued writing short stories and attempted a few novels through his early twenties until he stopped to focus on his computer animation ambitions. He studied English at a Minnesota college during that time.

He learned the art of computer animation and went on to work on twenty feature films, a television show, and a AAA video game as a visual effects artist over thirteen years.

Dean currently teaches animation for visual effects in Orlando, Florida. Inspired by his favorite authors, Stephen King, Ray Bradbury, Richard Matheson and H. P. Lovecraft, Dean began writing novels and short stories again in 2018 to thrill and delight a new generation of horror fans.

ACKNOWLEDGMENTS

Thank you to my wife and family who supported me, and who continue to do so, through many long hours of writing.

Thank you to my friends and relatives, some of whom have passed away, who inspired me and supported my crazy ideas. Thank you for putting up with me!

Thank you to everyone who worked with me to get this book out on time!

Thank you to all my supporters!

Printed in Great Britain
by Amazon